Clifford P. Allen

Pilgrimage of Mary Commandery

no. 36, K.T. of Pennsylvania to the twenty-fifth triennial conclave of the Grand

encampment U.S. at Denver, Colorado

Clifford P. Allen

Pilgrimage of Mary Commandery
no. 36, K.T. of Pennsylvania to the twenty-fifth triennial conclave of the Grand encampment U.S. at Denver, Colorado

ISBN/EAN: 9783337293703

Printed in Europe, USA, Canada, Australia, Japan

Cover: Foto ©Andreas Hilbeck / pixelio.de

More available books at **www.hansebooks.com**

PILGRIMAGE

OF

Mary Commandery, No. 36

K. T. of PENNSYLVANIA

TO THE

Twenty=Fifth Triennial Conclave

OF THE

GRAND ENCAMPMENT U. S.

AT

DENVER, COLORADO

PHILADELPHIA

1892

Friday, July 15th, 1892.

CLEAR SKY and warm sun ushered in this most important day in the history of those who intended to take part in the pilgrimage of Mary Commandery, to the Triennial Conclave of Knights Templar, at Denver, Colorado. The more important, because of the short cut we intended to make to Denver by way of the Pacific Coast.

At an early hour there was a scurrying to and fro of heavy wagons and light carriages, as the trunks, boxes, ladies and other impediments began to accumulate at Broad Street Station. By 9 A. M. the vestibuled train, intended for our use, and composed of the combination smoking and baggage car Columbus, the dining car Capitol, drawing-room sleeper Ixion and Cat sleeper Frankfort, was backed into the station, and soon not only crowded, but literally packed with the pilgrims and their very numerous friends and well wishers. All were eager to inspect their accommodations, wish them a pleasant journey, and give them a parting God-speed. The Committee of Ways and Means had their hands full between answering questions, seeing that the necessary evils were on board for the commissary department and amusement bureau, and fastening the side badges with the name of the Commandery on the sides of the cars. This latter duty had been promised to be attended to by the railroad officials, but was found, at the last moment, to have been neglected by them. Fortunately they had been put in the baggage car, so that willing hands were able to soon have them stretched and tied temporarily in position, that we might not go forth upon our eight thousand mile journey, unknown and untagged like ordinary travelers.

In bright contrast to our departure for Erie in May of last year, we were cheered by the presence of many Sir Knights of Mary, as well as their ladies, who were loath to tear themselves away until the final parting made it actually necessary.

Precisely at 9.30 A. M. the conductor's call of "all aboard" sounded. There was a crushing and dodging time in and around the narrow passages about the drawing rooms, between those inside who were anxious to get out and those outside who had no desire to be left. A few farewell cheers and waves of the hand ensued and our pilgrimage was fairly commenced.

Through the liberality of Mr. C. A. Lane, an immense basket of roses had been sent to Mrs. Allen, containing corsage bouquets for each of the ladies on the expedition. These were at once distributed, and lent a brighter complexion to the interior of the ladies' car.

After the start, our first employment was to compare the numbers of the sections with that upon our voluminous tickets, and make sure of the location of our local habitations for the coming thirty-one days. This was very soon effected, and grips, parcels, umbrellas and bags stowed away in the most convenient places. Introductions of those hitherto unacquainted and renewals of interrupted friendships were then the order of the day, and were easily accomplished in the smooth passage of our heavy train over the perfect road-bed of the Pennsylvania.

Up in the baggage car, our old friend and factotum, John Robbins, had been installed as presiding genius of the refrigerator, and had his department in working order as quickly as the locomotive. Mr. Thomas Purdy, whom we found later on to be the "Grand Master" of tourist agents, was rapidly made acquainted with those after whom he was ordained to see. Mr. J. Howard Speakman, who had been assigned to accompany us during the entire trip, was busily engaged in getting our trunks into such shape and familiarizing himself with the names thereon, as would enable him to answer all calls upon his patience at any time through the day or half of the night.

In the smoker the large wicker chairs were already occupied, and the library of ninety novels had been opened up on a convenient shelf in one end of the car. A number of the same kind of means of recreation had been brought along by the ladies of the party. It is deemed worthy of mention here, that such was the engrossing interest of the entire pilgrimage, it was unanimously agreed that not ten of the books had been read through by the combined efforts of all the readers.

Flashing upon our way past the numerous stations, without any halts, we were unexpectedly brought up, in the Lancaster cut-off, by a freight wreck which had occurred shortly before our arrival. We were, perforce, compelled to back the train twenty-two miles to Dillersville and take the main track to get around it, thus increasing our railroad mileage about fifty miles at the start. In consequence of this delay we ran into Harrisburg one and a half hours behind our scheduled time.

Harry Emmerling, our baby member, with his uncombined weight of three hundred and eighty pounds, had arrived promptly at the Philadelphia station with the rest, and had been assigned to a lower berth through the extreme unwillingness of any of the other participants to have him suspended over their heads for a whole month. Through the anxiety of Mr. Brocks, our

HARRY EMMERLING

commander-in-chief of the dining car, and his dusky staff, to make a good
impression with their first meal, our luncheon was a little late, but none the less
enjoyable on that account. When Emmerling came to take a seat at one of
the tables, it was found impossible for him to squeeze into the space alloted
to ordinary corporations. Brooks was obliged to rig up an impromptu table
in the passage outside for a day or two, which was afterward varied by the
service of his meals on one of the writing tables of the smoker. Here he was
excellently accommodated until future circumstances rendered any extra attention to his wants unnecessary. That there may be no mistake as to the kind
of fare we enjoyed throughout this trip, we append the bill of fare of the first
luncheon, with the assurance that it was no better than any that followed it.

MENU MARY COMMANDERY

LUNCHEON EN ROUTE JULY 15TH, 1892

·····SOUP·····
TOMATO WITH RICE

·····COLD MEATS·····
ROAST BEEF　　　　HAM SPECIAL　　　　SMOKED TONGUE
　　　SARDINES　　　　BAKED BEANS　　　LAMB'S TONGUE

CHOW-CHOW　　　　MIXED PICKLES　　　　OLIVES
　　WORCESTERSHIRE SAUCE　　　TOMATO CATSUP

SHRIMP SALAD

BAKED POTATOES　　　FRIED EGG PLANT　　　SARATOGA CHIPS
　　SUGAR CORN　　　　　　GREEN PEAS
　　　FRICASSEE OF CHICKEN

PLAIN BREAD　　　BROWN BREAD　　　GRAHAM BREAD

·····DESSERT·····
VANILLA ICE CREAM　　　　　　　PRESERVED FRUIT
　ASSORTED CAKES　　　GOLDEN GATE FRUIT
　　ENGLISH. GRAHAM AND OATMEAL WAFERS

BENT'S CRACKERS　　　　　　CHEESE
　　　COFFEE　　　　TEA

At Harrisburg we were joined by a fellow-voyager, Mr. B. F. Brown, of Lock Haven, who proved to be, in addition to a "jolly good fellow," an amateur photographer of no mean capacity, and a cigarette smoker. The latter trait was soon suppressed in him, but the photography was fostered and nursed into full bloom, and many of the cuts through this book are due to his industry and generosity. The diaries provided by the committee were very extensively pencilled during the first day, and in quite a number the practice was kept up until the last. Many of them bore a family resemblance at the end of the trip to that of George Kessler, which showed a heading on the first page of " Philadelphia, July 15th, 1892," and was guiltless of word or letter thereafter during the whole thirty-one days. Even this was suspected of having been made at home as a preliminary effort.

At 4 P. M. a can of ice-cream, which had been sent to the train through the forethought of Sir Jimmy and Mrs. Baird, was tapped, and its welcome and cooling contents discussed throughout the train. The weather had become warmer as the day advanced, and this occupation found favor in all eyes. At Altoona the arrival of three more of our party was heralded and Sirs Lee of Clearfield, Crist of Osceola Mills, and Spencer of Curwensville were welcomed with open arms. Mrs. Crist had come down to the city to start with us, but Crist had remained at home until the last minute.

Going up from Altoona the air became very much cooler, and the delightful view of the Horseshoe by daylight lost none of its attractions from that fact. Later on, the Conemaugh valley, together with Johnstown and some of the still apparent results of the great flood, claimed the attention of all the travelers. Dinner was served promptly at 6 P. M., and the now bracing atmosphere gave all good appetites for the meal.

At 9 P. M. we rolled into the depot at Pittsburgh and took on the last member of the expedition to report, Sir Wells, of Wellsville, Ohio. Heavy rain was falling at the time, and the prospects of still cooler weather were very encouraging. Only enough time was consumed here to change engines and supply the cars with ice and water. Out into the darkness we sped once more on our way, trusting implicitly in the engineer and his air-brakes. The long lines of coke-ovens which we passed continuously after leaving Pittsburgh, broke upon our view through the gloom of the night like a sort of individual Hades, each with its attendant imps. We were soon across the line into the Buckeye State, with the rain still pattering an accompaniment to the roar of the wheels.

The greatest curiosity visible through the darkness to-night was the McDonald oil field through which we passed. Natural gas flares were burning in all directions, and the gallows-like apparitions of the derricks loomed up from all quarters. We were informed that many of the latter were erected through the roofs of now deserted dwellings, in the cellars of which oil had been discovered. Through the mutual desire to not be the first to break up pleasant parties, it was a late hour when all the berths were made up and the occupants had turned in. It was eventually accomplished, and we endeavored to become acclimated to our new sleeping quarters.

Saturday, July 16th, 1892.

CLEAR weather and cool air prevailed this morning, and the blankets of the Pullman Company were a welcome addition in the night. All hands were on deck pretty early, many being unable to sleep much on the first attempt. Breakfast was ready promptly, but 7 A. M. seemed a long time coming. This was partly owing to the fact that we had to set our watches back an hour at Pittsburg to keep pace with the new railroad or Central time.

Our first stop to-day was made at Indianapolis at 8 A. M. Here a telegram was handed to us from the fraters of Ascalon Commandery No. 16 of St. Louis, tendering to us a reception at their Asylum this evening. Capt. Gen. Munch replied by wire and accepted the invitation on our behalf.

At Greencastle Junction another freight wreck ahead of us caused a stop for some little time. Advantage was taken of this to refasten our side badges in a substantial manner. In the course of a search for rope or twine at the small store of the Junction, the ancient German dame, who presided over its business affairs, was much astonished and amused at our statement, in reply to her queries, that we were taking a short trip to California. Sir Dill distinguished himself by attaching one of the tie-ropes to an opening in the wheel of the car, under the impression that it would get tighter as we journeyed further. The job was finally well done, in spite of the fact that the majority of the crowd were volunteer bosses and the workingmen in a small minority. The weather was all that could be desired, and the ladies took advantage of the stop to rest themselves by promenades on the station platform. Brown also inaugurated the photographic business by making a picture of the baby as well as a group of those who were taking the air on the platform.

Emmerling afforded the Hoosiers much amusement by offering to be photographed on the signal ladder with one of the ladies in his arms, as if rescuing her from a fire.

The road was at length cleared and we were soon again speeding across the level ground of Indiana. The first fireworks of the occasion were sprung about this time, and went off in the mouths of Zeitz and Emmerling, in the shape of red-fire cigars. They occasioned those gentlemen no little astonishment, and afforded much amusement to their particular friends.

Terre-Haute was reached at 9.45 A. M., and another short stay made there. From this point an almost uninterrupted line of corn-fields and rail fences, varied only by a view of the luncheon tables, followed us right into East St. Louis at 3.15 P. M. Some of the middle-aged in the party could recall the time when this thriving and busy little city was only a ferry landing, and part of the ground on which it now stands was the duelling ground of the fire-eaters among the St. Louis aristocracy. It went then by the name of Bloody Island, and was the scene of various encounters in that line.

The steel bridge over the Father of Waters was soon crossed, by many for the first time, and the cars tightly closed for the gaseous trip through the tunnel. This part of the trip was soon covered, and we emerged into daylight and the depot, from which point the street cars were made use of to reach the Southern Hotel. Here a parlor was secured for the ladies, from which, after leaving a portion of their wraps and grips, the party scattered in as many directions as their varied inclinations led, with the understanding that they were to rendezvous at the Southern again at 6 P. M. Shaw's Garden and Forest Park were the objective points of some, while others were content to ride back and forth on the cable and electric cars for a general view of the streets. The stores on Broadway also found admirers and shoppers, who laid in their first instalment of souvenirs, which included spoons of course. Barber shops were already the object of search parties, and anxious inquiries were made by the later arrivals therein as to which of the knights of the razor shaved the easiest.

After 6 P. M. all parties began to drift into the hotel in larger or smaller squads, until dinner was served at 6.45 P. M., in a private dining room. Ample justice was done to the meal, after which further developments were awaited. These turned up in various shapes. Purdy took a division to the races, which were advertised to be run under the glare of the electric light. Here, by the aid of several straight tips, with which articles we became familiar much nearer to home, some of the sportingly-inclined were enabled to blow in a few dollars. One of the sure tips the party had become possessed of came in at the tail end of the race. A second lost ingloriously by a nose, and the third actually dropped dead before reaching the finish.

At 9 P. M. a coach was secured, which took most of the ladies, together with Phillips, who had been suddenly taken ill at the hotel, back to the train. At 9.30 P. M. an escort from Ascalon Commandery arrived at the hotel with a band and escorted Mary's contingent, twenty-seven in number, to their asylum. There Emmerling was sent up first in the elevator, and strained it so badly that the remainder of the command were obliged to march up the stair-way. The line of march was direct to the banquet table, where the members of each commandery found seats, alternating with each other.

In a few minutes the remainder of the Ascalon Knights, who had been conferring the Red Cross upon five candidates, made their appearance and took possession of an adjoining table. Due attention having been given to the wants of the inner man, and the toothsome viands prepared by Mrs. Owen, Ascalon's caterer, fully discussed, a social exchange of remarks ensued. P. G. Commander Agler first made a speech of welcome to the pilgrims of Mary. The ball was then kept rolling on behalf of Ascalon, by Sirs Lamb, Rainwater, Mayo, Walsh and Richardson. Mary's share of the talk was sustained by Capt. Gen. Munch, Sirs Milligan, Johnson, Sobernheimer and Emmerling, followed by Sir Register, on behalf of Crusade No. 5, of Balti-more. Sir Mayo, being an honorary member of Mary, made touching allu-sions to that fact in his remarks. The fun was fast and furious until 11.10 P.M., at which time we found it necessary to be on the alert to make the train. Pop Millick, in his endeavors to get on the right side of the ladies, as usual, discovered that Mrs. Owen, who is called the mother of Ascalon Commandery, was a Philadelphia girl and had gone to the same school teacher as himself in the Quaker City. But we had to tear him away from his acquaintance, as our hosts had busses in waiting to convey us to the train. A number of them accompanied us that far and we parted with mutual cheers for Ascalon and Mary and wishes for a safe and pleasant journey. Some of the pilgrims had been to the theatre, but all were now returned. At 11.30 P. M. the train moved out promptly, and the weary sojourners were not long in seeking their berths.

DINING CAR

Sunday, July 17th, 1892.

THREE of our ladies were under the weather this morning from the buffeting around the berths, caused by the rough ride over the Missouri Pacific during the night. Even those who were too tired to be kept awake, and who slept through it all, could feel the soreness occasioned by sundry thumps against the wooden walls. The run this morning was along the shores of the muddy Missouri, with its constantly shifting channel and moth-eaten banks. The bluffs on either side of the river are always in process of wearing away by being undermined by the swift current when the water is high. Immense masses of earth then fall in and are washed away in turn, thus always keeping enough dirt in solution in the water to entitle the river to its name. There is enough of it goes down to give the Mississippi the same character after the Missouri joins it. Above the confluence with the latter river the former is as clear as any respectable stream.

We made our debut in Kansas City at 8 A. M. Our first discovery was of two tramps who had ridden on the iron braces under one of the sleeping cars from some point unknown. Their dust-covered condition did not excite any envy in our breasts because of the saving in railroad fare they had effected. Breakfast was not over when we reached the station, and we were side-tracked up the station yard until we had finished. The immense amount of trackage and railroad yard room attracted general attention.

After breakfast the entire party set out to have a look at the city, which is intersected by a very extensive system of cable cars. By transfers, a ride of eleven miles can be had for a nickel, so that we were enabled to cover the ground pretty thoroughly at wholesale rates. Various lines of cars run upon the same street until their turning-off point is reached. There the raising of an iron handle with a chain attached will send the car whizzing around the corner into its proper track, without any waiting or laborious tugging by a team of horses.

We knew it was Sunday, because it was printed on our itineraries, and because some of the party lit out to find a church. There was no other outward evidence of the fact in Kansas City. Business was proceeding serenely in most places, and in one locality that we passed they were digging and walling cellars for houses. The retail stores were generally open, and presented some unusual combinations to our sight. One in particular, just opposite the depot, afforded us an opportunity to purchase drugs, jewelry, tobacco and hardware, while at the same time you might scalp your railroad ticket. The latter business was a very prominent one, especially in that particular locality.

The policeman smoked on duty as calmly as if he were a locomotive, and the switchmen who lifted the cable cars around at their turning-points, were armed with red, white or blue police clubs, which they used as signals in place of flags. Base ball and horse races were advertised for to-day, and our ability to enjoy the means for amusement afforded us was only limited by our short stay in the city.

Troost Park was situated at the end of the Troost Avenue cable line, and the majority of the pilgrims found their way there at some time of the day. From one of the high points on the avenue an excellent birds-eye view of the city was had, as well as the river and the city's twin beyond it. In the park we found a menagerie of small size, of which the principal attraction was a prairie dog village in full blast. A supposed Mastodon, over which Milligan delivered an interesting lecture to the bystanders, was finally exposed by Blackwood, who had taken the whole lecture in as gospel. At the close he examined the monster critically, and exclaimed in an injured tone, "why, it is only a piece of limestone!" A switchback, erected on the grounds, was highly recommended in a grandiloquent circular as being highly moral, conducive to health, and patronized by all the crowned heads of Europe, who were highly honored by having all their names printed in the circular. The crowned heads were no inducement to our bald heads and they passed.

The streets of the city, where not black dirt, were paved with wooden blocks or asphalt, except between the cable car tracks, which were filled in with Belgian blocks and grass. The conductor wore as his badge of servitude an immense bell punch, suspended to his neck, of the weight of three pounds. One of the men whom we interviewed proved to be a Philadelphia boy from the 26th Ward, and we gladly answered his numerous inquiries for his friends in the Kilkenny district. The cable trains here all have plenty of accommodations for smokers, and all the western cities show a spirit of enlightenment in that respect that may in a century or two touch the hearts of the Quaker City autocrats of the car lines.

The city seems to have been located in a rather hilly spot. You cannot find a dead level anywhere. When we were not going up hill we were sure to be going down, and on one point, just above the car track on which we came into the station, the descent was quite of a blood-curdling nature, which gave rise to various speculations as to where we should land if the cable broke. From the end of the cable line at the station we took a ride on the elevated road over into Kansas City, in Kansas. This afforded a good view of the Armour packing houses and stock yards, as well as the river. The Kansas side of the river proved of little interest, except to prove to us that the story of the inhabitants being obliged to cross the river to whet their whistles was not true. A lad in a jewelry store into which we dropped, offered to steer us into three places in the same block where we could get all the beer we wanted. A horse-car took us back on the level ground, and passed a number of places on the Missouri side where you needed no steering to find the beer. The city possesses many fine blocks of buildings devoted to business purposes as well as residences. The flat system seems to be very much in vogue, and handsome specimens of that style of building were numerous and new. The city also has a couple of commanderies of Knights Templar, whom we saw after we got to Denver.

By 1 P. M. the party began to drift back into the depot for luncheon, but the train had been run out into the yards and did not appear until 1.30 P. M. Brooks' set-out suffered in consequence to a great extent. We left Kansas city on time at 2 P. M., while partaking of luncheon, and bade farewell to all its short-comings. Following the course of the Missouri, watching the low stage of its muddy current, and counting its innumerable sand-bars until 4 P. M., we arrived at Topeka. Here a delegation of Sir Knights, who, although they had only a half hour's notice of our coming, boarded our train at the station and expressed their regrets that we could not make a stop here to receive some attention at their hands. We were also sorry that we were unable to stay with them, so we could only mutually promise to see more of each other at the conclave to which they expected to go.

Directly after leaving Topeka a service of song was commenced under the leadership of Sir Shaw. The entire Moody and Sankey collection was about used up in the ceremonies, which were then wound up with the Star Spangled Banner. Some one suggested Ta-ra-ra-boom, but that was immediately frowned down.

Emporia was reached at 6.05 P. M., just as we had sat down to dinner. Here we were deprived of the further services of a genuine cowboy conductor and brakeman, who had been with us through the afternoon. The brakeman had smoked a loaded cigar for our benefit, while the conductor carried two home with him to smoke after supper in the bosom of his family. As we did not propose to return by this route we were a little reckless of consequences.

The landscape to-day has been enlivened by the sight of immense herds of cattle, which are brought here by long drives over the cattle trails of the lower country, and left to fatten up for the market. Occasionally we flashed by an emigrant camp by the side of some running water or spring. The prairie schooner or wagon drawn up beneath the shade of a tree, the team of horses picketed in the grass, the heads of the department busy over the culinary preparations by a camp-fire, with various frowzy-headed youngsters playing with the inevitable yellow dog, made up a picture which grew to be a familiar one to us before we had got far on our pilgrimage.

At Newton, Kansas, at 8.20 P. M., we were met by another delegation of Knights, from Newton Commandery, No. 9, headed by Generalissimo Sir Jas. McKee, who also regretted that we had not allotted time at this point that would give them an opportunity to fittingly receive the representatives of Mary Commandery. Capt. Gen. Munch thanked them kindly on our behalf for their good intentions. We explained to them that our schedule had to be strictly adhered to for the reason that so long as we were on time we were entitled to the right of way, and once thrown off it, we were at the mercy of everybody.

Advantage was taken of our short stay at the station by the Misses Graham and Miss Branson to inaugurate a series of foot races up and down the station platform, in which exercise they were encouraged by the plaudits of their fellow-travelers. The night had fallen quite cool. Car windows were closed down and berths made up at an early hour to seek repose from the exertions at Kansas City, the more so as it was Sunday night and we might not do as we listed as on other nights. Things were quiet in the smoker sooner than common, and Cas Lowry, who had developed a penchant for sleeping in one of the large wicker chairs in preference to his berth, was enabled to get to sleep early. Back in the cats' car they were enabled to do the thing up royally at night. Being all one kind of cat, they did not find it necessary to draw the curtains on any of the sections, and by leaving everything open got the benefit of air from the ventilators as well as the windows. Of a warm night this was found very advantageous.

Monday, July 18th, 1892.

UPON arising this morning we found that we had lost another hour during the night at Dodge City. As we had no time to go back and gather it up, the only resource we had was to drop it from the face of the earth and start afresh with our watches turned back. We had now got into the sage-brush country and had ample occupation in watching for prairie dogs. Their habitations were to be seen every few feet, but only the patient watcher was rewarded by an occasional sight of the round little animal himself. Before you could call the attention of your neighbor to him, either the train had flashed past or with a comical flourish of his tail and hind legs the little "varmint" had disappeared down the hole in his conical sand hill.

The jack-rabbit though was a more frequent sight, as he would be started up by the noise of the locomotive. Once roused, he stood not upon the order of his going, but went at once through the brush as though some forgotten business in the next county had just been recalled to his mind. He apparently forgot it again just as quickly, as he would squat beneath another bush so suddenly as to make you think your eyes had deceived you when you saw him in motion. He would drop on his hind-quarters first and apparently take a look around him before settling down in front. When he did get down he was indistinguishable from the surrounding brush and ground.

At an early hour we got a fair view of the top of Pike's Peak, clearly outlined against the background of sky. At the time it was said to be one hundred miles distant from our train. There are times, and we ran up against many of them, when you do not exactly care to express all that you think to one who is giving you free information. We found ourselves in that predicament pretty often during the next few days we spent in the rarefied atmosphere through which we traveled. When your attention is called to a mountain, or a range of them. to which you are satisfied in your own mind you might walk in a couple of hours, if it were not too hot, and you are coolly informed that they are distant anywhere from 80 to 120 miles, you often think much more than you like to say, especially if your informant is a total stranger and a little large for his size.

Owing to fast running during the night, we were ahead of time this morning, and able to enjoy a stop of twenty-five minutes at La Junta, Col. Here we commenced to air our knowledge of the Spanish language, and say La Hunta, which is the correct thing if you do not wish to be looked down upon as a tenderfoot. From this point all the way around to Frisco all the J's want to be pronounced as H's and all the finale E's like A. We did not expend any of the Commandery cash for this lesson in Spanish, and are therefore willing to impart it to others as freely as it was given to us.

Cowboys were as plentiful around La Junta as fleas on a dog, and much amusement was afforded our young lady travelers by the kite-shaped landscapes which were visible beneath them, owing to the excessive amount of horseback riding indulged in by the cowboys.

At 8.30 A. M. we had a fine view of the Spanish Peaks, together with the adjacent range of Rockies, upon which many patches of snow were still visible, in spite of the warmth of the midsummer sun. We also began to pass some adobe houses, built of sun-dried bricks, with which we were destined to become more familiar in the near future. Cattle were very numerous in this section, although we could not discern much sustenance for them. This was explained to us by showing us the bunches of mesquit grass which are interspersed through the sage brush. These tufts of grass are eagerly sought for and devoured by the cattle, which grow very fat from that food. Just beyond Coleridge we cross the boundary between Kansas and Colorado, and make our debut in the Centennial or Silver State.

Had we been on our way direct to Denver, we could have turned off at La Junta and reached Denver in a few hours ride, but many days were destined to elapse before we could get as near to our objective point as we were to-day. But we struck out to the Southwest, and at 10 A. M. reached Trinidad, Col., making quite a long stop at that point. Across a small river, just opposite our stopping-place, was a high, ragged looking rock called Simpson's Monument. It was so called because a Mr. Simpson, who was quoted as the founder of the city, was buried on top of it where he could have a good view of his handiwork when it became time for him to scratch out. His tomb of white stone of some kind was plainly visible from the station, from whence the camera fiends soon got a shot at it. They then took snaps at some of the Greasers or Mexicans who were lounging around, as well as a load of hay which had just come in with a team of oxen. An additional charm was lent to the picture when the girls climbed to the top of the load to be taken with it.

Trinidad is one of the bustling cities of Colorado. The mountains and canons around it are full of natural resources that are being rapidly developed, and will soon make the city a great manufacturing centre. The coal deposits

AN ADOBE HOUSE

are among the richest in the world, and only four miles away there are hundreds of coke-ovens in constant operation. Iron is found in unlimited quantities, as well as many other minerals. It is also an important wool market and shipping point for cattle and hides. Our view of it was limited, but we could see that it was well supplied with electric lights, street cars, and other modern improvements. It is elevated six thousand feet above the sea, and is said to have an exceptionally fine climate. We had left Kansas City at an elevation of 450 feet, and had risen constantly but gradually until we had attained to 6000 feet. Now we were going a little higher and going to be quicker about it, so they hooked on two powerful engines at this point to see that we succeeded in our efforts, and were supplied with two rations of cinders during the climbing operation.

Invitations were issued this morning to the ladies for a three o'clock tea in her stateroom by Mrs. Allen, and others to the gentlemen by Capt. Gen. Munch, for a "smoker" in the cats' car at the same hour.

It was only an additional sixteen hundred feet that we had to climb, but it might have been a little more if we had not dived into a tunnel at State Line and come out into the light at the other end in New Mexico. The view of the Spanish Peaks before going into the tunnel, which pierces the Raton mountains, was exceptionally fine. They are more regular in their proportions than any others around, rising gradually and regularly to a point, and justifying the old Indian name "twin breasts." At least that is the English of the Indian word, which we did not attempt to get our tongues around.

We got down to Raton at 11.20 A. M., and made another halt of fifteen minutes. A large brown bear, chained in the yard of a hotel in the station, gave the kodak carriers a chance to take a safe shot at a bear. They secured him in different positions; many more than they might have done had the bear been upon his native heath and unchained. We met here Dr. J. H. Franklin, a member of the Masonic Veteran Association, of Philadelphia, as we saw by the badge which he wore on his breast. He was glad to see several of his fellow-members so far from home, and blew them full, like so many of his migratory contemporaries, of the fact that he had now been domesticated here for several years and had found "the finest climate on earth."

At Raton are located the railroad car shops and round house, which are surrounded by quite a large town. There are also large coal mines near this point, and Colfax County is claimed to have located 800,000 acres of coal land. Gold, silver and copper are lying around in the vicinity, and may be had for the digging. Happening to speak here of Mr. Simpson as the founder of Trinidad, we were politely informed that it was a mistaken idea, as Trinidad was a Mexican settlement before Simpson's ancestors thought of migrating to the American shores.

Promptly at the appointed hour the ladies' tea and gents' smoker were inaugurated. Mrs. Allen was assisted in receiving her guests by Miss Haldeman and Miss Branson. The labor of waiting on the door was borne by two of the colored contingent from the dining car who were kindly loaned by Mr. Brooks. Such of the ladies as called without cards were politely but firmly refused admission by the guardians of the door until they had returned to their berths for the necessary pasteboard. The motion of the cars distributed the tea in about equal proportions, in the mouths and over the dresses of the participants, without distinction. Each of the ladies received a souvenir of the occasion.

Capt. Gen. Munch presided over the smoker. After having distributed among his guests a sufficient number of souvenir pipes and cigar-holders, together with an unlimited supply of tobacco and a white cap, he opened the ball with some happy introductory and congratulatory remarks. " Comrades" was then sung by George Kessler, the chorus being howled by all the rest of the smokers. A recitation by Milligan followed and was heartily applauded. The tree-trunk pipes, presented by Munch, had meanwhile pulled a number of teeth for the parties who let go of them in their enthusiasm, and were substituted by the cigar-holders. " My Maryland " was then sung by Register, and the chorus again rattled forth with a vim which drowned the noise of the train.

An interruption was caused at Las Vegas, by the arrival of a deputation from Las Vegas Commandery, No. 2, of New Mexico, headed by Sir Knight E. C. Forsythe, who also expressed their sorrow at our thoughtlessness in not allowing time at this point to have them show us some attention. Several of them promised to drive out to the Springs to-night and spend the evening with us.

Upon the resumption of the festivities of the smoker, McIntyre was persuaded to sing " The Bould McIntyre," in his own inimitable style. The clouds of smoke were getting too heavy for some of the non-smokers, and they were glad that the train rattled up to the Hot Springs as the song was finished. We were just one and a half hours ahead of time. A general break was made for the bath-houses, only to be subjected to a temporary but general disappointment. The proprietor or manager, in the face of his knowledge that we were to arrive, added to the fact that we bore the accumulations of four days travel, had allowed his stock of dry towels to run out. We were accordingly compelled to wait around and be photographed in various positions by Brown, Blackwood and Enochs, Jr., until the towels were dried. This did not consume much time and the party were soon accommodated with rooms and towels. Emmerling alone indulged in a mud bath, which proved of great benefit to him. He not only lost eleven pounds of his avoirdupois, but got rid of a game knee which had compelled him to use a cane for some time, but which he was able to discard from this time out. He had many callers after a bath of sufficient size had been found, and he had been immersed in the black, unctuous mud up to his neck. The numerous remarks fired at him kept him in a state of high glee. The mud shook as though a volcanic disturbance was going on beneath, but it was only the patient laughing.

The Hot Springs are about forty in number and range in temperature from 111° to 140° Fahrenheit. Their curative properties were known to the Mexicans and Indians many years before the government established an army hospital here nearly fifty years ago, and before the United States had acquired the territory on which it stood. They profess to cure most of the ills that human flesh is heir to, and probably do a great deal of good combined with the rarefied air of the elevated plateau of New Mexico and the breezes from the pine-clad mountains which surround the valley in which the springs are located.

An unlimited supply of the native burros was on hand at a stable close to the bath-houses, bearing both split and side saddles. The offers of the boys in charge to let you ride as long as you wished for twenty-five cents were freely accepted. The burro is a peculiar but patient animal, whose actions, upon this our first introduction to him, afforded us more amusement than anything we had yet struck. He was at home here in the land of his forefathers, and he accordingly did as he pleased. His huge ears are evidently not given him to hear with, but only by way of ornament, or a mark for his parents to recognize him by. This is evident by the manner in which he pays no attention to the commands, threats or objurgations of his rider. He moves not, except at his own sweet will, and sets his own pace, which is that of the snail. Some of the waiters from the car did succeed in getting up a race between them when headed for the stable, but the persuasive powers of a fence-rail could not hasten them an inch in the opposite direction. McIntyre's boy had a circus of his own for an hour with one mount, which could not be induced to pass the stable door by any earthly means. Milligan exhausted himself in the endeavor to get one out of a walk, first by sitting on his back and pounding him with his heels, then by getting ahead and pulling by the halter, and lastly, by boosting him in the rear. Being advised to pick him up and run with him, he declined and gave up his contract. A sharpened iron spike in the end of a stick is said to be the only means of waking up a burro, but even with that you must hunt all over him for a vulnerable spot.

The road from the baths up to the Montezuma Hotel is at an angle of about 40°, but some of those who walked up will be qualified that it is nearer 80°. Most took advantage of the stage which is constantly running and stops on the road at the bazaar of a sun-burned Sheenie, who poses as a Mexican, and keeps a curio shop. He will relieve you of your surplus cash in exchange for anything, from a string of Indian beads up to a Navajo blanket.

Our final destination was the Montezuma at which we were booked for dinner. The altitude of the Springs is seven thousand feet, and a seat on the hotel porch on this lovely summer afternoon was an enviable position, until the shades of evening had fallen, when it became entirely too cool to sit outside. The hotel is one of the large Western hostelries in which we are to be housed from time to time during our trip, and is reputed to be the best in the Rocky Mountains. It is certainly a fine stone building, elegantly finished, with appointments to correspond, and a most romantic location. The house, although on such high ground itself, is surrounded by still higher peaks on all sides but one. The one opening is the valley through which we made our entrance, and affords a magnificent view from the porch of the hotel, or better still from the observatory on top. Just before 6 P. M. Emmerling returned from his mud siesta and received a grand ovation, especially from his comrades in the Big Four combination, Henderson, Zeitz and Hemphill. Dinner was on the table directly after, and the entire party was able to do full justice to the meal, the more so as the long waits between the courses gave rise to many inquiries as to " whether anything had been heard about a coon falling dead in the kitchen." Fresh mountain trout was one of the attractions of the menu, and many of us looked for something outside of the small fry of the East. We were a little disappointed, however, as the reality put us in mind of an assertion we had often heard in regard to the Jersey mosquito, that "a good many of them would weigh a pound." The Pecos River, running through the Vegas to the left of the hotel, is claimed to be one of the best trouting streams in the country. We had no time to verify the assertion, although Millick's trunk was half full of trout lines, reels and flies.

The manager of the Montezuma, Mr. Clark D. Frost, kindly organized a hop for our benefit at 8 P. M., and furnished excellent music for the same. The dancing was enjoyed until a late hour, especially by Judge Milligan and Mrs. Branson. During a "hands around," Wells let go of Mrs. Branson's hand. The effect of this was to send that estimable lady flying through the bull fiddle of the orchestra, and exhibit the Judge in an entirely new act, that of standing on his neck. At another time the electric lights all went out, and it was whispered around for a time that "the rent of the hall was not paid." But it was only one of those periodical fits to which the electric is subject, and soon brightened up, when again all went " merry as a marriage bell." Munch, Kessler, Brown, Gorman, McIntyre, Schuehler, Spencer, Thomson, Cantlin, Sobernheimer, Bickel, Enochs and Shaw, testified by their agility on the floor, to the salubrious and enlivening effect of the hot baths.

About 10.30 P. M. the stage, whose trips were resumed for our benefit by the liberality of Mr. Frost, began to convey the pilgrims back to their quarters on the train. The cars had been backed so far down the glen that it was necessary for all to enter at the rear door and go through the cats' car. Several of the ladies started in ahead, but were scared out in quick time by an apparition, which, they said, looked like a gigantic white chicken. Upon investigation it was found to be only Pop Millick, in a brief night gown, standing in the aisle and leaning over into his berth. He was soon chased into bed and covered over, leaving the coast clear.

Some of the wakeful ones remained on the bridge over the Rio Gallinas, which ran along beside the track, until an early hour, singing the chorus and listening to some verses of Munch's composition to the tune of Ta-ra-ra-boom-de-aye. Each was appropriate to some event of the trip, and was sung upon the advent of the interested party into the glare of the electric light. The hits contained in the verses were received with every manifestation of delight. especially if they hit middling hard. We were very much under the impression that many of them had been toned down to a considerable extent when the song was added to the repertoire of the evening concerts. We found our berths made up to night with double courses of blankets, and were thankful enough therefor before morning.

Tuesday, July 19th, 1892.

HE train was supposed to leave the Springs at 2.25 A. M., and probably did so, but not many of us were cognizant of the fact. It should also have arrived at Santa Fé at 7.30 A. M., but did not reach that point until 8.15 A. M. From Las Vegas we had made another ascent, until we reached Glorieta, where our elevation was 7,500 feet. This is another pass through a spur of the Rockies, and the view of the mountains in the clear air of the early morning was a sight long to be remembered. At Lamy, the first station on the descending line, we entered upon a branch road for a trip of eighteen miles to Santa Fé. By the time we had reached that point breakfast was over, and we were ready to take immediate possession of the numerous coaches and carriages that had been secured by virtue of Milligan's negotiations.

The tour of the ancient city was then begun and proved fully as interesting as our anticipations had led us to expect. Santa Fé was one of the most unique spots we found on the whole tour. Its combination of ancient and modern buildings, adobe houses, old Spanish Mission, Mud Palace, with its rooms full of antiquities, the Plaza, the mixture of American and Mexican inhabitants, uniformed soldiers, curio stores and museums, the loitering and impassive burros looking still more diminutive under their loads of firewood and hay, the filagree jewelry manufacturers, all went to make up a picture the like of which we shall probably not see soon again, certainly not in as quick time as this was seen. The old Mission of San Miguel was the first objective point unto which the party streamed, after the usual donation of two bits. They overran the entire place, signed the register, tried the cabinet organ, tolled the old bell, examined the aged paintings over the altar, and invaded the precincts of the garden to talk with the priests who have charge of the church now. On either end of the ceiling of the church are the original oaken girders with their quaint carvings of a past age, while the centre has a comparatively new roof, the timbers in which are only one hundred and forty years old. The old bell stands down on the church floor, suspended by rawhide ropes in a frame of wood. The date A. D., 1356 is cast in its outside rim. The metal of the lower edge is about five inches thick, and the sound it gives forth is as clear and resonant as any of modern manufacture.

A number of adobe houses lie parallel with the old Mission walls, one of which is said to have been standing long before the church was built. It looked like it, and some of the Mexicans looked as though they might have been there still longer. A few of the dwellers in the adobe huts were churlish,

MUD PALACE

and drew the curtain of the little window when attempts were made to examine the interiors. Others, more liberal, invited the party inside and made a demand for ten cents each to let them out again. Outside the houses were a number of large, round brick ovens, used in a similar manner to our old Dutch ovens.

The bishop's ranch and residence, St. Michael's College, Academy, Cathedral of Santa Fé, St. Vincent's Asylum, and the fruit ranches surrounding the town were all interesting points. The curio shops, museums and jewelry stores all came in for a thorough investigation. J. Gold, with his curios, and the filagree manufacturer Spitz did a thriving business before the expedition brought up at the Governor's Palace. This building was erected in 1598, and has been since continuously occupied by Spanish, Pueblo, Mexican and American governors for almost 300 years. Two of its rooms are occupied by the Historical Society of New Mexico, and are filled to overflowing with relics, guarded by Governor Prince and his wife with zealous pride. In another room of the building the celebrated novel, "Ben Hur," was written by Gen. Lew. Wallace, while he was Governor of the Territory.

Purdy had telegraphed to the Governor before our arrival to know if he would receive the Commandery officially, and had received an answer in the affirmative. Our assemblage at the palace was in pursuance of that arrangement. The party was received in one of the large rooms by Governor and Mrs. L. Bradford Prince, and their niece, Miss Gilchrist, of Newark, N. J., who were assisted by Col. Pearson, the U. S. Commandant at the post here, and his charming wife. After all the pilgrims had been ranged in front of the receiving party, Governor Prince welcomed them in a speech in which he said :

Eminent Sir, Ladies and Gentlemen :—I am glad to extend to you a cordial welcome to our city and to New Mexico. This city should be peculiarly interesting to your party, because it is what I call a city of the Holy Faith. You will see here many evidences of the faith of those who were the first discoverers and settlers of the country. This room may be considered the historic room of the United States, as well as the building which contains it. You will also find, throughout New Mexico, interesting matters reminding you of the Holy Land, so much sought after by the Templars of olden times. You will find the same one and two storied buildings, built of the adobe or sun-dried bricks; the same threshing floors of earth, used now by the Pueblo Indians, that were used in the Holy Land. You will see, as mentioned in the Scriptures, the two women grinding at the mill, where one was taken and the other left, and the same old hand mills that were used at that time. Many other interesting reminders will also present themselves to your gaze. We welcome you as Templars and friends. The members of the Commandery at this place will endeavor to make your visit pleasant and agreeable. We also welcome you as citizens of Philadelphia, that City of Brotherly Love, of which we have heard so much. I saw but a short time ago that Philadelphia was settled in 1682, so this building was one hundred years old at that time. That was the year of the revolution of the Pueblos against Spanish rule at this place. I repeat that we are glad to see you as representatives from that part of our country. I have a map there on the window sill, which you can examine later on, upon which I could not find the location of Philadelphia, but we have heard much of you and the prosperity of your city. The map was printed, as you will see, in Boston. Boston is located upon it, but there is no Philadelphia. We have here some printed programs or lists of places in our neighborhood which we consider would be interesting to visit, if you have time to do so. They are forty-two in number, and we think if you saw forty-one of them, there would still be one point at which you could be sure that you had missed something. Here is also a pamphlet in which we endeavor to prove to you that the Rio Grande Valley was the original location of the Garden of Eden, and that Santa Fé was the central point of that delightful spot. I also desire to call your attention to the relics contained in this and the adjoining room, and hope that you will take time to examine them at your leisure. Again I extend you a cordial welcome to New Mexico and Santa Fé, and reiterate the hope that our people will make your visit a pleasant one.

Capt. Gen. Munch responded in fitting terms and introduced each individual member of the party, after which Mrs. Prince and her friends took great pleasure in explaining the history of some of the innumerable objects of vertu in the two rooms. They were not confined to relics of this section of the country, but were connected with history running back to mediæval Europe.

MEXICAN CRONES

The list handed us by the Governor of " what we could do in and around Santa Fé" would have consumed our entire holiday if carried out, and we were obliged to take the larger part of its assertions on faith. The cameras were in very active service during our short stay, and will doubtless turn out many interesting fac-similes of the places seen and explored. We noticed over one or two of the doorways of Mexican dwellings the emblem which denoted that death had been an unwelcome visitor. This consisted of two strips of some black and white stuffs intertwined and festooned over the door. This is, of course, similar to our emblems of crape, but is not removed after a funeral, being left to rot away in the weather. This is considered a safe-guard for the soul of the deceased from evil spirits. Col. Pearson had ordered the Tenth Infantry Band of the garrison to be stationed on the Plaza in front of the palace for our entertainment. and they gave us a serenade after the delivery of the speeches. The Plaza contains a soldier's monument, and there is one in another section of the city to the memory of Kit Carson, the celebrated scout. Eminent Commander W. S. Harroun, M. D., and Sirs Knaebel, Matthews, Cart, Berger, Robinson and Gildersleeve, of Santa Fé Commandery No. 1, were on hand during our stay and did all they could to make our visit agreeable. Sir Jack Frost, the lively editor of the Santa Fé *New Mexican* was also extremely solicitous that we should find the city all that we had heard claimed for it.

By 12.15 P. M. we were compelled to take leave of our hosts, with many thanks for their hospitalities and make our way back to the train. Crouching on the platform at the station were a couple of ancient Mexican crones, with their hands extended for the reception of stray dimes. One of them was said to be one hundred and ten years old, while the other was a giddy young damsel of not more than ninety or thereabouts. The skin of the elder was wrinkled and tanned until she looked more like a wild beast than anything human, but her hair was still abundant and as black as coal. We are glad to be able to state that they reaped a harvest that will make them comfortable for some time, unless they blow it in for some new clothes, of which they stood sadly in need. At 12.30 P. M., just as we were all safely housed in the train, a sudden shower of rain came down. This was something new for us, being the first we had seen since leaving Pittsburg, except about ten drops at the Hot Springs, although the signs of it had been visible all through the trip. We had found the dust thoroughly laid for us all the way out and were duly thankful therefor. Gorman had returned to the city for some order of filagree work and had not yet returned when the time came to leave. The whistle was blown several times for him and he drove up with the last blast. We were off at once and commenced climbing up grade again.

Our shower of rain lasted but a few minutes, but thunder storms were visible up in the mountains on each side of us. The usual water-courses down from the mountain sides were now raging torrents which cut and washed the sandy banks away like sugar. They were emptied as fast as they filled, as was evidenced by the appearance of some of the gullies where the storm had already passed. Jack-rabbits were again abundant, skipping out on either side of the track when scared up by the noise of the engine. A large wolf was espied in the brush as we passed.   He trotted leisurely ahead, glancing over his shoulder at the train, and did not appear in any hurry to get out of our road.

A short stop was made at Los Cerrilos.   We were surprised to learn that a large field of anthracite coal had been discovered here, and was now being worked for coal that would compare favorably in quality with any from our

INDIAN WOMEN

own state.   We ran across our first squaw here and bought up her stock in trade of specimens of turquois.   Inquiries in regard to her rings, necklace, shawls and other gewgaws, developed the fact that she was willing to sell anything or everything she had on.   At Wallace, at 3.20 P. M., we struck another crowd of Pueblos, of both sexes and all ages, from an adjacent village, who were also on the trade.   Topaz, turquois and Indian pottery comprised their stock, although some of the party bought their silver rings and necklaces of beads of Indian manufacture. One of the Indians was much interested in the size of Emmerling's stomach, and anxious to know if it contained one pappoose or two. Soon after starting again from Wallace we passed a large pueblo or village, upon the roof of one of whose houses were a number of small Indian children, confined by a fence at the edges, while the parents were at work in the fields. In fact, there was now a quick succession of Indian villages and towns, surrounded by fields in a very high state of cultivation, all watered by irrigating canals led in from the Rio Grande River, along whose bank we were now running. Greats herds of cattle, horses, sheep and goats were very frequent sights, all being the property of the Pueblo Indians. The wheat was ripe and the owners were busily engaged in harvesting it with the sickle, one of the last relics of a primitive age. The operation of threshing was also going on at one place on a hard earthen floor, by men armed with the old-fashioned flail. These instances were corroborative to some extent of the remarks made to us by Governor Prince.

A beautiful little antelope, lying dead beside the track, had evidently been struck by a train but a short time previous to our passing it. All the houses of the Pueblos were built of the adobe bricks, and were only one story in height. At Bernalillo, which we passed at 4 P. M., the collection of houses looked as though they might have been transplanted about the same time as the Mud Palace at Santa Fé, and been asleep ever since. It was hard to tell whether the inhabitants were Indians or Mexicans.

Albuquerque was reached at 4.20 P. M. Getting in ahead of time gave us a few minutes to stroll into the new town and look up souvenir spoons. The old town of Albuquerque is some two centuries of age, and lies to the westward of the new town, which was only laid out in 1880. The population in that year was 125. By a census taken last summer it had reached 10,000. The town has now a pushing, thriving appearance and many more substantial-looking blocks of stone buildings than would usually appertain to a place of that size. It is the chief wool market of the territory, and an enormous crop of that staple is handled every year, nearly eight millions of pounds being shipped from this point during last year. The Atlantic and Pacific Railroad, upon whose line we enter shortly after leaving here, maintains large shops and a hospital at this place. The government supports an Indian school, and there are fine church buildings for every denomination except the Baptists. By the kindness of Mr. C. D. Pitts, city editor of the *Morning Democrat*, we were furnished with the above statistics, together with a volume containing fine phototypes of the prominent buildings and residences. The information, of course, applies to the new town exclusively, the old town being one of the oldest in the territory and distinctively Mexican in its character. The Sandia Mountains to the northeast of the town and ranging along the road we had just come, make a picturesque back-ground to the scenery, and were just now the scene of a continuation of the thunder showers we had left behind us, if the black clouds rolling around their tops was any indication.

We were off again at 5 P. M. and struck out to the westward. Thirteen miles out we passed through the large Indian village of Isleta, belonging still to the Pueblos, containing all the signs of thrift that the residences of that people had shown along the Rio Grande, together with the same sawed off and hammered down specimens of humanity. We passed through Rio Puerco at 6.40 P. M. All along the tracks this afternoon were scattered the carcasses of cattle which had been struck and killed by trains, and our whistle was heard very often in its efforts to scare living steers from the same fate.

Having again picked up some time, a stop of twenty minutes was made at the large Indian village of Laguna, about sixty miles out from Albuquerque. It was nearly dusk when we reached it, but a brisk barter in beads, rings and pottery throve as long as we could see. The entire population of the village was out as was also that of the train, and it was no easy matter to separate them and get our complement on the train when our whistle sounded.

The concert in the smoking car to-night was well attended, and kept up until after 10 P. M., the night being cool and the weather fair. The ladies in attendance on the concert, in a little while monopolized the instruments, and soon became greater adepts in their use than the men.

While we were stopped at Laguna, our baggage-master, Howard Speakman, gathered and divided among us some specimens of a fine red and white variegated stone which he claimed was petrified wood. It has more the appearance of a fine porphyry.

Wednesday, July 20th, 1892.

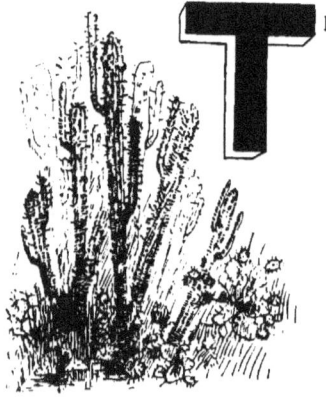

THE dividing line between New Mexico and Arizona was crossed about the middle watch of the night, when no one was watching except the train crew. The first intimation of the dawn that most of us received that we were in the new territory, was when the train was halted on the centre of the bridge over the Canon Diablo, to give us a view of that great work of nature. The Canon is an immense zig-zag break in the yellow limestone, reaching as far as we could see in either direction. The bottom was 225 feet below the railroad bridge, which is over five hundred feet long. The deep chasm is enclosed on either side by mighty buttressed rocks of a deep yellow color, which were carved into grotesque shapes of all kinds, evidently by the action of swirling waters in some very remote age. The Canon is said to have remains of the habitations of the ancient cliff or dwellers of this portion of the country, but this we had not time to investigate. The train was held on the bridge for twenty minutes to give all who were awake a good view up and down the Canon, when we again sped away Westward.

The weather this morning was fine, with a cool, crisp air, which had a bracing and appetizing effect, which put Brooks in a good humor with the party, although he was never seen in a bad one. Rain had still been beforehand with us and there was no dust. We had ascended from Albuquerque over two thousand feet higher than that point in the night to the point where we crossed the Continental Divide, and had come down again about the same distance, just east of the Canon Diablo. Now we were climbing again toward Flagstaff, which is nearly seven thousand feet above sea level. From that station we shall descend pretty steadily to the Needles, and will not rise nearly as high again between there and the Pacific Coast.

The San Francisco Mountains, with several lofty peaks among them, have been in plain view all the morning, on which snow is again evident. To the right of them is a range known as the Coconino Mountains, which have extinct volcanoes among them, and whose canons also contain many relics of the cliff-dwellers, as well as the still earlier cave-dwellers. A fine growth of timber occupied the lands on each side of us this morning, until we reached Flagstaff, at 7.50 A. M. A large sawmill at that point was busily engaged in converting some of the timber into marketable sizes.

Invitations were issued this morning, by Miss Sadie Branson and Miss Bertha Graham, to a progressive euchre party in the dining car this afternoon.

We arrived at Williams Station at 9.10 A. M., and made a stop of forty minutes, during which the train was iced up and watered. Several single peaks of considerable height appeared to be in quite close proximity to us here. The nearest of these was Bill Williams Mountain. Bill was presumably one of the early settlers of this region, whose name is thought worthy of being perpetuated. A buck Indian had a young fawn for sale cheap at five dollars, but no customers could be found for any live stock. Many of the ladies would have liked to own the little spotted pet, but could not carry it through to the Pacific and back again.

When we left Williams', at 9.50 A. M., we had a descent of 1,600 feet to make in the next few miles. The railroad managed to overcome it by means of a couple of dozen grapevine twists, and landed us safely in the bottom lands.

The thermometer in the smoker marked 66° at Flagstaff. From here we began to go down into the valley at a very sudden rate, and were not long in finding warmer air. On the way we passed through a rocky pass known as Johnson's Canon. A dark looking hole on the right of the track was said to be unfathomable. It was called the Bottomless Pit, and will probably be utilized at some future day by one of these Western railroads as an air-line to China, when the people get reconciled to and wish to import more Chinese.

At 10.40 P. M. we struck the desert again, with its monotonous growth of sage-brush, greaseweed, sand and conglomerate. The mountain ranges in the back-ground, along which we ran all day, were the only relief to the landscape, except the prairie dog hills along the track and scattered through the brush. Letter writing and card playing were exertions sufficient to occupy the travellers' time this morning. It had been a matter of education to learn to write while the train was in motion, so that the words would be intelligible to others than the writer. When we first started writing it was only possible when the motion of the train had ceased. Then the writing tables were full of industrious scribblers. But we gradually got to learn that by holding the manuscript on a book or card in the hand, clear of any other support, it was possible to write fairly well. We left Peach Springs at 12.05 P. M. The sun was now blazing hot and the mercury in the smoker marked 95°. Still no one seemed to suffer with the heat, because there was no humidity in the atmosphere and no perspiration on the part of the traveller. It was worst in the dining car at luncheon time, because we were stirring up our first taste of dust, and were unable to raise the window sash. A short halt was made at Hackberry, at 1.55 P. M. There were numerous Indians about the station, and Blackwood started for them with the kodak. A squaw who struck his fancy saw the camera pointed at her and started to run with Blackwood in pursuit. On the second lap around the station building she found the photographer gaining upon her, and made a dive under the station platform, from which refuge no amount of persuasion could dislodge her to have her picture taken.

The progressive euchre party went into blast at 2.30 P. M. and continued all the afternoon. The air outside the car windows was like that from a furnace, but the heat was not sufficiently felt inside to drive any of the players from the game.

The mountain ranges to the north of us this afternoon were those enclosing the Grand Canon of the Colorado. At Peach Springs we were only distant from them twenty-five miles, but, being a warm afternoon, it was, thought best not to stop the train until we walked over and took a view. The walls of the Marble Canon, the deepest portion of the Grand Canon, are over 6,500 feet in height.

We crossed the Colorado river and entered Colorado at the Needles, at 4.30 P. M. These are three tall columns, apparently of a red sandstone, standing upon the California side of the river and looking, at some little distance, like a stone gateway, but the road passes to the right of them with a very sharp turn, and runs along the river bank. The Colorado at this point is a wild and turbulent stream, or had been made so by recent rains. The track crossed on a fine iron bridge, eighty-five feet above the water, and with a single span of 660 feet.

At 4.40 P. M. we pulled up at Needles station. Many Indians were congregated at the station. Not the staid and hard-working Pueblos of the Rio Grande Valley, but Mojaves from the reservation near at hand of that nation, gaudy in paint, blankets and long hair, with an occasional plug hat as a covering. Gay squaws, in green shawls and red petticoats, with beaded moccasins lent color to the scene. But all of them seemed to have an unconquerable aversion to the cameras levelled at them, and their counterfeit presentments were only secured by stratagem. The Big Four combination tried hard to get up flirtations with the dusky daughters of the reservation, but the time was evidently too short for their fascinations to take effect. The thermometer at this station stood at 108° in the shade, and we were comforted by the remark of some of the inhabitants that this was rather a cool day for them, the mercury having a habit of climbing up to 120° when it took a notion. They told us a yarn there about a U. S. soldier who had been stationed here for some years and had died. He went duly to his appointed berth in Hades, but as we were informed by apparently reliable witnesses, came back in a couple of days for his blankets, having found the climate too chilly for him. The only thing to cast a doubt upon the reliability of this story, in our minds, was the extreme improbability of anybody wanting to come back to the Needles for any consideration, after having once got away. We got acquainted here with an old

Chinese doctor, Wee Ching by name, but Anglicized into Willie Ching. He was no particular lover of the Indians, but said he doctored Americans, Indians, Chinese, Mexicans, railroad men, horses, dogs, cats and pigs, with strict impartiality. He was a jovial old soul, and wide awake, in spite of his half-sleepy eyes.

A quiet remark from one tough-looking animal, leaning against the garden fence at the station, to an equally hard specimen of his confreres, had a disquieting effect on some of his hearers. He merely wondered how the party would feel if that train were held up in the cut below and some of them relieved of "them diamonds they had on." Either of the speakers looked fully equal to the part of taking a hand in the hold-up.

At the Needles we had come down to less than 500 feet elevation, having descended more than six thousand feet between Flagstaff and the Needles. At Goff's, less than thirty miles further on, we had added another two thousand feet to our height, and found it much cooler, being obliged to sleep under the the blanket as usual. The euchre players kept on the even tenor of their way, finished their games, and distributed their prizes in time to be out of Brooks' way in time for dinner. The first prizes fell to the lot of Register and Mrs. Blackwood, while the seconds were awarded to Brooks and Mrs. Johnson. After dinner, while resting from the arduous labor of disposing of that meal, we were treated to some gorgeous effects in a view of the sun as it disappeared behind a mass of clouds and the mountain range at the same time. The varied colors and changes were indescribable, and were watched with intense interest by all. We were crossing a section of the great Mojave Desert, which upsets all our preconceived notions about deserts. The luxuriant growth of a species of cactus, called the Yucca Palm, has been a surprise to us all. Many of the specimens are from eight to ten feet in height, with curiously distorted branches, full of bright yellow flowers. All around the base of them is the sage brush, with many varieties of smaller cacti interspersed through it, many of which also bear colored flowers. So that the desert is really a curious garden to the Eastern traveller.

At 9 P. M., the usual concert was inaugurated in the smoker, and enlivened by songs and recitations from Munch, Gorman, Milligan, Cantlin, Hemphill and John Robbins. Munch sang the new version of Ta-ra-ra-boom, to which he added verses each day, as occasion afforded. The Ladies' Kazoo Band contributed its full share to the merriment of the evening, and was only deterred from further efforts and the performers forced to fly, at a late hour, by the breaking of several little glass bombs. The effect of these was first taken cognizance of by young McIntyre, who, in an excited voice, exclaimed to his father, "My pop! do you smell?" It was time to seek rest and it was sought to a great extent.

Thursday, July 21st, 1892.

AN BERNARDINO, CAL., was our first stop at 7 A. M. The railroad running time had changed at Barstow at midnight to Pacific time, giving us an additonal hour's sleep. Harmon Johnson is said to have used up his extra hour and celebrated the event by having a Knights Templar parade of his own around Barstow in his night garb as a pilgrim penitent. We give the report for what it is worth, the parade having had few spectators. Although the air was so hot through the desert yesterday afternoon, the blanket was very acceptable by bed-time and the air this morning was a delightful contrast to that of yesterday afternoon, the mercury in the smoker standing at 68 degrees.

Our train had been climbing the eastern slope of the San Bernardino Mountains this morning early, looking backward at the sage-brush and the cacti of the Mojave desert. Just before our advent into San Bernardino we had attained the summit of 4000 ft., and emerging from the Cajon Pass, had opened our eyes at the transition to an entirely different country. Orange groves, vineyards, fruits and flowers make the valley spread before us a bright green spotted carpet and a relief to the eyes. The dark foliage of the orange groves in particular has a cool and inviting appearance and our car windows are crowded by eager admirers. The grape vines running over the ground and lying so close to it are first taken for sweet potato vines and we can hardly be convinced that we are wrong.

Across the valley from San Bernardino Station was visible in the bright morning sun, on the side of one of the mountains, a large arrow head as perfectly formed as if cut by hand, and extending in actual length a quarter of a mile. The mountain side was seven miles away but the arrow head was plainly visible as if just across the street. The valley is said to have been first settled by Mormon emigrants who had been sent out by Brigham Young with directions to travel in this direction until they should see this Heaven sent sign. He told them the location would be a fruitful valley, designed especially for their use and such they found it or made it by their labors. An empty baggage truck at the station was utilized to give Emmerling an appetite for his breakfast by an early morning ride after the close confinement of the previous day.

We passed through Riverside at 7.45 A. M., and the glimpse we got of its orange groves, irrigating canals and the flowers planted along the curbs outside of its footwalks gave promise of future delights on the occasion of our later stop at this place.

We had now reached the country where the alfalfa grass takes the place of our grass for feeding four-footed stock of all kinds. This is a species of clover

ROSE EUSH RIVERSIDE

and grows very heavy. It is claimed to take root from eight to ten feet deep and the crop is a continuous one in this section, averaging five crops in a year. It is possible that the roots are fully of the length reported as the virgin soil in Southern California is of wonderful depth. In the gulches and cuts made by water courses in the rainy season it is visible to a distance of from twenty to thirty feet, offering quite a contrast to our own State where as many inches make a first-class farm.

Mountains were in sight all along our left and, back by the pass through which we had gained the valley, "Old Baldy," with patches of snow was standing guard over the entrance. We passed through Santa Ana at 9.05 A. M.

Fruit drying was in full progress at and near this town. The ground was covered with wooden frames or racks full of halved fruit drying in the sun. We at first took them for yellow peaches but found later on that they were apricots. Improvised camps built of small tree trunks, covered with boughs and foliage were set up in each orchard. Under this shelter small regiments of men, women and children were busily engaged in preparing the fruit, only pausing in their work long enough to give us a salute or wave of the hand as we passed.

About this time one of the new California brakemen, that we had taken on at San Bernardino, got pretty hot under the collar because one of our red fire cigars shot out its refulgent rays while in his mouth and nearly startled him into falling out the baggage car door. But we are getting used to such scenes now and soon had him cooled down again.

At 9.40 A. M. we passed the ancient Franciscan Mission of San Juan de Capistrano or St. John Beheaded. It was founded by Father Serra, the leader of the Franciscan Missionaries in 1776. It is apparently in a ruinous condition now so far as we could see, the roof being off and a portion of the walls having fallen in. Our road ran now for a long distance between immense cattle ranches on either side of the track, some of which feed from 30,000 to 40,000 head of stock. Along each side of the railroad, about twenty feet distant from the road bed was a ploughed strip of ground eight or ten feet in width. This followed the track up hill and down or across the level and was a mystery to us. Bright green patches springing up here and there in it led us to believe that something was planted in it. Inquiry developed the fact that the ploughed strip was only a fire guard to prevent fires which might arise from sparks along the track from spreading into the grass of the ranges. The green patches were wild mustard which springs up everywhere and cannot be got rid of.

At 10 A. M. we got our first view of the Pacific Ocean and gave it an enthusiastic reception. Our ride for the remainder of this day ran along its shores, being only occasionally shut off from it by a cut through the hills. Many wild flowers grew along the tracks, which were eagerly gathered whenever it was necessary for stops to be made. One in particular, which was a general favorite, looked like an ice plant and its red berries and stem were covered with what looked like little dew drops which glistened in the morning sun like diamond points. We tried to preserve some of its branches but they soon withered. Several groups of rocks out in the ocean, were passed on which seals were congregated and could be seen sunning themselves. Some of the rocks were snow white with the guano of the innumerable birds which made them a resting place.

It had been intended to leave our train at San Diego and cross on the ferry boat to Coronado Beach. This programme was changed when San Diego was reached, for the worse as it turned out, and the train ran over the Coronado Beach Railroad direct to the hotel. The engine which undertook the contract to pull us around there was spavined, ringboned and had a bad case of asthma. She would snort, puff and wheeze on a dead level and a little rise in the grade would bring her to a standstill until more water was boiled and a fresh start taken. Along the meadows large salt works were in operation, making that necessary of life by the process of evaporation. Many wild flowers grew in the sand along the beach track together with curious cacti of different shapes. Some of them ran along the sand like vines to a great length, taking root every few inches.

All good things in this world come finally to an end as did our ride at 1.30 P. M. We were four and a half hours behind time, of which three had been consumed in making the twenty-four miles necessary to get around the curve of the beach. Purdy had secured our room cards at San Diego and distributed them among us, so that we were soon domiciled at the hotel and our baggage brought to us.

The Coronado is one of the grand Pacific coast hotels and its appearance more striking than any of the others from the great difference in its style of architecture. It is built right down to an asphalt and board walk which marks the high water limit of the Pacific, whose ceaseless surf thunders day and night in the waking ears of the occupants of the house. Its rooms are said to number 750, but no one undertook to count them as the opportunities for being lost in the act were numberless. The porches on the ocean side for three floors were enclosed with sash which could be opened at will, giving unlimited chances for sun-baths or moonlight promenades. There is a large circular room for theatrical or concert performances with a large stage and a conical vaulted ceiling over the whole running up three stories. The theatre also faces the ocean and is used as a ball-room. The parlors and sitting rooms are numerous and elegant in their appointments.

The inner court yard is a scene of tropical beauty and a joy to the lover of floriculture. It was studded with palms, cacti, lemon, orange and banana trees, while the flowers of the temperate zones were cultivated to such a size as to stagger belief. There are rose geraniums twenty feet high with stems as thick as a good sized tree. Heliotropes from ten to twelve feet high with a mass of foliage and bloom that would fill an ordinary room. Passion vines that extend over a distance of 150 feet and up to the third floor, bearing flowers and blossoms in hundreds. In the central plat of tropical plants a covey of quail have been domesticated and at this time had young ones which scuttled through the grass like animated little balls of yellow yarn. The grounds on the outside of the house also contain many curious plants and trees and are kept in excellent condition, although still unfinished on one side of the house. Banana, pomegranate, date and fig trees flourish, and a walk around the entire circumference of the house makes a good constitutional before breakfast. A Mary badge reached the soft spot in the heart of the old German gardener so that he could not do too much for the ladies of our party. He robbed his rose bushes

GARDEN IN CORONADO

and lemon trees and gave us many specimens of a curious flower which he called the Dutchman's pipe. It not only represented perfectly the pipe and stem but had a perfect tobacco pouch depending from it which could be opened.

Luncheon was awaiting our arrival and we only stopped long enough for a wash-up before enjoying it. Afterward strolls through the gardens and grounds of the hotel were in order until a later hour when most of the party gravitated to the warm salt water bathing pool. This was built on the beach front several hundred yards below the hotel and you could bathe in it or take to the surf or change from one to the other as you saw fit. Those who tried the ocean did not stay long as they found the air very chilly. There were several in the party who had taken in Atlantic City on the Sunday before our start and now took a dip here, so that they had bathed in the Atlantic and Pacific Oceans inside of the two weeks. The centre of attraction in the pool was a toboggan slide which was there erected. This was at least twenty feet high and set at an angle of about 70°, curving out at the bottom onto a horizontal plane. The slide and its raised edges of about six inches were covered smoothly with sheet copper and two small jets of water kept running down it at the top. It was only necessary to walk up the stairs, throw your legs over the top and let go, to feel your "innards" come up in your neck, but you hardly had time to feel them before you were shot out horizontally into the deep water where you made a prodigious hole and splash. This was a new racket and the opportunity was eagerly embraced by all the men and some of the girls to enjoy a fresh sensation. The fun was fast and furious for a couple of hours and was added to by a floating cask with a horse's head attached, which everybody made attempts to ride. If you succeeded in getting it balanced finally, you were kindly assisted over its head and ducked. The water was kept at such a temperature that your stay might be indefinitely prolonged without any bad results.

A museum building between the hotel and the bathing pool, filled with curiosities consisting largely of fossil remains, served to while away some little time. A maze or labyrinth over on the other side, near the station of the steam road which ran to the San Diego ferry, was also extensively patronized. It was formed of evergreen hedges, the devious paths by which the centre was reached were difficult to follow and the road out was still harder to find. Robinson went in with a party and thought he had solved the problem when he took a newspaper along and dropped a small piece at each turn of the road. But some one behind him picked up all his land-marks and they all broke through the bushes as the shortest cut to the outside.

Some of our pilgrims made trips to San Diego during the afternoon and evening. A narrow gauge steam road runs from the hotel station to the upper end of the beach, whence large ferry boats cross over to San Diego. There is quite a town on the beach through which the railroad runs, with some substantial residences, any number of fine gardens and all the streets lined with shade trees. It has also several hotels in addition to the Coronado, electric lights

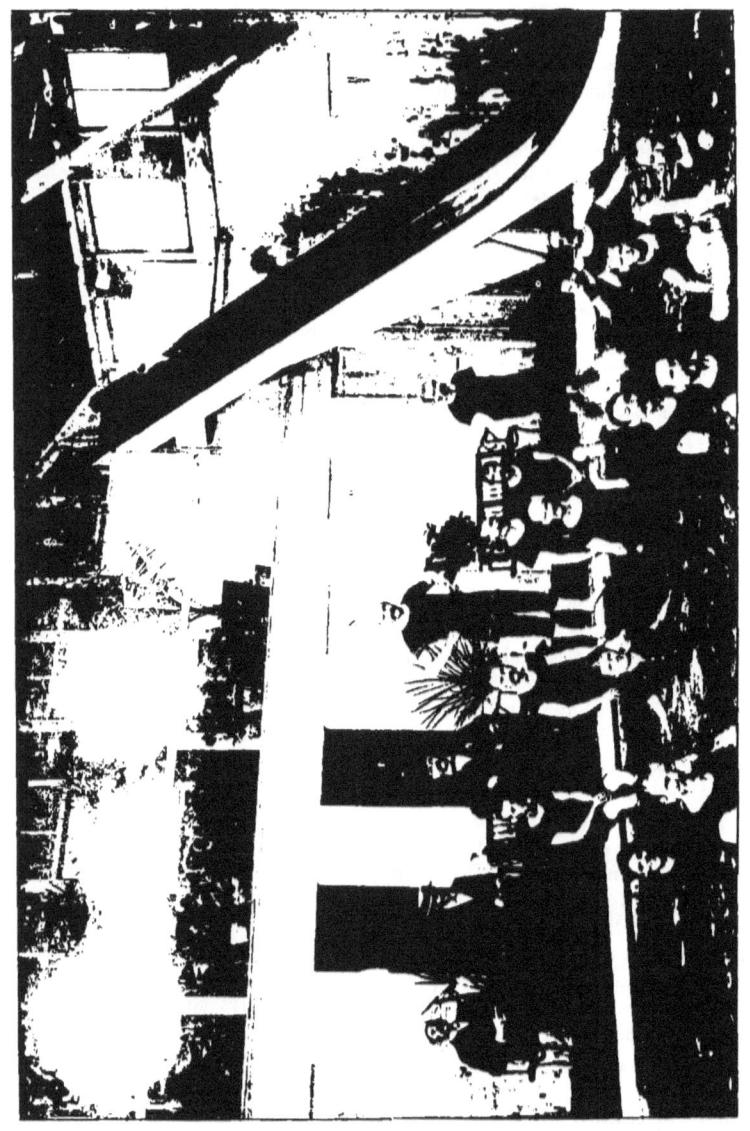

SWIMMING POOL

and a water system, with a number of factories and an extensive dry-dock. All this where four or five years ago there was a sandy waste. The Bay of San Diego is one of the largest and finest harbors in the world. It is thirteen miles long and almost entirely land-locked, affording room and safe anchorage for the navies of the world without having had a dollar of Government funds spent upon it.

San Diego, like most of the older settlements in California, has its old and new towns. The old town is a relic of the Spanish and Mexican rule and has its plaza and rows of adobe houses with a few of modern construction. The adobe is a brick of about twice the size of one our own made of the adobe clay, which is very tenacious, and baked in the sun. The walls of these houses are from two to three feet thick, laid in mud and plastered over on both sides with the same useful material. Some of them have been modernized, covered with cement and topped out with ornamental wood work, making a neat and substantial house. The thickness of the walls of the old adobes keeps out dampness as well as heat and allows for the ravages of time. The roofs are put on horizontal timbers, with several wooden spouts inserted to carry off water. These project out over the sidewalk and apparently make walking in the street a necessity when it rains hard. The roofs are sometimes of clay like the walls, sometimes thatched and often of tiles, the latter being hollow and laid in the first course with the hollow side up and the second course straddling them with the round side up.

The new town or city of San Diego is a thriving and bustling city of modern appearance. It has large business blocks, broad thoroughfares, horse, cable, and electric street cars, a goodly fleet of shipping at its wharves and every sign of business prosperity. It owes its sudden rise to the finishing of the Santa Fé Railroad system over which we have come and from a population in 1885 of four thousand has jumped in seven years to one of over thirty thousand. It slopes gradually upward from the shore of the bay and makes a very pretty appearance as you come over in the ferry boat from Coronado. The great land boom, which all Southern California cities seem destined to pass through at some period of their existence, has been on hand here, and the bottom thereof having fallen out as usual, the city has been left on a solid and real basis.

We led a quiet life around the hotel during the evening. It was too cool to sit outside without warmer clothing than we had been wearing and too much trouble to hunt out heavier ones. Sir Knights Morgan, Powers and Jackson, of San Diego Commandery No. 25, called at the Coronado after dinner, and spent the evening in efforts to assist the boys to pass away the time. The ten-pin alleys were assailed, and no boys being on hand to "set-em-up," the party took turns at either end of the alleys. Munch, Kessler and Schuehler soon showed the fruits of their Mænnerchor training, and forced their competitors, including our visitors, to acknowledge that they were not in it. Lafferty put up a fair game, but Millick, Dill, Sheeler, Phillips, Hemphill, Zeitz and Sam Thomson were simply "rotten." When they got tired of setting them up and knocking them down again, the pool tables became the centre of attraction for some hours later. Many of the ladies joined in this game as they did in everything else that went on while they were around. The evening hop which had been going on in the theatre ball-room had attracted them, and some few of the men for a time, but the majority of the men-folks claimed to be too tired to dance, and so went to rolling ten-pins.

The first really good opportunity to write home was taken advantage of in the hotel writing-room by many of the party. A glance outside at the moonlight playing on the waves of the Pacific, and a glimpse of the revolving light on Point Loma, five hundred feet above the ocean, and we were ready to try the luxury of a soft bed for the first time for a week. Sleep came easily after the labors of the day, and was unbroken even by the pounding of the surf on the beach.

Friday, July 22d, 1892.

LATE rising was the general rule this morning, some of the worst of the sinners getting down nearly late enough to get shut out from breakfast. An iron pier in front of the museum, of which the outer half had fallen down, contained a solitary fisherman. The early risers naturally drifted in his direction to investigate the size of his catch. He was only after his breakfast, and when he had captured a couple of good king-fish, he rolled up his line and departed. Our visitors of last evening had suggested to us a trip into Old Mexico, which could be reached by a railroad trip of nineteen miles. Arrangements had accordingly been made with agent of the Coronado Beach Railroad to run two special cars for us to National City, and attach them to the regular train that ran down to the Mexican village of Tiajuana, as we understood.

After breakfast there was little straying beyond the hotel grounds until 10 A. M., the hour that had been set for the departure of our train. Then there was a gathering of the clans, with the exceptions only of Mrs. Fairlamb and Miss Haldeman, who were to spend the day with friends in San Diego, into two roomy cars, and our special sped around the sandy spit to National City, into which we pulled at 11 A. M., and were switched onto the regular train at once.

This is a sort of suburb of San Diego, at which the California Pacific has located its shops. It seemed to be a town of considerable size and energy, with a number of manufacturing plants located within its limits. An olive oil mill has been established here, furnishing a market for olives grown in the lower counties of the state. The railroad to Mexico did not pay much attention to grade levels, but followed the wagon road up hill and down as it happened to go, and did not stick at any rise, however steep. It passed through a highly cultivated section of country, which, we were informed had been opened up within the last four years only, and owed its fine appearance to the introduction of irrigation. The groves of fruit trees already bearing, of which a great number were olives, were a matter of wonder when the time was taken into consideration.

Our programme at first included a visit to the Sweetwater Dam, wherein is confined the water that supplies the irrigating canals, as well as the water system of National City, but want of time and the fear of losing our luncheon made us cut it off. It is esteemed a great piece of engineering, and would probably have been more interesting to us than Tiajuana. But we wanted to be able to say that we had been in Mexico, and Tiajuana carried the day. When we reached the end of the road we found that we had a half-mile still to go to reach the village, and the route was through as fine a bed of Jersey sand as ever a mosquito flew over. Carriages were found sufficient to accommodate the ladies, and a portion of the men, but the balance had to foot it. Billy Dill was sorry he did not walk in the first place, as the team that was drawing him did not go far until one of them balked and kicked him over the side of the wagon, tearing the whole bosom out of his pants and straining his back badly.

At the village the first onslaught was made on the Custom House. Here the inspector in charge was kept busy stamping his official seal on the backs of cards and the corners of handkerchiefs. From there the crowd drifted into the Post Office, and bought the office out of two-cent postal cards, at the rate of two for a nickel. These were hastily written upon, directed to our homes, and mailed from the Mexican Post Office. Neddy McDowell stood his silk umbrella against the table on which he was directing his postal, and when he picked it up again it was not there. Some Greaser had fallen in love with and appropriated it. As soon as Ned reached home he started in to learn enough Spanish to do justice to his feelings when he meets that Greaser again. The latter gentry were a tough and surly looking lot as they stood around the doors of the stores and saloons, with their broad-brimmed sombreros, spurred boots, and seven-shooters belted to their waists, and seemed fully capable of worse robbery than lifting umbrellas.

The stores were also invaded for memorials of our visit, and did a thriving business in souvenir spoons and Mexican curios of various kinds. Here the omnipresent Hebrew confronted you as at nearly every place we had stopped at in this Western country. If you wanted to buy anything you ran up against a hooked nose at every turn, and any one who has something to sell can always find a like customer to buy if there is anything in it. We were at length obliged to chase the would-be purchasers out of the stores to get back to the train on time, notwithstanding we aroused the ire of the merchants by so doing. After settling with the coon who was generalissimo of the carriage brigade, we made an attempt to buy the Mexican Sombrero which he wore. So many bids were made that the market was ruined and our attempts to barter rendered ineffectual. The hat weighed a matter of four pounds, principally made up of silver ornaments, and was valued accordingly.

At the station were some fine specimens of the pepper tree. It was a new species to nearly all of us, and all broke branches of its fragrant blossoms or berries as mementos. Lee, who has been in this section of the land before, bought some of the Mexican sweetmeats called tomala, and brought it into the cars for the party to eat. The composition consists of hashed meat that has been cooked in olive oil, mixed with corn-meal, cayenne pepper and raisins, the whole being tied up in corn-husks. Lee explained the manner of eating it, illustrating the same by his own actions, and seemed to enjoy it. It was more than the rest could do, as it looked and tasted like a compound of yellow soap and cayenne. Brown took a swallow of it, went out on the car platform and waited patiently for it to come up, but it was too heavy and remained a weight on his conscience. We all came to the conclusion that a liking for tomala was a taste that had to be acquired. On the way back, Dr. Morgan boarded the train with a bottle of olives that had been packed right here, from some of the many groves we were passing through. These met with a much better reception, and tasted very different from the "spoiled plum" variety so generally met with on our eastern tables. The Doctor took leave of us at National City, but his olives remained with us.

The return trip to the Coronado was safely accomplished at 2 P. M. Luncheon was awaiting us, and was immediately attacked in the dining room of the hotel, which is in itself a dream of beauty, with its panelled walls and ceiling. It affords plenty of variety to gaze upon and study up, while the waiters make up their minds which return train to take from the kitchen. The table decorations of flowers afford another distraction at similar times. Great vases and bowls of roses, always fresh and of immense size and variety, are found on each table. The inroads made upon them at the departure of guests from the meal caused no apparent loss in size.

A rendezvous was ordered for all hands in the pool at 4 P. M., for a farewell slide down the toboggan. Advantage was taken of the intermediate time to visit the Botanical Gardens on the line of the narrow guage, about a mile from the hotel. The head gardener here was very obliging and full of information. In one of his greenhouses was apparently sufficient smilax to reach Philadelphia if tied together. The ordinary flowers of our home gardens, such as verbenas and the like, he characterized as "only weeds," as he well might in the midst of the profusion of tropical beauty growing around him. It was out of the season for roses, he said, but we might have loaded our baggage car with the grand specimens that were in bloom. A corps of Chinamen were engaged in trimming flowers and hedges and deluging the beds with water. Harmon Johnson nearly pumped the gardener dry of information, to be transplanted for use to the banks of the Schuylkill.

An Ostrich farm, which now boasted of only four of that long-legged and long-necked species of feather foundry, came in for its share of visitors, while some who concluded they did not stand in need of any further ablutions, made their way over to San Diego again. At 4 P. M. the warm water tank was alive with pilgrims. The toboggan was descended singly, in doubles, triples and whole trains, which made the water fly when the impact with it came. Purdy, Brooks and Backus were regular water dogs, and took the ordinary sliding-board head first. This feat was attempted on the toboggan by Milligan, and resulted in a pair of skinned elbows. It was after 6 P. M. when the last straggler came out of the pool, and all cast regretful glances back at it as they departed.

Baggage had been ordered to be ready in the rooms by 6 P. M., so that Howard could have plenty of time to get it to the train. Dinner was partaken of with the customary appetite, and preparations made for departure, with a general feeling that we could well have put in a little more time at this stop. We began to straggle toward the cars about dusk, but the main body did not move until 9 P. M., and boarded the ferry-boat by the glare of the electric light. The ride across the bay was more than cool, and the shelter of the cabins very welcome. Our landing on the other side was close to the train, so that we were soon able to stow away our incumbrances in the berths and start out to take a trip up town in the horse-cars to see San Diego by night. After a long wait for a car, on what McDowell suggested might be a tri-weekly line, because it tried to run once a week, we secured a couple and rode up into the business parts of the city. Some of the spoony people had no San Diego samples of their hobby as yet, and the stores were all closed. Finding a window lit up with a stock of spoons in it, the living quarters of the proprietor were hunted out and invaded, when he was forced to get out of bed and open up the store to as much business as he had probably done all day. His stock of Mexican opals was large and reasonable, and suffered accordingly.

An excavation for cable cars, a company of militia being drilled on the street under the electric lights, and some sort of new fangled street sweeper at its work were about all the sights we could see at the late hour at which we made our return trip to the wharf. The train was lying out on one of the piers with but a narrow path intervening between it and a cold salt-water bath. Everybody must have walked very straight when they came in at night, as we heard of no involuntary duckings in the morning.

Saturday, July 23d, 1892.

RUNNING into the greatest orange growing country and the finest example of what irrigation has produced in Southern California, we found our train coming to a halt at Riverside at 7 A. M., a half hour before our scheduled time. We stopped beside one of the main canals through which the water, that makes the desert to blossom like the rose, was ruuning in a swift stream. Right abreast of us was a grove of English walnut trees, loaded down with fruit that was not yet ripe. Next to it was a field of alfalfa grass, with its tangled and matted mass of foliage almost impenetrable to the feet when you attempted to walk into it.

We finished our breakfast on the train, while the carriages that had been telegraphed for to enable us to take the famous Magnolia Drive, awaited our pleasure. The air was a little warm, and Emmerling brought a big chair from the smoker out under the walnut trees. Here he found it so comfortable, and the ripple of the running water so soothing, that he decided to spend his morning there rather than to take the drive. Lafferty elected to stay with him for company, but the others were soon stowed in the comfortable carriages provided for them, and found themselves behind as good road stock as could be found in the country.

What can we say of the surprises and delights of that drive? If naught else remained of our recollections of California, the Magnolia Drive would be a bright memorial of our trip, until the night of life shall fold its dark wings around us. Our curiosity had been aroused and our imaginations set to work for many months by the accounts we had heard and read of the beauties of this place, but the reality was so far in advance of our most advanced ideas that we feel that any attempt at a description of them must fall flat.

We first drove through the business part of the town, together with one or two other avenues of considerable extent before striking the Magnolia. When we did get into it and encountered its successive surprises, exclamations of delight were heard from all quarters. As the various carriages would meet or overtake one another, eager questions would be hurled from one to the other

MAGNOLIA DRIVE

such as " Have you seen so and so?" or " Did you drive into Mr. ———'s ranch?" or " Where did you get the oranges?" The entrances to many of the ranches were a drive in themselves, so far do the houses set back from the road. The city is said to occupy 25,000 acres of land. Including the business part of the place the population is only about 4000. This distribution of ground gives some of the ranches a good opportunity to make show places of their residences.

The name of Magnolia Drive is not given because of the number of trees of that species. There are only three magnolias planted to mark each mile of the drive, which is hard and firm, and kept well watered by numerous sprinkling carts employed for that purpose. One side is bordered by the Eucalyptus tree, which is an importation from Australia, and grows quickly to a height of from eighty to a hundred feet. It is also known as the fever tree, and considered a safeguard against malaria. The other side is guarded by gigantic palms, which are here in such countless numbers as to give the entire landscape a tropical aspect. In the centre is an avenue down which the horse-cars run for a distance of seven miles, with a driving avenue on each side. The three are divided by two rows of pepper trees. This is one of the most graceful and beautiful trees of the coast. It has the smell of pepper and bears the fruit of the pepper, but will not make that condiment, and is of no value commercially.

The pepper trees have grown to such a size as to interfere with one another, and gangs of men were now employed in removing every alternate tree. While the avenue looked equally as well, if not better where the work had been accomplished, it seemed a pity to see so many fine trees with their beautiful foliage ruthlessly cut down and chopped into firewood.

Nowhere on earth, we judged, has the art of hedge-growing and trimming been brought to such perfection as we witnessed at Riverside. Fences were so few as to cause remark when one was seen. Everything on the street line was enclosed with hedges, cut into all kinds of fantastic devices, and kept trimmed at such height as the owner's fancy dictated. One green wall that we observed particularly was nearly forty feet to the top. Urns of all conceivable shapes, columns, arches, spades, clubs, hearts and diamonds, hitching-posts and gates all done in dark green, alive and growing, meet the eye at every turn. Chinese laborers, with their conical bamboo hats, were engaged here and there with long shears, trimming off the straggling new growth. This is necessary to be done five times in the year, so quick is the enforced growth in this country.

Back of all is the dark green foliage of the multitude of orange trees, with the bright yellow clusters of fruit in its midst. The orange harvest was virtually over at the time of our visit, but many of the trees were still full of fruit, and the ground beneath them was covered with it. A slight frost had touched much of it and rendered it unmarketable, although we could not see that it had made it unpalatable. A drive into an open gateway, with one word of request, would gain you the privilege of gathering as many branches full of fruit as you could carry, as the interior of the carriages soon bore evidence. Close to the dwellings on the orange ranches were the packing houses, in which labor was now suspended, but which witnessed busy scenes a few weeks since. The Chinese apparently bear the brunt of the labor in this section, the white man finding his time fully occupied in bossing the job. The ranch of Mr. Everett, containing eighty acres of orange trees, is one of the most beautiful in Riverside, and its owner may be justified in taking pride in

HEDGE FENCE AT RIVERSIDE

his possessions. All through California we were awakened to the fact that when a man has made his fortune, built himself a fine house and beautified his grounds with trees or flowers, or possibly fine statuary until they become a feast to the eyes, he does not plant them with steel traps or station a man behind a convenient tree with a gun, to fill any intruder with shot as in the East, but throws wide his gate and places thereon the inscription, "These grounds open to the public." This is indicative of the feeling of the average Western man, whose heart is as big within him as the fruits of the country in which he lives. Century Plants are seen in immense numbers inside and outside the gardens. Just within the gates at the entrance to the ranch of Mr.

Gilliland, we had the pleasure of seeing one in bloom. The stalk on which the flower or blossom appeared was at least thirty feet high, with a spread of the curious branches about four feet in diameter. This gentleman's house

CENTURY PLANT

was built of adobe bricks, but had been so architecturally improved as to make one lose sight of that fact. The residence of Mr. S. C. Evans, the pioneer irrigator of Riverside, is also one of the finest on the avenue. One can scarcely imagine his feelings as he now looks around upon the results of his first experiment in the visible prosperity of such a community as this garden city.

As a striking contrast in background to all these enchanting tropical scenes immediately under our eyes ran the lofty range of Coquomoca Mountains with seemingly impossible patches of snow lying in the gulches and hollows near their summits. Circling around over the valleys, in their inimitably lazy, wheeling mode of flight, were many buzzards on the lookout for something to die, that they might have a square meal. All along the drive, deep in the

OSTRICH PEN AT RIVERSIDE

recesses of the shrubbery, we heard the whistle of the mocking bird as he called to his mate. Before going back to the train we drove to a small ostrich pen, surrounded by a high board fence. A light entrance fee gained us admission to the enclosure wherein eight of the ungainly birds crowded up to the low fence which confined them still further. They were very tame and apparently hungry. Several large bunches of red beets, lying convenient in a shed, were confiscated and fed to the birds. It was curious to watch half of a beet disappear at a gulp in the cavernous bill and then trace its course down the long neck into the depths of the Ostrichville suburbs. The food would go down in front of the neck until near the bottom, when it took a turn and passed over the back of the neck into the body.

What an excellent chance it would be for a man who likes to taste his whiskey all the way down, if he could secure an ostrich neck. He would also be able to start the water on its road to put the fire out before the whiskey got half way to the bottom. The ostriches were not particular as to diet, snatching at beets, oranges, finger rings, coat buttons and the trimming of the ladies' hats with strict impartiality. They seemed sociable enough, but a glance at the ugly looking great toe, which looked capable of ripping up a dog, made us satisfied to fraternize with them over the top of the rail fence. The owner came in and pulled some of the smaller grey feathers from the birds to present to each of the ladies. In the little shop attached to the place they had feathers, ostrich eggs plain and decorated but all blown, together with photos of the birds for sale. Several availed themselves of the chance to secure eggs which would, as McIntyre remarked, induce a man to make more than one bite of a "sherry and egg" in the morning. On our way back to the station we passed again through the built-up portion of the city, among whose features were especially noticeable, the Glenwood Hotel, Loring Opera House, Rubidoux Club, First National Bank and the Riverside High School.

More than a half million boxes of oranges have been shipped within a year from this point, and with the number of young trees now being set out, it is almost impossible to predict the future of the trade. There was said to be a tree here which bore thirty-five boxes of oranges in a year, full sized boxes as we were careful to inquire. In addition to the oranges, there are likewise large shipments of lemons, olives, walnuts and other fruits. When we consider that these industries have been created out of almost a desert land in six or eight years by the aid of the water alone, the result seems marvelous.

There are two water supply companies, the Riverside and the Gage, deriving their supply both from the Santa Ana River and from artesian wells. The city water supply is taken from the latter, sent down from such a height as to give sufficient pressure for business and fire purposes. The city has an assessed valuation of five millions of dollars and no city debt. The County of San Bernardino, in which it lies, is in the same enviable condition as regards debt. The famous Temescal tin mines are located twelve miles southeast of the city and are now in active operation after being in litigation for a number of years. We arrived back at the train, which had been pulled up to the station platform, at 11.40 A. M., laden with trophies of palm leaves, oranges, olives and English walnuts which were hung up in the baggage and sleeping cars as ornaments. We bade farewell to Riverside at 12 M., just as Brooks made his stereotyped announcement of "first call for luncheon." Our run was along the range of San Bernardino Mountains. In addition to the pleasure of viewing the scenery, every one was full of reminiscences of and interrogatories about the scenes we had just witnessed in Riverside.

The mountain ranges hereabouts are generally seen in three ranges. First the foot-hills, then a range of mountains with a still higher range in the background, extending on every side and apparently shutting us into a basin to which there was no visible outlet. But the railroad finds a valley to go through or a pass to go over, or in default of either, dives into a hole in the ground like a gopher, and comes out on the other side. The rivers or what were the rivers in this section of the State are, at this season of the year, mere beds of dry gravel and stone with wagon roads running down them in all directions. The men who own the irrigating canals go up in the mountains, head off the springs which would supply the rivers, bring that necessary fluid down in canals, aqueducts or flumes which are sometimes carried across wide valleys on trestles a couple of hundred feet in the air, and distribute the same to those who desire to use and are willing to pay for it. Consequently the river bed is a bed of rest for seven or eight months in the year, being used only in the rainy season to carry off the surplus. The names of stations this afternoon are of decidedly Spanish appearance. Such as Ozusa, Duarte, San Dimas, Santa Anita and Sierra Madre. The latter was situated upon the ranch of "Lucky" Baldwin, through whose domain the road ran. In addition to miles of oranges, lemons and vineyards, the "bonanza king" here raises some of the finest horses in the country. Many fine specimens were visible from the car windows and served to excite the envy of the horsemen on the train.

At 3 P. M. we arrived in Pasadena and were side-tracked directly at the station. This city is emphatically a city of residences of which the surrounding grounds are ornamented with choice plants and roses innumerable. They said here the flower season was over, but we would be pleased to have ours over in such guise at all times. Palm trees, magnolias, century plants, fig trees, twisted live oaks, pepper trees, umbrella trees and another collection of ornamental evergreens were the attractions of the gardens here, interspersed with every color and variety of roses. The Raymond hotel lies upon an eminence about a mile from the station and in plain sight. Gorman kept several carriages running thither during the afternoon for the accommodation of the ladies. From the elevation upon which it stood the view in every direction was simply enchanting, while the garden surrounding the hotel was perfect in its beauty. While the hotel was now closed, as was the one at the station, there was a corps of gardeners on hand to see that the grounds were kept in order. The road out there was lined with handsome villas, prominent among which is one belonging to Professor Lowe, formerly of Norristown.

The horse cars also ran out to the hotel and far out in the opposite direction. A ride on them revealed a number of fruit farms on which the drying of apricots was going on at a great rate. The apricots of Southern California have been a source of great comfort to all the pilgrims and many of those grown around Pasadena stood little chance of being dried after the advent of our party this afternoon. A fine stone building on the line of our ride in the horse cars was labelled Public Library and a free reading room was attached thereto.

The temperature was very pleasant in Pasadena this afternoon, growing quite cool during the evening. The climate here is claimed to be one of the most equable on the continent, the mercury having a range of about 20° only and the mean temperature for the summer months being 67°. It is only twenty-five miles to the seashore and but four miles to the Sierra Madres, where you can get up into the air a distance of eight thousand feet. Farming goes on

AN UMBRELLA TREE

the year round as the country produces everything known in the line of vegetation. Apples, guavas, grapes, strawberries, pears, peaches, apricots, oranges, limes, lemons, pomegranates, currants, bananas, figs, walnuts, chestnuts and other fruits grow equally well. Six crops a year of the alfalfa provide fodder for the live stock. We saw many specimens of the cork tree growing in the yards of the dwelling houses.

There are two large wineries within a short distance of the city, but the town itself is a Prohibition one. You cannot buy a glass of beer at any price but the boys were steered onto several places where you could buy a cracker and a piece of cheese of open hearted dealers who would magnanimously make you a present of a glass of beer.

A game of base ball on the plaza, or what goes for a plaza, was surrounded by a deep fringe of the admirers of the respective clubs, both on foot and in carriages. A goodly representation of the pilgrims was attracted thereby, and as usual, freely interjected unsolicited advice into the players. A departure from the usual Eastern process of charging fifty cents to go inside the fence to see a game, was the passing around of a hat when the game came near the finish.

Several members of the Pasadena Commandery met us at the station upon our arrival and Sir E. C. Jones gave us numerous invites to call at his store on the main street. Shaw, Enochs and Allen found an old friend and neighbor in the person of Dr. Rosenberger, who was running a drug store here.

It was Saturday night, and the crowded state of the barber shops interfered seriously with the scraping which most of the members of Mary seem to feel the necessity of at stated intervals. It was curious to note the advice given by the first shaved, as old stagers in the city, to select certain shops on the main street. One would say, go to the shop with the three barbers and try the little coon with the wart on his nose, he is the best in town. The opposition line would recommend the long-legged yellow fellow at the shop where they gave baths, until finally all were fixed up for Sunday.

A brass band, stationed on the plaza directly facing the train, discoursed fair music all the evening This was not done out of compliment to us, but is a regular Saturday night diversion. Playing euchre and cribbage with lemonade accompaniment was the extent of our excesses for the evening. With some letter writing, which could be easily accomplished with the train at parade rest, these amusements served to fill in the time until berths were turned down. We learned later on that the sons of Old John Brown were living close by the route of our car ride this afternoon. We should have liked nothing better than to have called upon them, but got the information when we were many miles away. Our train remained on the siding until daylight. The quiet night served a good purpose in locating some of the snorers in the cats' car, a matter which had been debatable when mixed up with the clatter of the train.

Sunday, July 24th, 1892.

WAY from Pasadena at 5 A. M., before any one but the engineer, fireman and Jimmy Baird were up. Jimmy and Tom Henderson were evidently born when the sign of the owl was in the ascendant. They lie around in the daytime, blinking and napping in the easy chairs of the smoker when their victims will allow it. At 3 A. M. Baird will awaken and grope his way into the rear car to arouse Henderson, or *vice versa*, awaking Bickel and a half dozen more in the act. Then they will prowl through the train to the baggage car and rest until the train stops. This is the signal to go outside and hammer under the windows of the cars, especially Emmerling's. They did not come within reach of the club which Harry kept for them, so that he could only take satisfaction in words of which he was neither sparing or choice.

A short morning run of one and a half hours brought us to Redondo Beach. As soon as the train stopped a large basket containing boutonnieres for all hands was handed on board. This was the gift of Mr. Schafer, the proprietor of the Casino on the beach opposite which we had come to an anchor. A long pier projected out into the ocean just above us, with a pavilion or store at the inside end where you could hire fishing lines and poles. Schuehler went out before breakfast, and claimed to have caught three fish upon his return. The story fell for the want of confirmation, as no evidence could be secured corroborative of such an exploit.

By 9 A. M., after the arrival of some of the excursion trains from Los Angeles, the line of poles along the side and on the end of the pier resembled a Louisiana cane-brake. The fish caught, smelts and young herring, from four to six inches long, were as carefully treasured as the fishing experts hoard their mountain trout. Emmerling fished for two hours without result, while conductor Backus caught one. Pop Millick looked longingly at the array of poles and lines, but a Sunday fishing bout would have ruined his reputation in West Philadelphia forever. You could easily tell the hired poles from those that were held in fee simple, from the fact that the former were painted in red,

white and blue rings, so that they could not pass their owner at the pier head without detection. McIntyre and his boy had one for a long spell, but as Scotch herring are not found on this shore, they got no bites. Redondo is only four years old, but has already made great strides in that time. The long pier is a terminus for the Santa Fé road and a shipping point for the city of Los Angeles. Vessels and steamships of large size load and unload at the pier, and from the appearance of things, a large amount of freight was in transit. The Redondo hotel, a little way up the beach, is a large and very finely finished building. Unlike most sea-coast houses, it has quite a large garden on a sunny slope. Along the top is a broad cement walk, communicating with the beach by a high flight of cement steps. It has also a fine board walk, with numerous pavilions along the edge of the beach. The surf is not heavy, but there is a corresponding absence of undertow and the advantage of being able to bathe the year round, as report goes.

The pier end of the beach will be a rival to Coney Island in a few years, if the attractions keep on increasing. The Casino has a good dancing floor for which a fine orchestra furnished music all the morning. At one end of it was a tent containing a circus, whose performers were ponies, dogs and monkeys. A marine merry-go-round was in operation beyond the other end, on which were fastened a number of boats with sails set, which furnished the motive power with the aid of the fine sea breeze which constantly blew.

Mr. Schafer made us perfectly at home under the shelter of his immense pavilion, and did all he could to render our short stay a pleasant one. A gang of fishermen were hauling a shore net in front of the place from early morning, bringing in at each haul many fine kingfish or barb. John Robbins secured some fine ones which were consigned to the dining car and furnished a fresh fish breakfast for the colored contingent. An immense quantity of the small mackerel and smelts were dragged ashore with the net each time and left on the sand to be scrambled for by the excursionists. One woman, of evident French extraction, took off shoes and stockings and was foremost in each rush after fish with a gusto that aroused the enthusiasm of the lookers on. This was the more pronounced because she took extra precautions to prevent the possibility of any of her feminine toggery getting even damp.

At 11.05 A. M. we took our departure for Santa Monica by way of Los Angeles. It was customary for the committee to count noses upon leaving any place to see that none were left behind. There were such crowds on and about the railroad track here that it was feared to back the train down in front of the Casino, from which point it had been moved as soon as the excursion trains began to come in, on account of accidents. The train was held for five minutes and, from a cursory examination all were thought to be on board. Upon marking off a list, after the train started, it was found we were two short and the absentees were Pop Millick and Enochs, Sr. Purdy telegraphed from Los Angeles to have them sent on, their tickets being in the possession of our conductor Backus, but an answer was returned that they had already left for Santa Monica by the other road running to that place. It afterwards transpired that the two delinquents were sitting with their backs to the shore, so much interested in the antics of two Creole girls who were floating in the surf, that neither time nor train had any room in their minds. What further adventures befell them before they rejoined us at Santa Monica, no amount of interrogation would induce them to divulge, except that they witnessed a balloon ascension at Redondo which we missed.

Our road ran through another highly cultivated valley. Although it was Sunday, Chinamen in every direction were engaged in digging, hoeing, ploughing or hanging out the family wash. Pumpkins, squashes and melons grow so thickly along the public roads, outside the fences, as to barely leave room for teams to pass. Many groves of the Eucalyptus tree had been planted along the route but whether from a sanitary point of view we could not tell. Los Angeles was reached at 11.50 A. M. Our train was shifted to several different depots while here and we did not get away again until 12.53 P. M.

Major J. S. Lauck, Travelling Passenger Agent of the California Pacific came on board and delivered an invitation from Golden Gate Commandery No. 16, of San Francisco, to partake of their hospitality, in their asylum at that city, on the evening of Monday, August 1st. The invitation was accepted by Capt. Gen. Munch by wire, supplemented by letter. Several members of Cœur de Lion Commandery No. 9, of Los Angeles also called on us and tendered their services during our stay at this point as well as Santa Monica. When we reached the latter place at 1 P. M., Sir T. H. Ward, of Coeur de Lion also boarded the train and extended to us the hospitality of his Commandery for the morrow at Los Angeles.

It transpired, in the course of conversation, that Coeur de Lion had sent an invitation to the Knights of Mary more than two months since to spend some time fraternally with them. Her fraters had been surprised and not a little hurt at not receiving any reply to the same, which was very natural under the circumstances. A very few words served to convince our frater that no such invitation had ever reached the hands of our committee and matters were soon straightened out.

After luncheon, rooms were secured at the Arcadia Hotel, as headquarters for the ladies, although the train was but a stone's throw distant. The attractions of the beach were then inspected. The crowd upon the sand and congregated under a large wooden pavilion was something immense. Numerous excursion trains ran here from Los Angeles, as at Redondo, and each one brought its full quota of holiday seekers. The surf here was much better than at Redondo and the crowd were enjoying it in liberal numbers. Jerusalem had apparently come out of bondage for the day and you could not throw a stone without hitting a score of Jews.

Our party early discovered the fact that the elite did not bathe until after 4 P. M. and put in the time lying around the sand or sitting in the shade until that hour, so that they might not be confounded with the ordinary sea-shore visitor. This is another of the spots which claim to have surf-bathing during the entire year. It was very enjoyable at the present time, the undertow being scarcely perceptible, although the surf was good.

About 3.15 P. M. the prodigal sons who had left us at Redondo Beach returned to the bosom of the family and were received with open arms. We did not kill any fatted calf, but Millick was inclined to kill somebody on his own hook until convinced that he had not been intentionally left behind. There was no danger of his being left anywhere during the continuance of this trip. A balloon ascension was to be made from the beach below the hotel this afternoon and for two hours the managers of the affair were at work filling the big bag with gas or hot air or smoke made by burning gasoline in a hole in the ground. Just before it was fully distended and the premiere danseuse in abbreviated skirts and corduroy pants, who was to ascend with it, had been promenading around it for half an hour, too much of the inflammable material was thrown into the hole and caused a grand explosion. The balloon was rent apart, threshed around among the spectators for a short period and collapsed, as did the crowd that had gathered around it. Nobody was hurt fortunately, although several of our pilgrims were in the front rank as usual. Carriages were in demand with which the surrounding country was pretty well explored. The shore line is a bold bluff, rising abruptly from a broad expanse of sandy beach, along which you can drive for miles. The town itself extends about two miles along this road and contains many handsome residences, surrounded by fine grounds. One of the finest of these belongs to Senator Jones of Nevada, who was the first projector of the place, or rather gave it its first impetus by building a railroad as an outlet from some of his mines to this point. The town enjoyed a great boom for a time but its business glory has subsided to a great extent.

There is a Soldier's Home three miles out, from which many of the pensioners were mingling with the crowds around the hotel to-day. A line of cars ran out to that place from a point above the hotel.

We were booked for dinner at the Arcadia and towards 6 P. M. the party began to rendezvous on the hotel porch. Brown improved the opportunity to group them at the end of the porch and take a photograph just about the time the light was getting a little dim. At 6.30 P. M. dinner was announced and the party marched in couples, making a circuit of the table before taking their seats, the orchestra being stationed outside the door to furnish music for the march. The table was most elegantly decorated with large vases of flowers, a boutonniere at each plate and trailing vines of smilax winding in and out around the dishes the whole length of the board. The dinner was served in regular courses from soup to black coffee.

After dinner was over the majority were content to lounge around the hotel porch and take their rest or smoke. Quite a number hunted up a church somewhere and went in to the services. Being unacquainted with the town, they had to skirmish around until they found the sacred edifice and were naturally a little late in arriving. They were reminded of their remissness by the preacher who stopped short in his sermon and gave them a sound lecture on the heinous crime of coming in late and disturbing the services.

One of our small bombs, dropped from the porch into the window of a billiard room where some young Jews were intent on knocking the balls around, created quite a commotion. One after another rushed into the room, carefully examining the gas-fixtures all around it, until finally one waiter donned his coat and flew up the road post-haste for a plumber.

A number of the cats had made their calculations for a trip up to Los Angeles after dinner, but found there was no return train at a late enough hour to suit their purposes. All hands accordingly retired on the train at an early hour, where the labors of the day rendered them an easy prey to the god of sleep.

Monday, July 25th, 1892.

HE morning came with the weather cloudy and very foggy. It appears that this is a usual thing on the Coast although it only lasts for an hour or two, although they get more rain here than a little further inland. The Coast range of mountains, lying about two miles in shore and rising to an elevation of from two to four thousand feet, catches the clouds and fogs as they drift in from the ocean and manages to rob them of their moisture before getting across. The consequence is that the mountains are full of excellent streams of water, from which the Coast cities derive their water supply. That of Santa Monica is brought down in this way, in iron pipes, from a point six hundred feet above the level of the town. and the force is sufficient to send a stream over the highest buildings.

We were off at 7 A. M., in the midst of breakfast, for the run to Los Angeles. The old Spanish title was La Puebla de la Reina de los Angeles, literally the town of the Queen of the Angels. This being too much of a mouthful for the people, after the country was Americanized, was cut down to the last two words. We passed through the same highly cultivated belt that we had gone over on our way down. The groves of Eucalyptus are especially noticeable, many plots of ground being fenced around with them. It is a noble fence when each picket, so to speak, is a stick a hundred feet high and as straight and well tapered as a ship's mast. It is hard to tell when you leave the country and get into the city, the suburbs of charming villas and ranches, with numerous orange groves extending far out from the business portion of the city. We finally ran into the depot at Los Angeles at 7.45 A. M., breakfast being still disposed of by the second brigade, which did not finish until 8.30 A. M. At 9 A. M. the Committee of Cœur de Lion came upon the scene and we surrendered ourselves unconditionally to their orders. They consisted of Sirs T. H. Ward, who is Grand Warden of California, Morgan, Holton, Orme, Teed, Van Doren, Field, Bray and Boynton. They had chartered two cars on the electric road, which soon arrived in charge of Superintendent A. W. Barrett, who went along and took charge of the cars, switching them off when not needed. The first stop was made at the County Court House, an imposing structure just finished and occupied. Sir Ward, who is also County Clerk, was in his element here and showed us through the entire building, displaying the very complete methods of filing records of all kinds as well as his curiosity shop of relics pertaining to cases in the criminal courts. These include a whole arsenal of pistols, knives and bludgeons that have been used with murderous intent, and much other bric-a-brac. The party were taken in the elevator to the observatory on the roof, where a magnificent view of the garden and orchard-studded country rewarded them. Sir Gibson, Sheriff of the County and a typical Western sheriff in appearance, took a squad over into the jail and locked them in for a few minutes with a tougher looking lot of fellow citizens, inside of iron cages, than they would have cared to meet outside. The cars were then taken again for a ride through the residence portion of the city. Some of the last to get up to the roof were left behind and followed in one of the regular cars.

Although Los Angeles was founded more than a hundred years since, its growth as a city has been achieved within a dozen years back and unexampled results accomplished in that short time. From a collection of adobe huts it has bloomed into a great metropolis. With hardly twelve thousand inhabitants in 1880, its population has reached hard on to a hundred thousand now. It is divided east and west by Main Street, and north and south by First Street. South of First Street, in the residence quarter, the streets are paved with asphalt while north of that street, in the business portion of the city, the streets are all finely paved with Belgian blocks. Electric lights are strung in every direction, while cable, electric and horse cars transfer you to any desired quarter. The main streets had an aspect of business activity that we had not witnessed since leaving St. Louis. The business blocks, both wholesale and retail, comprise many imposing buildings and evidences of prosperity show on every hand. The city is cosmopolitan in the nationality of its inhabitants to an unusual extent and embraces representatives of almost all nations.

On our way we were joined by Major Walter S. Moore, Chief of the Fire Department, who is a brother of our frater Gilbert S. Moore, and who continued with us on our rounds. The flowers in every direction were marvellous, both for size and abundance. Many of the two-storied houses had rose bushes running to the roof, which bore a very large yellow rose in unlimited numbers. When the limit of the electric road was reached the cars were abandoned temporarily for a walk through some of the avenues where the private residences and their surroundings were of the most costly character. The magnificent grounds attached to the residence of Judge Silent were traversed with gratitude for the opportunity to witness such a display of flowers and plants. Miss Chapin here secured the husk off the blossom which matures into a bunch of bananas, as a trophy. The irrigating canals are carried along close up to the front fences or stone copings of all the finest houses, with lateral branches leading into the grounds. The rush of bright, clear and cold water almost tempted us, during the warm walk, to take off our shoes and stockings and wade up the canals. By 10 A. M. the clouds had all dispersed and the sun had got down to active business. The cars were awaiting us at another point and our ride was resumed as far as the Westminster Hotel, at which we were to partake of luncheon. This is another of the large hotels to which the country is addicted, and we were ready to enjoy the rest which it afforded us. The rooms secured for the use of the ladies were at the end of a labyrinth of passages on the second floor, which needed a pilot to lay out the course necessary to find them. A good wash-up first occupied our attention and we were then ready for the meal which was in waiting for us. The service in the dining-room was rendered by girls who did their work both quickly and well. Emmerling made his appearance for lunch-eon, decorated with a magnolia blossom as large as a dinner plate, which did not look out of place on his broad expanse of bosom and amused the girls very much. It was hard work far some of the pilgrims to tear themselves away from the attractions of the girls after those of the meal had been disposed of. They lingered long over the dessert and partook of all kinds to lengthen out their time. After luncheon many of the party took to the retail stores on Spring Street, where ten years ago it was all adobe buildings, to do some shopping. Others hunted up Chinatown, which is an inseparable adjunct of all the Coast cities, to see what might be seen. Some of them tried hard to learn the art of "hitting the pipe" or taking an opium smoke. They also visited the Joss house and watched the country Chinese who came in to burn a few Joss sticks or incense to old Joss and offer up their prayers. One Chinese store was visited whose owner was the father of three interesting children, of which the youngest was named Benjamin Harrison as a front name. Of course the girls had to take advantage of their first chance to fondle a genuine Chinese baby.

The Committee returned to the depot with some of our party as the time drew near for us to leave, regretting that we had not appropriated more time to view their stirring city and we were more than regretful on that score our-selves. When the baggage car was visited we found that they had put therein several boxes of oranges for our use on the trip. In front of the grand station of the California Pacific, in which our train rested, were two immense palms, of which we endeavored to discover the age. No one seemed to know, but it was evident from their height and the ripened leaves or shucks that had fallen down against the stems in layers, that they had been there for a long time.

We were a little behind time in getting away, owing to the minutes con-sumed in taking leave of our kind hosts and returning our thanks for the favors shown us. We got off, however, in good shape at 3.05 P. M. We soon reached the Los Angeles River and were surprised to find some water in it. Our route lay up the San Fernando Valley through scenes of surpassing loveli-ness. Orange and olive groves lined the way on either side, as well as suburban residences for a long distance out of Los Angeles. At 4 P. M. we stopped at San Fernando station. The San Fernando tunnel, under the range of mountains of that name, was just ahead. We had to wait until they brought out a gang of track repairers, before we could go through. They had timed their labors by the regular trains, not knowing of the coming of our special. The tunnel is one and a half miles through, and before we entered at 4.15 P. M., all windows, doors and ventilators were closed to keep out the gas and smoke.

Our dishwasher, Buzzard, happened to be sitting out on one of the car steps enjoying the landscape and was shut out there. After we got through he was admitted to the car again, half choked and wholly scared. Zeitz, who is also one of the owls who go hoo-hoo-ing around in the early dawn, was found asleep when the train came again into the daylight and was promptly brought to consciousness with a shower-bath of ice-water; for which he threatened dire vengeance on the morrow.

At Saugus we turned on to the Ventura division of the Southern Pacific for the run down the Santa Barbara valley, which proved to be one of the most enjoyable and picturesque rides of our whole trip. We first ran through a rich grazing country on which the great herds of cattle were numbered by thousands. At one point, on a steep hill side, up which you would hardly imagine any one would attempt to ride a horse, we saw in reality a picture that we had often seen on paper. Two cowboys had lassoed a steer by one front and one hind leg and thrown him to the ground. Each rider sat up straight on his mustang, which had braced all four feet against the pull of the lasso in regular picture style. We could not tell what fault the steer had been guilty of, but he was a pitiable sight as he bled from nose and mouth, the rest of the large herd looking stolidly on.

The grazing grounds were followed by a succession of highly cultivated ranches. One of these beyond Camulos was pointed out to us as the home of "Ramona," the heroine of one of Helen Hunt Jackson's novels. Their descriptions of the scenery and surroundings of these Southern California homesteads are strikingly realistic. The houses are principally of adobe, while the outhouses for hands were often mere shelters built of cornstalks with thatched roofs. Dams and irrigating canals again held sway over the country, while wagon tracks ran up the dry river beds. At Santa Paula we were surprised to find indications of the oil business and still more so to learn that oil was piped there from numerous wells on Sulphur Mountain, only four miles away. A pipe-line also extends to Ventura.

At 6.30 P. M. we came in sight of the ocean again and from that time the view was a succession of delightful pictures. Oftentimes with barely room for the train to pass between the craggy rocks on the right, towering above us, and the edge of the steep bluff which overhangs the sandy beach below and along which the track ran, the ride seemed really hazardous. While we have seen no rain in this country, it must rain here sometimes in earnest, as the washouts in the face of the bluffs were terrific. Large masses of rock had been hurled into the ocean and the seas broke over them with great volume and force. Some of the gullies in the bluff came right up to the ties on which our road was laid and while their rugged sides and edges were very picturesque to look upon, we thought they might have been filled in to advantage with some of the stone ballast going to waste in the crags above.

A short stop was made at San Buenaventura station, just after passing through one field of 2800 acres planted entirely in beans of the old-fashioned kind. This was said to be a venture of some Boston man. For a long stretch there was but little show of a beach below the bluff, but the ground gradually got lower and the stretch of sand was wider. Flock after flock of snipe was put up by the train and flew out over the water. In the distance were visible the islands of Santa Rosa and Santa Cruz, during all our ride along the coast. Towards evening we could see the sea-fog rolling up around their bases and it gradually grew into a wall that shut them from our sight altogether. A grand sunset into the ocean was eagerly watched for until, just before the sun was about to dip behind the horizon, the train took a big sheer to starboard and shut the sun from view behind a projecting headland. It could not, however, shut out the gorgeous colors in the surrounding skies, with the enjoyment of which we were forced to be content.

At Santa Barbara at 7.30 P. M. we were side tracked beside a large vine-yard at the lower station, of which the city boasts two. A committee consisting of Sir Knights D. B. Hassinger, J. H. Austin, J. W. Hiller of St. Omer Commandery No. 30 and Judge Norway of Ventura, promptly boarded our train and tendered us the hospitalities of Santa Barbara. As soon as dinner was over, all but a few of the pilgrims sallied forth to see what they could of the city by night, returning in squads up to a late hour.

Tuesday, July 26th, 1892.

ROUSED punctually at 5 A.M. by the noise of tin horns, supplemented by pounding on the sides of the cars with cobblestones. The owls had been as good as their word and taken satisfaction for their treatment of yesterday at the tunnel. Santa Barbara is another of the old Spanish mission settlements dating back to 1786. Up until five years ago it was little known except as a quiet country town of little importance and one that bothered itself little about the outside world At that time the Southern Pacific pushed its branch through to and twelve miles beyond this point. The advent of the cars was a turning point in the character of the city, which now is hustling for trade and has become a great resort for tourists from the East and parties who are looking up health resorts. Mrs. Fairlamb and Miss Haldeman had found friends here also and had gone to spend the time with them.

Breakfast was over before 9 A. M., at which hour the Committee of Knights were on hand with the teams which were to take us around Santa Barbara. One of these was a six-in-hand Yosemite coach on which all the ladies were perched with Munch up beside the driver, armed with a long tin horn, as bugler. Four-in-hands were good enough for the rest of us, especially when the leaders were any way skittish. The first drive was to the old Mission of Santa Barbara, which was visible from the train as it nestled on a slope of the foot-hills back of the city. Here we were hospitably received and shown all there was to be seen through the buildings. The Chapel, with its several altars and old paintings, was first taken in and then the little cemetery outside the side door. Up over the doorway, plastered into the outside stucco of the building, were a couple of skulls with the attendant cross-bones, ghastly relics of some old timers of the monastery. Two stone tombs or chests against the side of the walls probably contained the remains of some of the more prominent brethren, but the most of the graves were indistinguishable from the surrounding soil. None were marked in any manner to tell of the occupants. The heavy stone walls of the chapel, which have stood now for more than a hundred years, seem

fit to last as long as the mountain range which confronts them, while some of the bony Franciscans, who were attending to their duties in cloister and garden, looked as though they might be as old as the walls. The Father Superior, however, was fat and jolly looking and seemed pleased to have our names in the convent register. Up through a stone staircase, imbedded in the wall, we ascended until the belfry of the old tower was reached, from which a fine view of the rich and peaceful valley was had. The roofs were covered with the reversed tiles before mentioned and from their vantage the ladies could look into the promised land of the convent garden. This part of the institution is tabooed to the gentler sex, and the only females who have been allowed to slip into its hallowed precincts, as we are informed, were Mrs. President Harrison and Princess Louise of England. After taking leave of the fathers we were driven back into the city and down State Street to the livery stable to secure another four-in-hand, as we were a little crowded and one of the drivers thought he was carrying too much live weight. One of the old-time stage coaches came down from the mountains, as we passed down the street, with its load of inside and outside passengers, the leathern boot behind for baggage and the four horses galloping down the asphalt. The whole outfit was covered with dust from top to bottom and afforded a fine contrast to our train of vestibuled Pullmans.

The new carriage was soon obtained and filled with outcasts from the others and we were off to see the surrounding country. Past the poorhouse, for which they have little use in this fruitful valley, and an old salt lake or saline spring to which, at one time, a large extent of the country around was forced to send for its supply of that useful condiment, we came to an English walnut grove, belonging to Sir Hassinger, who was with us, from which he harvested last year twelve tons of nuts. A pretty good return from a plantation which needs now but the gathering of the crop.

Coming down one of the steep declivities with a sharp turn at the foot of it, one of the coaches which had a defective brake, made its team hustle ahead in quick time. Pop Millick was on the box and held on manfully until the driver was able to pull them up again. Although a lover of a fast horse, he does not enjoy too much of a good thing.

A Chinese trucker had driven up to the train this morning and disposed of some of his wares to Brooks for the use of the dining car. Mentioning this fact to Sir Hiller, he informed us that' all the truck raisers in the neighborhood were Chinamen and that one of them served his household of thirty people with all the vegetables they needed the year round, outside of strawberries and potatoes, for one dollar per week. The one at the cars was evidently not the same man, as he asked Brooks about Philadelphia prices for all he had to dispose of. His vegetables were all good and fresh ; he had a fine, stout pair of horses, good harness and a heavy wagon, painted sky blue all over. He spoke very fair English and, in response to some of the many questions poked at him about the color of his vehicle, remarked, " I paint him myself ! How you like him ?"

All the morning clouds had been rolling around on and below the tops of the Santa Inez mountains, looking like big wreaths of smoke among the tree tops. At one point what we took for clouds was said to be the steam which

arose from some hot springs, away up the mountain side, above the suburb of Montecito, which forms a part of the city. No irrigation is required in the valley here, except for orange groves. Many horses were grazing in the meadows, most of which are raised here. Hemphill's eyes glistened when one of the committee told us of having purchased thirty head of good horses for $1,100. After seeing many minor points of interest, our drivers finally brought up on the ranch of Mr. Alfred McKee, whereon is situated the celebrated big grape-vine which is one of the sights of Santa Barbara. The vine is of the same stock as originally brought here by the Franciscan fathers and the grapes not considered as good as some of those grown in the new vineyards. It is principally celebrated for its size and the amount of fruit it bears. It is supported on a trellis seventy-five feet square, the trunk measures sixty-seven inches in circumference and six tons of grapes have been picked from it in one season. While inspecting and admiring the vine, particular attention was given to a couple of trees laden with ripe apricots, whose flavor was unrivalled by any we had yet seen.

One of the ladies was taken ill here, from riding on top of the Yosemite coach, and compelled to remain a few hours under the care of Mr. and Mrs. McKee, who were unremitting in their kindness and did all that was possible to care for the sick one and those who remained with her. McKee's ranch is not a vineyard proper, but set out with oranges and lemons, particular attention being paid to the latter as the greater source of profit ; English walnuts, bananas and figs are also raised, as well as an infinite variety of rare and curious flowers. One of these, called the red-hot poker, we had seen before but had not heard it named. It resembles its namesake in all but the length very much, the hot end of the poker being graduated from a cherry red down to a dull yellow, like the genuine article.

The coaches returned to the city by another route, passing down the asphalt pavement of State Street through the business part of the city to the Arlington Hotel, where luncheon was served. The manager had the table set in the form of a hollow square in honor of the occasion and, what was more to the purpose, served a first-class luncheon. After luncheon the party broke up into squads and visited whatever sections of the city they desired. Shopping was in order as usual, rides on the horse cars along the broad avenue of State Street and more carriage rides were also indulged in. Sir Hassinger received many callers at his place of business and spent most of his time in fraternizing with them. Any attempt to make a purchase from him was rather unsuccessful from the fact that he was disposed to give away whatever you wanted to buy. Some of the party made their way down to the beach, where more fine sea bathing was to be had. There were a number of the visitors to the city down there, among whom was a good looking widow into whose good graces Pop Millick soon ingratiated himself. He had hardly time to get well established and congratulate himself thereon, before Harmon Johnson came upon the scene and cut him out completely.

By 6.20 P. M., all had drifted back to the train for dinner and the guests of Mrs. McKee had been returned in an easy carriage. A band of Italian minstrels had been engaged on the main street during the afternoon to come down to the train in the evening and give us some music. They made their appearance after dinner and entertained us for a time while we promenaded the station platform, until it was suggested that we have a drill of those who intended to parade at Denver. The idea was well received and Capt.-General Munch drilled us in the marching movements, under the bright glare of the electric light, for nearly an hour. The platform was both long and very wide so that we did not need to go off it nor even to change our slippers for shoes. The usual concert took place in the smoker to-night after the drill and our fraters of St. Omer, who had called to take leave of us, remained until our starting time to enjoy the fun. While it was at its heighth a bump against the front platform announced the arrival of a fresh locomotive and at 10 P. M. we were off for the North, having bid farewell to our hosts of the day. It was a good deal later when the smoker was left finally to its own solitude.

Wednesday, July 27th, 1892.

E HAD heard and read much and often of the Tehachapi Loop and were on deck at 5 A. M., so as not to lose anything of so renowned a view. We learned this morning that, sometime after leaving Santa Barbara, the train had dashed into a flock of sheep huddled together on the track and had killed forty-five of them. At 5.15 A. M. we had only arrived at Mojave station, having lost time during our night run. Just above the station at Mojave a large warehouse had taken fire in the night and the ruins were still burning. The water tanks of the cars were filled here with water which is led down from the mountains in pipes and we have again a plentiful supply. We have trouble in one or the other, and sometimes both, of the sleepers wherever we make a long stop and the engine leaves us. The tanks are under the cars and the air supply is necessary to force the water up into the spigots. If the pressure is not put on before the engine leaves or is wasted by unnecessary turning of the cocks we are sometimes put to it to get enough water for our use, even if the tanks are full. The dining-car people are wiser and have their tanks overhead, the space under the car being fully utilized for the refrigerators.

We are running this morning through a corner of the Mojave desert and find it furnished with the usual supply of cacti, sage brush and greaseweed bushes. Jack rabbits, prairie dogs and gophers furnish the usual variety to the scenery. Some of the larger cacti, known as the Yucca palm, would have been noble ornaments for some of the Philadelphia gardens. They grow to a height of from twelve to twenty feet and send out branches without any preconceived idea of regularity, but in just such directions as you do not look for them to grow. They look like gnarled and knotted trees, being from eight to ten inches in diameter and bear numbers of bright yellow flowers. Many other varieties of lower stature were scattered among the bushes of sage brush and took to themselves many curious shapes and combinations. As we approach the mountains, the ground begins to rise into little hills and detached buttes of earth, which finally merge into a low range of hills that end in the mountains.

The clay buttes assume peculiar forms, rising from one to four or five hundred feet, and their sides washed in gullies and channels by the rains give variety to the view. As soon as we left Mojave we began to go up grade and were soon climbing at the rate of 160 feet to the mile. All the way up the mountains, the space between which was of a good width, the land was well cultivated, much of it being planted in immense fields of wheat. Some of it had been cut and stacked, but the harvest was still in progress by means of traction machines which cut, threshed and bagged the grain at one operation.

The tin horn was missing this morning, having probably been lost yesterday by bugler Munch, and the owls will have to hunt up some other weapon of offence. Emmerling had found a section of gum hose at Santa Barbara, about four feet in length, which he took to bed with him as a means of retaliation on those who waked him up. It proved very efficacious and a source of much astonishment to those around whom he got a chance to wind its flexible length.

Tehachapi Summit was gained at 6.15 A. M. and our train side-tracked to allow the passage of a regular train coming in the opposite direction. Nine-tenths of the buildings on either side of the track were saloons. They were all closed up yet, because everybody was asleep except the proprietor of one good-sized combination store. He had never heard of a souvenir spoon, but sold us some of the worst smelling sulphur matches that could be found on top of ground. After the south-bound train had passed, we started on our way down the northern slope of the mountains, but had not gone but a little way before a young bull stopped the train by standing in the middle of the track. He was a sturdy young bovine and seemed inclined to dispute the right of way with the iron horse, paying no attention to the shrieks of its whistle. The gleam in his eye was not inviting enough for any one to get out and chase him and we waited until he at length thought better of the matter, when he walked to one side of the track where he stood and watched us pass by.

Going down toward the Loop there was a succession of wild views, grand in the extreme when visible to us. We were running down the more than steep grades at what seemed a terrific rate of speed, with rocks half a mile above our heads on one side and an abyss on the outside of the train of more than that depth with nothing but good luck between us and the bottom ; the few trees in the way not counting if we had once run off the the track. At every two or three turns we would dive into a hole like our friend the prairie dog but, unlike him, we came out on the opposite side. There were twenty-six tunnels between the summit and Caliente and we did not miss any of them.

At one point a jack-rabbit was scared up, which started down the narrow trail abreast of the track, seemingly in an attempt to race with the train. He kept up pretty well, to the great amusement of those watching him, until the train fouled him by going straight across a filled in cut, while he went down one side and up the other and got left. Breakfast was entirely neglected in the absorbing interest taken in the scenery. The train seemed to be dancing a jig along the mountain sides, so much did it turn and wind about. The track we had been on, the one we were on and the one we intended to be on were all generally visible at the same time on different levels

The train was stopped for a few minutes on the edge of a sheer descent of several thousand feet to give us a view of Caliente just three miles distant across the valley, but we had to travel fourteen miles to get down to its level. Finally at 6.50 A. M. the train twisted its tail and gave a last flourish as it ran under itself and dived into a hole in the ground, which looked before we reached it like a jumping-off place to the Antipodes. It was only another tunnel and we soon emerged from its depths and squared away for Caliente which we reached at 7.35 A.M. The place appeared to be more of a starting point for numerous stage-lines, than to have any special importance of its own.

The running from here on was more level and we started in to make up some of our lost time on the schedule as well as to get even with Brooks' bill of fare for the morning meal. We had not yet finished the wrestle with the latter when we pulled in to Bakersfield at 8.15 A. M. Before the train had stopped a committee of Sir Knights consisting of Judges Conklin and Brundage and Dr. Cook had boarded it and invited the pilgrims to take a ride about Bakersfield and inspect the country. Judge Conklin represented Bodie, No. 15, of Bakersfield and was a Past Grand Master of the State. He was presiding over the Superior Court and had adjourned its hour of meeting until 2 P. M. in order to be with us this morning. Judge Brundage was from Coeur de Lion No. 9, of Los Angeles, while Dr. Cook was a member of Arizona Commandery, No. 1, of Arizona. Mr. J. H. Little of the Kern County Land Co. was also anxious that we should see the possibilities of the land hereabouts.

Carriages were soon in readiness and the pilgrims, with the Committee, stowed away therein. The first drive was over a rough and rather hilly, dusty road which apparently ran a great risk of dwindling down to a squirrel track and running up a tree. Our wonder was not so much as to where we were bound for, but rather why we were going there, until we wound up at what was called by our hosts, Panorama View. We wondered no longer but drank in the scene and were thankful. Down in the valley far beneath us flowed as much of the River Kern as the canal people had left to it. On either side of it, following its silver thread in its windings, spread out a garden country, fair and green in the sunlight and extending for miles. A little turn to the left and the eye took in at one sweep the town of Bakersfield, which embraces several outlying colonies.

Two years ago the town was literally swept from the face of the earth by a fire which destroyed everything, the entire population having been compelled to camp out. To-day, not a vestige of that fire remains. The town is rebuilt on wide, handsome streets, lined with substantial brick dwellings and business houses of modern style. It has now a population of 3000 white and 1200 Chinese inhabitants, which is expected to more than double in the next five years.

While driving away from the panoramic bluff, we were startled by a number of explosions and heavy clouds, apparently of smoke, hanging in the air ahead of us. We were re-assured by the doctor and informed that it was merely parties blasting for gravel. The top soil for four or five feet down was blown off with dynamite and the bed of gravel laid bare to be carted out. The clouds were only dust but they hung a long while in the rarefied air of the valley. It was a trifle hazy this morning and we were unable to see Mt. Whitney which, although two hundred miles distant, can be seen distinctly on a clear day. This beats the record so far as we have gone.

We were driven now across the prairie to see some of the industrial works now being prosecuted and to get a glimpse of some of the irrigating canals. Our drivers took us down through a dirt canon to try our nerves and succeeded in rattling some of us when short turns were made on the steep grades with the fresh four-in-hands behind which we travelled. At one point a small army of Chinamen was engaged in making a heavy cut for a new railroad, while several similar detachments were digging fresh canals. They were nearly all equipped with the bamboo hat, like an inverted wash-basin. Their quarters were a regular encampment near a spring or some running stream where the cooking gang were now hard at work preparing their noonday meal. Men were carrying water and other articles suspended from the Chinese yoke which fitted across their shoulders. They were all well acquainted with us and answered to the name of John as readily and pleasantly as John Keen.

A similar crowd of Mongolians were working an asphaltum mine on one portion of the prairie, the product of which was being refined in a large new building at another point on our route. While boring for the asphalt, a vein of lubricating oil had been struck and was now being worked with great profit. At several places we crossed the main irrigating canals, one of which the Calloway, is thirty-three miles long, one hundred and twenty feet wide at the top, eighty feet at the bottom and has a depth in some places of six feet. Several others are nearly as large, there being in Kern River valley a length of over three hundred miles of main canals, with nearly two thousand miles of lateral branches. The valley is nearly as level as a floor and we saw there two canals, not over four feet apart, in which the water ran in different directions. In their length of over four miles there was but eight inches difference in the grade. The water rents are not high, the charges varying from one to two dollars per acre annually. The alfalfa grass is grown here to a large extent, more than 85,000 acres being planted with it. Three crops a year are cut from it and during the balance of the year the immense herds of cattle brought in from the plains are pastured and fattened on it. Horses are kept in green pastures the year round.

The two judges and the doctor had some great yarns about the growth of some of the vegetable productions of the valley ; stories very apropos of what we have been informed was the country of " little matches and big liars," that is California.   We took in most of the doctor's stories until he tried one on us about a head of cabbage that was grown here and reached the size of seven feet in diameter.   That cabbage stuck in our throats and is there yet.   We thought perhaps he was giving us another when he said that sometimes the winds blew so hard and so suddenly as to leave the gopher holes sticking eighteen inches in the air.   This we found afterwards to be a fact because the gopher, of which we saw plenty on our drive, coats the burrow which it makes in the ground with mud. When this gets hard, the dirt can be removed from around it, leaving it stand-ing like a tube eight or ten inches high.   Judge Conklin likewise got off a corker about his potatoes, which are sold in this country by the ton.

A drive through the business part of the town gave the spoon fiends a chance, as well as other shoppers.   The opportunity was also taken advantage of to show us an exhibit in Drury's drug store of some canned, or rather bot-tled fruits that are being selected to send to the exposition at Chicago next year.   If we should attempt to size up some of the exhibits in those jars, we should acquire a regular California reputation and will therefore leave them to be seen at Chicago.   Drury also had a jar of rattlesnake skins with rattles attached, but no stuffing in, at one dollar each.

One saloon on the main street had a huge sign out which gave some-what contradictory advice to this effect.   "Save your money for the World's Fair ! while you are here drink Buffalo beer."   At Dr. Cook's house, which we passed several times, we saw a young fawn which had been captured but a few weeks, but would follow any one about like a young dog.

Our time was now drawing to a close, which compelled us to return to the train.   Here we took leave of our entertainers with many expressions of our thanks and boarded the cars again.   A telegram was found at the station from Fresno, our next stop, saying that the Sir Knights at that place would have car-riages in waiting for us upon our arrival for a drive around Fresno.   We were a little late and did not get off until 11.15 A. M.

In the three hours we had put in at Bakersfield we had received consider-able information to digest at our leisure, which was supplemented by numerous pamphlets which Mr. Little had distributed throughout the train.

Soon after leaving Bakersfield we were shown, at some distance across the prairie, what looked very much like a large lake.   After admiring the immense sheet of water sufficiently, we were informed that it was not a lake at all, but only the effect of mirage.   We begin to feel that we are getting into a very bad section of the country when we cannot even believe what we see, to say nothing of what we hear.   Just before reaching Tulare, at 12.40 P. M., a large section of the prairie was seen on fire.   This was undoubtedly real, as there could be no imitation about the volume of smoke and fire that rolled up from it. The country was dead level and we scratched out over it from forty to fifty miles an hour without any trouble. The natives rush from both sides to read the side badges on our cars and cheer us as we fly past. Numerous camps of Chinese section laborers at work on the railroad are passed, the most of the occupants being now engaged on luncheon like ourselves. The sun seems pretty warm, but there is a cool air blowing. The mercury only indicates 83°, which is not doing badly for a section of the country of which even the railroad men predicted that "the backs of our necks would be roasted." At Goshen at 1 P. M. The wheat crops along our road are still being harvested and we see some astonishing machines which they are using in that process. One reaper, or whatever its name might be, looked like a frame house on the move and had twenty-eight horses attached. The driver was stuck up in front on a telegraph pole, or something similar, with a seat on the end of it. Another was drawn by thirty horses and all that we saw, cut, threshed and bagged the grain, dropping three bags at a time when filled. In some places the straw was being burned as soon as threshed out.

At Kingsburg were immense warehouses for the storage of wheat, of which large quantities are annually shipped from this station. Irrigation is also used here for fruit raising, it not being needed in the wheat fields. Water is secured for the purpose not only from the ditches, but also by means of windmills set up over wells out of which they pump the water. Just beyond the town we crossed the King's River which also had some water in it, a sight to which we were again becoming slowly accustomed. Many vineyards now began to show up along the road. The vines grow or are trained low down to the ground, looking more like sweet potatoes than grape vines. One vineyard was fenced in for more than a mile with a hedge of crab-apple trees, whose bright colored and plentiful show of fruit possessed a most pleasing effect.

As a result of fast running we picked up our lost time and arrived at Fresno at 2 P. M. Sir Knights Silleck, Williams, Baker, Maupin, Anderson and Congar, of Fresno Commandery No. 29, were on hand and extended us a cordial welcome. Presently teams began to arrive at the station until more than enough were on hand to accommodate the entire party. Sir Knights would drive up with their double teams, load up four or six of our party and, handing over the lines, direct us to follow our leaders of whom a half dozen stayed with us as guides to the wineries which we were desired to visit. How many miles of grapevines we drove through that afternoon would be hard to calculate, as would the number of large bunches of grapes our conductors cut for us to see, although still unripe. Some of our party too, vandal like, would jump out and secure six or seven-pound bunches of white grapes for the pleasure of gazing upon them. Plenty of pear and apple trees lined the sides of the roads, laden with ripe fruit, under which the carriages would be driven with injunctions to help ourselves. Orders were strictly obeyed in this case and the trees despoiled at will, as the pears were ripe and good tasted. Five or six wineries were visited during the afternoon and, if all the wine set out to be sampled had been consumed, the party would have had a big load on and the horses a double one. 120,000 gallons of wine in one vault was a common exhibit with the wineries and all had vault after vault to show us into. They have thousands of acres planted in vines and other thousands in which they raise grains to utilize the ground until they are ready to set it out in vines. The irrigating canals line the sides of the roads as usual, but the water in this section is chiefly derived from flowing artesian wells from two to five hundred feet

FRESNO DRIVE

deep. We had noticed numerous derricks as we came up the railroad but thought they might be trying for oil.

The approach to the Las Palmas winery is through an avenue of palm trees lining each side of the avenue for a distance of nearly a mile and giving the roadway a grand tropical appearance. Another avenue of equal length, which gave entrance to another winery, had great oleander bushes planted between the large trees on each side. These were now loaded down with huge bunches of flowers both red and white. The effect was indescribable and called forth continual exclamations of pleasure from inside the carriages, but did not hinder the occupants from securing fine bunches of the bloom. The main roads were all lined with beautiful umbrella and fig trees, in addition to the fruit trees. The graceful foliage of the former was much admired, but the green figs did not seem to agree as well with the taste of the party as the sugar-cured article. We have had them set before us several times mashed or broken up and smothered in cream, but we have concluded that a liking for fresh figs is another taste that must be acquired. It adds very much to the appearance of the country to see that, where the space is utilized to so great an extent for vines and grain, such

OLEANDER AVENUE

a plenty is left to display flowers and ornamental trees. Most of the roads were deep with dust and all of us were deeply coated with it outside, but the majority found plenty of the wherewithal to wash down that which lodged in their throats. The teams were all first-class and did not seem to suffer any for want of water, of which they were not given a drop throughout the afternoon. Some of them, we were told, were in the habit of traveling their eighty miles per day and only taking a drink at each end of the route. Mrs. Allen, who had been taken ill at Santa Barbara, did not feel equal to the ride this afternoon and was kindly taken in charge by the good lady of Sir Knight Williams and cared for while we were away.

It was late for dinner when we arrived back at the train, after making a circuit of the city on our return from the country. The city possesses many fine private residences which have elegant gardens. The business portion of the city also comprises fine blocks. The streets are wide and one of them is spanned by an arch which is evidently a legacy from the Tilden and Hendricks campaign for President. Electric lights are everywhere and street-car lines afford the necessary transportation.

After dinner we roamed across the railroad tracks to the Chinatown suburb, inspecting the stores and making vain attempts to borrow a pipe and buy some opium. A Chinaman would come in and buy his ten cents worth of dope before our eyes, but the dealer would swear the next moment that he had not a taste of opium in the store. One merchant was kept busy by the boys, counting up the proceeds of imaginary sales on his counting machine, an instrument just like the ancient abacus. With the aid of this machine, John is a rival for some of the lightning calculators. Some of the almond-eyed heathen were very anxious to find out the distance to Philadelphia and what kind of a harbor it was for Chinamen. At 8 P. M. the lines were formed to march to the asylum of Fresno No. 29, in response to an invitation from the fraters of that Command-ery to spend the evening with them. Everybody was invited and all responded with the exception of the big four, who were found missing when the asylum was reached, only a few blocks away. They had probably gravitated towards Chinatown under the influence of some stronger attraction. The asylum was well filled with the Sir Knights and their families and some time was spent in fraternizing with them and getting their signatures in Mary's traveling register. At the request of the committee the line of march was then taken up for the banquet room, where all were seated at tables laden with fruits, wines, flowers, cream and cakes. After a season of refreshment a number of short speeches were made on behalf of each Commandery and by some of the citizens of Fresno. One of the latter, a Rev. Mr. Anderson, was anything but compli-mentary in his remarks to the Knights of Fresno Commandery, who had so exerted themselves to exemplify to us the fraternal lessons of Knight Templar-ism. Miss Daisy Sharp also favored us with a recitation.

The evening was right royally spent until 9.45 P. M., at which time we were compelled to take leave and return to the train, pretty well laden down with the contents of the table that we could not eat or drink while there. Fresno has the reputation of having once raised the largest sweet potato in the world, which is said to have weighed forty pounds. That sweet potato does not compare with the size of the hearts in the Fresno Knights and their ladies.

We parted at the station at 10 P.M. when our train pulled out for Monte-rey, with many cheers for Fresno Commandery. The party did not seem in any hurry to retire to-night, although all were fatigued by the exertions of the day. The smoker was well occupied until 11 P.M. when the crowd began to ebb away and was soon sleeping the sleep of the just.

RAN THIS morning onto siding at Del Monte station at 6.30. We were on schedule time but were not yet ready to quit the train, because Brooks owed us a breakfast. Long before the meal was over, coaches were in waiting to take us up to the hotel, where we were to remain until to-morrow morning. The station is just at the foot of the hotel grounds, which fact induced many to walk up and take note of the grove of ancient oaks and pines that surrounds the hotel itself. The gnarled and twisted old live oaks with their grotesque shapes contrasted strangely with the tall and perfectly straight pines which towered far above their heads. The surroundings of this house unlike most of the large hotels we have visited, must have taken ages to arrive at the size they have attained.

The Del Monte stands with its back to the ocean, about a half mile distant, and faces the south. It is another of the colossal houses with which we are being made familiar on this coast, rectangular in shape and not as pleasing to the eye as Del Coronado, with its graceful curves. It is very handsomely fitted up and the interior of all the larger rooms. office, parlors, reading, ball, billiard and dining-rooms is painted a snowy white. This shows no sign of tarnish from the fact that the climate is too cool to be healthy for flies. A feature of the hotel are the approaches to the rooms on the two wings on either side of the main building. These are in the form of twin inclined planes. One of these descends to the rooms of the first floor, while the other ascends to those of the third floor. the second being on the level of the office, without the use of stairs.

The house is surrounded by gardens containing flower and plant-beds of every conceivable design and variety of color. The beds in many instances are designed to imitate woven rugs or carpets and, with the dazzling colors of growing plants and the mosses possible to be had here, seem to outdo the carpet designs themselves. The gardens proper contain 126 acres and to our party were an everlasting source of wonder and admiration. A section, known as the Arizona garden, was set apart for the display of the wonderful variety of cacti we had seen while crossing the desert as well as many more whose first acquaintance we made here. Interspersed witn various rocky formations and sandy pathways, it seemed like a section of another country set down in the midst of the brilliant verdure which surrounded it.

Immense greenhouses, with beds surrounding them, kept up the supply and variety for the parterres around the hotel or furnished you with bouquets to order. The finest roses we have ever seen in one bunch came from these grounds. Surrounding all the walks were the velvety green lawns which, as we notice all through this country, have to be not only sprinkled every day but actually soaked with water to keep them in good condition. The Chinaman, with his gum boots and sprinklers spraying in all directions, has been our steady company throughout the State, while his twin brothers sit around the brilliant borders, patiently snipping away with their shears all day.

We found here another and much more complete maze, with borders of cypress bushes growing higher than your head and covering perhaps a couple of acres. It was laid out by an intricate pattern and more than difficult to find your way out of, with no holes broken through to evade the penalty of getting lost.

Croquet and tennis grounds abound and a beautiful little lake, with row-boat attachments and some Japanese water-fowl of rather combative instincts, helps to fill out the perfect picture. The Club House, which stands at some little distance from the front of the hotel, is a tasteful structure and is surrounded by more beautiful flower carpets than the main building. Club House is only a Western synonym for the bar and sporting rooms. This particular institution queered itself on the first morning by taxing Jimmy Baird a cart wheel dollar for two drinks, a ginger ale and a three cent cigar. He would not have minded the train being held up by foot pads, but to be skinned according to law was too much.

We had no sooner been installed into the hotel and roomed, than the baggage was on hand. Nearly everybody secured clean clothes and made a break for the salt water bathing pool down at the beach. It was found rather cool for surf bathing, which is claimed to be indulged in all the year round at most of these watering places and our party infinitely preferred the heated salt water pools. This bath-house had four pools about forty feet square each, surrounded by dressing rooms and the whole decorated with tropical plants and hanging baskets of flowers. For an hour or two the tanks were the scene of hilarious enjoyment, especially to Charley Shaw, who made a dive into one of the pools and came up minus his upper teeth. All efforts made to recover them failed, until the water was drawn off the pool in the afternoon, when Charley recovered his lost property and good looks.

The interior court yard or hollow square within the hotel buildings was also a mass of brilliant color around the borders, formed principally of geraniums which grew to a large size. Great numbers of brilliantly plumaged humming birds, some of which were not much larger than bumble bees, were continually hovering over then and extracting their sweets. The centre beds were occupied by palm gardens and a circular arbor covered with cypress vines.

At 12.30 P.M. luncheon was on the boards and was dispatched in quick time to get ready for the seventeen mile drive which was set down for 1.30 P.M. At that hour the carriages were on hand and were quickly filled. John Keen was a little under the weather and unable to go along, while Mrs. Keen stayed at home to nurse him.

We first drove into Monterey and through a portion of that historical town. The old town seems to have had no laying out, but is traversed by narrow, crooked lanes, dotted with relics of the ancient Spanish rule. The old Spanish hotel is now a deserted looking two storied structure of adobe with white plastered walls and board shutters. If it had any inhabitants they were all enjoying a siesta. What had been the old State House, in the palmy days when Monterey was the capital of the State, is now the common jail and, but for the iron bars in the windows, would not seem capable of confining any modern criminals for a great while. Another ancient building was pointed out as the first theatre in California. The Cathedral and the ruined walls of the ancient Mission also came in for a share of attention.

We were fortunate in having secured the services of a very intelligent driver, whose stock of information was above the average and whose useful, as well as quaint, remarks served to instruct and amuse us during the afternoon. A monument to Padre Serra, the leader of the Franciscan Mission movement to these shores, is on a gentle elevation just outside the town. Also the remains of an old fort with one gun still pointing into the air. The last building on the right of the road as we drove out of the town was a saloon. On its sign which extended across the footway was the legend " The last chance." After we passed we read on the reverse, " The first chance," so it was good for a drink going either way.

Our road led us first through groves of live oak which, with its pendant mosses, looked like a section transplanted from some of the Southern States. Our driver informed us that there were twenty-eight distinct varieties of oak in these grounds, the ride taking us almost entirely through or around the Del Monte reservation of 7000 acres. Whether it was something in the air of the place or a fresh streak of acquired laziness on our part in this new country, we could not tell, but it was almost impossible to keep awake and enjoy the scenery around us. One would get to nodding, in spite of the imminent risk of falling out of the carriage. Robinson, who was sandwiched between Foster and Allen, could lay over on either shoulder and sleep safely, while his outside guards were compelled to keep their eyes open or fall overboard.

Along the Bay of Monterey we wound by a smooth macadamized road, watching the breakers foam over the immense masses of black rock which lined the shore and seemed to have been placed there for the especial purpose of making a picturesque coast. Farther out shoals of porpoises darted through the waves, following one another in graceful curves as sheep take a stream of water. Several collections of the rudest kind of huts, with fish drying scaffolds attached, denoted the abiding places of the Chinese who follow the fishing industry for a livelihood. They could be seen off shore in their boats, in pursuit of the pompano and barracouta, while around the huts were their wives and children drying the fruits of their skill or engaged in preparing abalone and other shells for sale to the tourists. We stopped at one shanty and did our best to deplete the young Chinese wife's stock of shells and admired her family of four little Johns.

Plenty of wild ducks were skimming over the face of the waters or paddling around in flocks looking for food. Quail also very frequently ran across the road in front of our team from one thicket to another. Our attention was called to a point of rocks far ahead of us, on which we could apparently see an overgrown ostrich about forty feet high. It was an excellent representation but we found, upon a second inspection, that it was only one of the many shapes into which the gnarled and twisted cypresses had grown, while the resemblance was less marked as we drew nearer. The shore side of our ride drew most attention as we followed its windings around towards Cypress Point. The rocks were the acme of picturesque beauty, being black with age, bold and rugged in contour and covered with all varieties of weeds and moss, whose long ribands sailed lazily up and down on the long rollers as they rose and fell. Several islands or rather large rocks were covered with guano deposits and their high parts black with the birds who had made them.

Pelicans were plenty with their long bills and immense pouches pendant thereto, in which they were busily engaged depositing the fish that they picked up. At several different points there were collections of seals massed on the rocks. These are not the fur seal of commerce, but what is known as the hair or Harp seal. They are protected by law at this, as well as other points, on the coast and allowed to propagate and enjoy their rocky homes in peace.

Shorewards we are hemmed in by sand-hills along which many wild flowers are growing, one of which, the sand verbena, is very dainty and very plentiful. Every little while in the sand we see large deposits of that material of a snowy whiteness, which we are informed is pure silica. After turning Midway Point, with its lone and hoary old cypress sentinel, we enter upon a stretch of two and a half miles dotted with the same growth of trees, whose fantastic shapes remind one strongly of some of Doré's illustrations to Dante's Inferno. Our four-in-hand expert insists stubbornly that these trees are not a genuine cypress, but a species of juniper tree. He also volunteered the information that one of them was undoubtedly from 800 to 1000 years old when

Moses was picked up adrift by Pharoah's daughter. They all certainly look as if they had been clinging to their rocky foundations for ages.

Our Jehu also claimed that the pines, which are also plentiful in these woods, are a species within themselves and a growth peculiar to this section. We had certainly never observed any before with the peculiarity to which he called our attention. This was the fact that the pine cones grew against the main trunk or beside the limbs and not out on the twigs or branches as is usual with pine trees.

Emerging from the cypress growth, the beautiful view of El Carmelo Bay opened before us, with the light house on Point del Soeur in the distance. The shore itself is unusually wild and rocky, and worn by the action of the waves into rounded buttresses and black caverns into which the waters dash with a hollow roar. Back from the shore, on the opposite side of the Bay, where the Santa Lucia Mountains were visible, the fog was rolling around and below their tops like wreaths of smoke. Beyond Pebble Beach, with its tinted collection of stones giving Gorman a chance to fill his coat pockets without moving a foot, we struck another collection of Chinese fisher huts. Almost adjoining an enterprising showman had put up a tent in which to establish a show of a genuine "Buffalo" with several other curiosities. This affords a melancholy commentary on the prodigal recklessness which stripped the country of the herds that were but a few years ago deemed countless and inexhaustible.

Our road now turned towards Monterey again, striking into the county road which we found rougher and dustier than the great Macadam drive we had hitherto been on. We also found some pretty steep hills to climb. At the top of one of these called the Summit, we halted for a grand view. In front of us laid the Hotel Del Monte, Old Monterey, together with the Bay of Monterey and beyond all the majestically rolling Pacific. Back of us were the deep blue waters of Carmelo Bay and the farther shore with its background of mountain ranges.

Soon we dashed down the steep hill and reached another section of the old town. Spanish signs on stores and fences are frequent, while the boys gabble in a language unintelligible to our ears. Around many of the gardens, in which nestle adobe houses, are adobe walls with coverings of the ancient reversed tiles we have noticed before. Over the little paths leading from the gates to the front doors are many arches formed of jaw bones from the whale, a curious but lasting ornament. These are the remains of the whale fishery at this point, an industry that has been carried on for many years by Norwegian fishermen who go out in boats and capture the leviathan of the deep, tow him ashore onto the beach and try out the oil. Whales are said to come into the bays occasionally at this season, but none performed for our benefit.

A sweep around a sharp corner and we are again whirling through the forest trees surrounding the Del Monte, at whose front portal we are landed again at 5 P. M. The sleepy feeling culminated as soon as we landed in numerous naps, in more or less comfortable positions, by the majority of the party before the doors were opened for dinner at 6.30 P. M.

The celerity with which we were served at this meal was something phenomenal and unaccountable as well until we found that the waiters had orders to rush us through in order to attend to a large number of new arrivals who had come in on the evening train. Gorman and others, who became possessed of the information, managed to occupy the attention of their waiters for a much longer time than they otherwise would if things had taken their regular course.

Rest was in demand after dinner and many sought it by dozing in the main hall around the blazing log fire in the open fire-place. Outside on the porches, overcoats were in demand as they had been during the drive this afternoon. The shuffle boards on the front portico were generously patronized all the evening, in the endeavor to remain out of doors and keep warm at the same time. The ten-pin contingent hunted up the alleys over at the Club House, where Kessler managed to have a finger caught and mashed between the balls, as one of the China boys rolled another ball down the gutter against them. All hands retired tolerably early and slept under a stack of coverlets that would have been kicked off in a hurry at home.

Friday, July 29th, 1892.

REAKFAST was got over in a straggling manner this morning, the earliest risers having sufficient time to take a farewell stroll through the gardens in the cool morning air. The baggage was ordered to be in readiness at 6 A. M. to give the porters some chance and to allow Speakman to get it on the train before starting time. Everybody was on board at 8.30 A. M. and we departed at that hour with the same feeling that had possessed us at other places ; that more time might have been pleasurably and profitably spent at this point. Our ride this morning was through another fruitful country in which, although there was a great growth of wheat, particular attention seemed to be paid to trucking. Some of the potato patches through which we passed can only be classed as prodigious.

Santa Cruz was our objective point, which we reached at 10.15 A. M. The train stopped at the foot of a steep bluff, on which was perched the Sea Beach Hotel. We had only to climb several flights of steps and take possession of the house at the invitation of Sir Knight John T. Sullivan, the proprietor. We had hardly recovered our wind before the same courteous frater invited us to take a ride and see Santa Cruz in the right way. Sir Gamble and other Knights of Watsonville Commandery were present at our arrival, bade us a cordial welcome and tendered their services to help us make the most of our few hours stay. Our train had deserted us here and gone around to San José by the route we had come, leaving us to rejoin it at that point by a trip over the Narrow Gauge road which passed by the Big Trees. Hemphill had gone back to the train after some of his chattels not thinking of its leaving. When he knew that it was off for good it was running at a pretty high rate of speed. He made a jump for it and fortunately escaped without accident. After a wash and an investigation by some of the curious minded into the mysteries of Santa Cruz rum punches, we were taken possession of by Sir Sullivan and installed into the carriages of his providing, with as much solicitude on his part as if we were guests of his for a month. Our first stop was at the Santa Cruz Mountain Winery. The vaults of this institution are dug from the solid rock, a kind of conglomerate of which the bluffs along the coast appear to be formed, and extend over or rather under about a square of ground. The temperature in them does not vary more than one degree from 45° the year round. Samples of all the various kinds of liquid refreshments that are here produced were brought forth and pressed upon us. A new wrinkle to the samplers was introduced under the name of Strawberry Brandy and found instant favor. It was pronounced very good by all who imbibed it, and a number of cases purchased for shipment to home. A further drive through the city revealed many beautiful dwellings and fine gardens, although all the flowers in Santa Cruz had been destroyed four years ago by a frost which strayed this way. Our host Sullivan showed us many fine specimens of the Lady Washington geraniums which were now nine feet high and had been raised from seed inside of two years. The main stems were as thick as a man's wrist and still growing.

Vineyards were planted on all the sunny slopes. One of them on the side of a hill, that seemed just about steep enough for goat travel, our hosts assured us had been planted with a crow-bar, which was necessary to make holes in the rock for the roots of the vines. They were growing as luxuriantly as any of their neighbors. A long drive through the town and along the bluffs of the bay shore ensued. The shore here is cut and carved by the action of the waves into many picturesque patterns and rugged designs. In one place a natural bridge has been formed, and at a number of others there are spout holes in the surface with cavities under, into which the sea rushes and sends a column high into the air through the holes. Our route led us to a light-house away up the shore, and we returned by another course, passing on the road a sort of Ocean Grove establishment, with a large building called the Christian Tabernacle in the centre, and a regular camp-meeting array of tents on every side. We understood that several different denominations have similar places of meeting in Santa Cruz, which they occupy at different seasons. Devotional exercises were in progress in the main building as we passed, and sundry savory smells arising from the tent dwellings, denoted that somebody had a weather eye for the temporal wants of the community. The San Lorenzo River, which we crossed in our progress, had plenty of water in it, although not so extensive a stream as some of the empty ones we passed in the South. We were back to the Sea Beach at 12.30 P. M. sharp set for luncheon. Here we had another bright array of girls to wait upon us, and quick and excellent service we received to a fine luncheon. A large wicker or bamboo chair, with a hooded back or overhang, which completely hid the occupant from view, was a feature of this place, both on the hotel porches and the sand of the beach at the bath-houses. After luncheon the balmy air on the porches and a cigar superinduced cat naps, for which those chairs were exactly built. But woe to him who put faith enough in his fellow-man to indulge in that luxury. He was instantly laid over on his back on the porch floor. Once turned down he was as helpless as a turned turtle, and only released by his tormentors when the rush of blood to

NATURAL BRIDGE—SANTA CRUZ

the head threatened apoplexy. Emmerling was a favorite mark for the sport, but it took the united strength of two or three either to turn him down or lift him up again. ' The position was more undignified than uncomfortable.

Santa Cruz lies at one end of the crescent formed by the Bay of Monterey, directly opposite and facing Monterey, which is at the other. The bay is not a bay, strictly speaking, but an almost semi-circular indentation of the coast. Santa Cruz is the most popular and fashionable seaside resort in the state, and is known as the Newport of California. It has one of the finest beaches we have ever seen but the surf is not heavy. The view from the porch of the Sea Beach commands every possible feature of scenery. The Beach, the long swell on the waters of the broad expanse of the bay, with the old town of Monterey in the far distance, the flower gardens of the hotel and adjacent houses, the city rising from the beach back, the foot hills dotted all over with green vine- . yard growths and the mountain ranges towering back of all to keep off the bleak winds of the North, furnishing a temperature ranging from $52°$ in winter to $62°$ in summer. At a long pier, running out into the bay just above the hotel, a number of fishing boats were lying, each being rigged with a huge lateen sail of the true Mediterranean type. Many of the same craft were skimming over the water under the impetus of these sails and it was a mystery to those used to the fore and aft rig how they managed to trim them to the wind. An invitation from the Electric Car Co., to take a ride over their route after luncheon was accepted by forty of the party who appropriated the two cars sent for their accommodation at 2 P. M. The trolley system extends all through the city and out along the bluffs on which we had ridden this morning as well as along the beach to the bathing houses. The main street seemed to be bustling with trade and a number of manufacturing interests were also passed during our ride. The city is the county seat of Santa Cruz county and quite a railroad centre. It appears to be plentifully supplied with churches, judging from the spires, and has all other modern improvements.

A few of the party tried the bathing but the icy water soon drove them out onto the sand, whence the cool and bracing air sent them into their clothes again. The cars were back with the excursionists shortly before 3 P. M. After thanking Sir Sullivan and our other entertainers, we took our leave of them and wended our way to the Narrow Gauge Depot. Our train had not yet arrived and when it did come, it struck us as a strange contrast to the gilded and upholstered Pullmans we had been occupying so many days, but we concluded we might scratch through a few hours in it. At 3.05 P. M. we bade farewell to Santa Cruz and started up the valley of the dashing little San Lorenzo River.

The route crossed the Santa Cruz mountains through as wildly picturesque a region as any we had yet seen. Deep gorges on the one side with high cliffs on the other, made up the prospect when we had left the river and turned up along Boulder Creek. The situation was reversed as we ascended, the mountains towering to a lesser height above us and the depth of the gorge being fearful to look down upon. The creek was well named, as boulders of every shape and tonnage lay thick in the rushing waters. Yet we looked down occasionally upon a peaceful farming scene or a small hamlet whenever enough level ground could be found on which to locate.

At 3.15 P. M. our train halted at Big Trees Station. A board enclosure made necessary the handing over of a fee of one dime to gain admittance to the grove. A number of visitors were already on the ground, having come out from San José in carriages. Among them we found our friend Col. Moore of Los Angeles. He had been sent as a delegate to some convention in San José and had taken advantage of the chance to visit the trees. The grove is quite an extensive one and has many trees that would be considered large with us, outside of those that give the name to the station. The largest of the show trees has a sign with the name of "Giant" thereon and is surrounded by a picket fence, over which we lifted two small boys and got them to run a line around the tree near its base. The measurement was found to be fifty-seven feet.

The "Fremont," near the entrance of the grove, has been burned out hollow at the bottom for many years. In the space thus produced, forty of our party were introduced and stood comfortably at one time, leaving room for half a dozen more if they would have brushed against the charred wood. Notwith-standing the amount of heart taken out of the tree, there was still sufficient of the trunk left to carry sustenance to the top, which was as green and flourish-ing as any of the other trees. The inside of the cavity was plastered with vis-iting cards bearing names from all quarters and one or two of our party dis-covered their own cards that had been put up in 1883. Each of these trees was nearly 400 feet in height and as straight as a ramrod, as were all the other trees of their species in the grove. They are of the Sequoia or redwood growth, but the foliage resembles the pine in every way. Many of the other trees reached a diameter of six to eight feet, but seemed insignificant besides their larger companions. A dance floor about twenty feet square was said to rest upon the trunk of one tree that had been cut down.

Pieces of bark from the big trees were on sale, together with photographs and other bric-a-brac. The bark makes capital pin cushions and is equal to emery for keeping those useful articles bright. Shaw bought a sample of the bark which Enochs, after measurement, reckoned up as costing him eighty cents per square foot. Some of the bark specimens were from eighteen to twenty inches thick and of a deep red color. These are cut from the larger trees in the Mariposa valley. Brown gathered a number of the party in front of the Giant and trained the camera on them for a large picture with the tree as a back-ground.

At 4 P.M. the bell rang and the train was re-occupied after much persua-sion and repeated calls. Our road still ran along the wild mountain scenery with the tumbling waters of the creek in the defile below. We had to run through several tunnels, one of which was a mile in length. At a station where we met another passenger train and a long freight train, it was quite a problem of railroad engineering as to how we were to pass both, with the limited side track accommodations. Some of the freight cars were loaded with bitumen and samples were gathered therefrom, with a view of testing its qualities as a chewing gum. With the stain taken out it might have worked all right. The two trains were finally passed by splitting them up and we continued our wild mountain journey without further interruption, although some of the sharp curves apparently made sudden stops possible. In many places vineyards were planted on slopes of the mountain sides that seemed almost impossible to climb. At 5.15 P. M. we got our first view of Mount Hamilton, with the Lick Observatory on its top, a shining white object that must be visible for a long distance. As we descended into the Santa Clara valley, the vista of vineyards, orchards and gardens opened up to our view was a new revelation. Fruit drying was progressing on an extensive scale. For miles the ground was yellow with apricots, split open and drying in the sun on frames laid on the ground. Several large canneries were passed in which people were intent on preserving the same kind of fruit. Orchards of all kinds merged into one another on each side of the railroad right into San José, at whose Narrow Gauge Depot we stopped at 5.33 P. M. Carriages were in waiting to convey us to the Hotel Vendome, where we were to hang up till to-morrow night. As we drove through the city, we passed the Catholic College of Notre Dame, standing in an enclosure of ten acres on one of the main streets. At the intersection of two of the thoroughfares was an iron tower or arch, springing from the four corners and meeting in the centre. At the top, which must have been a hundred feet from the ground, was a cluster of electric lights. It was a pretty good distance to the Vendome, but we arrived in time to wash and dress for dinner, our baggage having come by our own train and preceded us to our rooms.

The Vendome is another of the large Pacific hostelries, though smaller than the Del Monte or the Coronado. It is set back from the street in the midst of some very old oaks, whose attractions are supplemented by those of more modern and ornamental trees like the pepper, poplar and fig. Bright parterres of flowers fill out the intermediate spaces, which are divided by asphalt walks, and complete the picture from the street, of which the Queen Anne front of the hotel forms a fine background. The interior is tastefully decorated and finely furnished. In the large rotunda in front of the office, a general lounging place, was an immense open fire-place in which a large wood fire was burning upon our arrival. In the evenings and mornings this is a necessity. The air is so chilly as to make a light overcoat very agreeable. Most of the ladies of the party stayed indoors to-night, but some exploring parties were out to see what could be seen of the city by electric light.

Saturday, July 30th, 1892.

QUIET morning followed a quiet night and few early risers were on hand to greet the morning sun. Axford had been prowling around the greenhouses in the gray dawn and discovered that the gardener was a Germantown man, with whom he soon got on good terms. A number of the pilgrims were unfortunate enough to come down too late for breakfast and were shut out from that meal. Many visits were paid to our train this morning when it was found to be located only two blocks away at the Broad Gauge Depot. It was a stopping-place on the road to the stores which were being overhauled by the shoppers, as well as a haven of rest for the weary pilgrim who was eternally hunting out the sights and sounds of a strange place. The electric cars ran from in front of the hotel all around the city and, by exchanges, a complete circuit could be made. San José possesses some fine buildings, among which are conspicuous the Court House, State Normal School and City Hall. The Court House in particular will bear comparison with similar buildings in cities of much larger size.

Purdy had a great time this morning, endeavoring to find out who were or were not going up Mount Hamilton to the Lick Observatory. He finally settled on fifty who would make the trip and secured carriages for their use. Emmerling, Dill, Lafferty and Millick started up the shuffle-boards on the hotel porch as experts, and gradually drew in McDowell, McIntyre, Keen, Register and a number of ladies to learn them the game.

Mrs. Sir Knight McKee kindly brought her carriage to the hotel and took a party of ladies for a drive, repeating the favor in the afternoon for some of those who did not go up the mountain. Luncheon was served at an earlier hour than usual to allow the excursionists to get away in good time. At 12.30 P. M. the carriages were driven up to the door and a merry and noisy crowd set off for the trip. The Observatory is only thirteen miles away in an air line, but just double that amount of riding is necessary to reach it. The founder of the institution, Mr. James Lick, whose remains lie buried under the column on which the great telescope rests, had the county supervisors agree to build this road at a certain easy grade, as a means of access to the Observatory, shortly before his death.

Sir Charles L. Patton, of Golden Gate Commandery No. 16, of San Francisco, called in the afternoon and took several of the party out for a drive through the city and followed it up with a trip to Santa Clara. He is an old Philadelphian and he and Pop Millick soon discovered that they were mutually interested in Patton's Aunt Hannah. For three mortal hours the others in the carriage were regaled with a recital of Aunt Hannah's excellent traits and Patton's strict injunctions, repeated a hundred fold, to Millick, not to neglect to call on the old lady on his return and give her all the news from California.

They went the rounds of peach, cherry, apricot and prune orchards. The latter is one of the main industries of the county; more than half of all the prune trees in America growing in the Santa Clara valley. They were eager to get a sight of the first prune orchard and a little disappointed when they found a prune was only a plum, while on the tree.

The Santa Clara College, which was taken in en route, is a Catholic educational institution located upon the site of another old Mission, that of Santa Clara, and is celebrated for the thoroughness of the instruction there imparted. The old Mission building is still used as a chapel and the garden surrounding it contains many rare and beautiful plants. The return trip to San José was made by way of the famous Alameda Avenue, which was formerly bordered by large willow trees throughout its entire length of three miles, which had been planted by the Franciscan Fathers. These were all cut down a couple of years ago, to suit the convenience of the electric road which now occupies the avenue, so that it is now no more than any other country road.

By this time Patton had pretty nearly killed the old mare, but he declared his intention of still driving her out to his ranch, some seven miles, and back again this evening.

Upon reaching the Vendome, committees were found in waiting to make arrangements for receptions in San Francisco on Monday and Tuesday evenings next. Sir William Edwards, on the part of Golden Gate, No. 16, and Sirs Wells, Doane, Flint, Slack and Jas. Edwards in behalf of California, No. 1. The preliminaries necessary were soon fixed upon and the evening was spent in pleasant intercourse with the Knights who had come so far out of their way to welcome their fraters in a strange land. Mrs. Wells and Mrs. Jas. Edwards, who were stopping at the hotel, also succeeded, with the help of their lady friends, in making the evening pass very pleasantly for those of our ladies who had refrained from taking the mountain trip. Foster and Lee had gone on ahead this afternoon to hunt up some friends in San Francisco, while Axford accompanied them, intending to stop in Oakland.

The Observatory excursionists, who left the Vendome at 12.30 P. M., enjoyed a very interesting ride up the mountains. Passing first through a section of the orchards for which the country is famous, they mounted the foothills with their slopes laid off in vineyards. Thence over the first mountain range, gorgeous in its wonderful growth of shrubbery and the infinite variety of wild flowers. This brought them to Smith's Creek, from which point their arrival was telephoned back to the Vendome. A halt was made there to partake of an imitation dinner at six bits per capita. McIntyre re-christened the house as the Hotel de Starve. They had a new kind of soup called egg broth, which had evidently been made by floating egg shells on top of hot water.

From Smith's Creek the actual mountain climbing begins. Passing up the broad road, every curve and turn brought a wider field of vision. The view of the garden-like valley of Santa Clara, fair to behold, was supplemented by a sight of the waters of San Francisco Bay, to the Northward and Westward by the Pacific. From the top it is said to be possible, on a clear day, to see Mt. Shasta, four hundred miles distant, if your eyes are good enough. Prof. Whitney, the boss telescopist, claims that from this place more of the earth's surface is visible than from any other known point on the globe. We will not argue the question with him, but be satisfied with the grand series of panoramic views afforded us on our way over the two ranges of mountains and up the component part of the third, on which the Lick Observatory is perched, named Mount Hamilton. At the last curve in front of the building a halt was made at the edge of a sheer descent of two thousand feet. This abyss has been named the Oh ! My ! that being the invariable exclamation uttered by all lady tourists upon their first look down the precipice.

In the neighborhood of two hundred and fifty persons were at the summit on this evening, the stage company having brought several other parties and a number of private teams having made the ascent as well. It was necessary to sit around the walls in line to await your turn to get a peep in the large telescope. Meanwhile you had a chance to examine the wonderful mechanism by which the sides and roof were worked, and could take a squint through the smaller glasses. The whole dome turned at the behest of the operator as easily as you could open a window sash, and the floor was raised and lowered at his will.

The large glass was trained on the moon, and afforded a fine view of that luminary, the only disappointment expressed being the lament of Mrs. Johnson that she could not see the man therein. The planet Mars was shining like a ruddy beacon light, but the astronomers would not bring the telescope to bear upon it, as they were at this time busily engaged in trying to open up communication with the Marsians by means of somebody's ostensible irrigating ditches dug in that planet. They probably did not want any of our party to get in the first word, for fear we might learn some new fangled method of painting this planet red.

Another and smaller telescope was pointed at Saturn and his rings, the beauty of which was greatly admired. Harmon Johnson begged for a view of Venus, but it was impossible to accommodate him. The moonlight ride down the mountains, with the three hundred and sixty-seven turns in the road and

4,200 feet of descent to the level of San José, was most thrilling as the teams dashed around the sharp curves, giving the drivers a gay chance to display their ability to handle the ribbons. At the first change of horses, a bottle of Santa Cruz strawberry brandy was tested and found very beneficial, and a great aid towards keeping out the cold. Songs, ancient and modern, in all possible metres, served to while the time away and keep everybody in good humor. The drive which consumed five and a half hours in going up was cut down to three and a half on the return trip. The Vendome was regained at 12.30 A. M., with everybody looking as though they had come through a light snow storm, so covered with dust were their clothes.

The wood fire in the big open fire-place had been built up afresh in expectation of our arrival, and everybody crowded within the circle of heat from its welcome blaze. The hotel also set out a nice lunch of crab salad with some cold cuts for the excursionists, which put them in a good humor with all the world and the Vendome Hotel. All had come back very much fatigued with the fifty-two miles of carriage riding, but they would not have missed the experience for a great deal more inconvenience. The mountaineers arrived at the train at 1.30 A. M., and, finding those who had preceded them at about 10.30 P. M. sleeping the sleep of the innocent, proceeded to herald their arrival by firing off packs of shooting crackers and other sleep-inducing pastimes. But they were too tired to keep it up long, and were soon in their little beds.

There are many other attractions around San José that we might have visited if time had permitted. There are soda springs, alum springs and other mineral springs within easy driving distances. The Almaden quicksilver mines are but a dozen miles away, and are said to be the largest deposit of that useful article in the country. The Methodist University is another point of attraction for visitors which we did not have time to see, but hope to be able to take in at some future time with the others.

Sunday, July 31, 1892.

HE train pulled out of San José at 6 A. M., with very few of the pilgrims on deck. When the smoker had gradually filled up, some one who felt the need of a little recreation, stirred up the combative disposition of the Big Four combination, until they had several battles royal among themselves and with others. By the time Brooks' "first call for breakfast" had sounded they had secured enough exercise to give them a fair appetite. Sirs Edwards, Doane, Wilkie and Judge Slack, had made an early start and reached our train in time to go up to San Francisco with us. Riding up the valley this morning we saw on every hand fresh evidences of the fertility of the soil. Orchards, vineyards, wheat fields, potato patches, vegetable gardens, hay ranches and hop yards testify to the varied productiveness of the soil. Even the orange is beginning to be planted in this section, and flowers attain somewhat the size of those in the southern tier of counties. We saw specimens of the lemon trifolia, bushes we call them, but here that name must give way to trees, from twelve to eighteen feet high, with stems from four to six inches through.

Coasting along the shore of San Francisco Bay for a long distance, we finally reached Oakland station at 8 A. M., but remained on the cars until 9.30 A. M., in order that all might finish breakfast and go across the bay in a body. Our train was then run out onto the Oakland mole to take the ferry boat at the end thereof. The mole extends a distance of nine miles out into the bay. As a concession for the privilege of building the same, it was stipulated that no fare should be collected by the railroad company for riding over that portion of its road. The officials informed us that every advantage was taken by the public of this treat, more especially by the boys, who were riding back and forth at all hours, and could not be molested or deprived of their right to a seat, even by regular passengers.

At the end of the pier we boarded a double-decked ferry boat for a four mile ride across the bay. The morning was cool and the air decidedly fresh, so much so that many remained in the cabins, which are not pens on either side of the boat like our own, but elegant saloons which embrace the entire

width of the steamer and are richly furnished. The boat ride was our first
experience of that kind on this trip since we left Coronado, and was heartily
enjoyed. The delightfully fresh air, with the attendant views of the shipping,
the islands in the bay, the always open Golden Gate and the bank above bank
of built up terraces of houses on the opposite shore were all eagerly scanned
and stored up in the recesses of our memories. These are already beginning
to be overcrowded, as we find it difficult to separate or locate the many and
varied experiences through which we have passed, without considerable thought
and study. Half way across we ran into a belated section of the morning fog,
which gave us a sensation like the sudden entrance into a refrigerator. Emmerling and Millick, having left their overcoats on the train, were under the necessity of borrowing a shawl from some of the ladies in which they enveloped
themselves. When the baby had secured his share of the shawl, Millick's
dividend was very small.

Carriages were in waiting on the city side, and we were soon rattled up to
our quarters at the Palace Hotel. Many of the members of the Denver Club,
who had preceded us a part of a day in their arrival from the North, stood
around the inner court of the hotel and saluted us with the air of old residents
as we alighted. Our rooms had been assigned to us while on the train, and
the boys at once showed us our proper location.

The first reminder that we had friends abroad came in the shape of a basket
of flowers, sent to the room of each lady of the party, with the compliments
of Golden Gate Commandery, together with an invitation to a reception by
the ladies of our San Francisco fraters in the hotel parlors on Monday afternoon. These attentions, coming as they did immediately upon our landing in,
as we thought, a city of entire strangers, three thousand miles from home,
certainly warmed the cockles of our hearts and gave a new significance to the
lessons we receive night after night with perhaps little appreciation of their
true meaning.

The Palace forms another link in the chain of big things which has been
forged for us through California. The exterior, although rich in design and
massive in proportions, has become dingy with time and does not make the
impression on one that the brilliant and lofty interior court and galleries
produce at the first glance. Tier upon tier of corridors, supported by clustered
columns and enclosed by massive balustrades and iron rail above with clusters
of electric globes, the top balustrade of all surmounted by large vases containing palms and other exotics, form a picture that can be conjured up in the
mind's eye at any time; so deep an impression upon you does the first sight
make. The whole is covered in by an arched roof of iron and plate glass and
the interior kept as bright as paint and Chinamen can make it. The parlors,
drawing rooms, dining rooms, grill room, billiard and bar rooms are each
studies in themselves and marvels of fine interior decorations and furnishing.
The private apartments, of which the house contains 865, have all the appoint-

ments, which the comfort of modern travelers demands, complete within themselves and are of unusually large size. The dining room, with its heavily panelled ceiling, is lighted by incandescent lights sunk in the ribs of the ceiling, twenty-five feet above the head and, altogether, the visitor finds much to admire and study before going outside the massive portals of the Palace. Our first care was to look after the furnishing of the luncheon tables which we shared with the Denver Club. Some few of the party, immediately upon our arrival, made a bee line for some of the churches in the neighborhood and improved the opportunity by finishing the naps of which they had been cut short last night. More took advantage of information publicly and privately obtained and determined to wait until to-night and go to the theatres, which promised to be in full blast. A determined reporter for the Chronicle gave some of the party no peace until he had run them into a tintype gallery around the corner, to procure a picture from which he could have manufactured a lot of caricatures which he printed in the morning issue as their portraits. These will doubtless turn up again in the first issue of the paper after there is another hanging match in the city.

After luncheon, the Haight street cable cars, running on Market street in front of the hotel, were boarded for a trip to Golden Gate Park. The route was nearly level for half a mile and then we began to go up stairs. One terrace after another was ascended, each the length of a block, with a level space at the top of each of the width of a street, until we must have gone up at least twenty-five and began to wonder what would be the effect if the rope broke and the brakes did not hold. But we reached the top finally and, making a descent of a block or two, were landed at the park entrance. At the end of the track, the car ran upon a turn table which revolved by the aid of the cable itself and started the car down upon the other track. The mechanical appliances and smooth running of all the Western cable cars seem as far in advance of our Philadelphia jerk-em-alongs, as the railroad train is superior to the Conestoga wagon.

Everybody in San Francisco seemed intent upon the same errand as ourselves, judging from the number of people in the park. A short distance from the entrance was a grand band stand, from which a first class band was discoursing music, to the gratification of thousands of listeners. These were mainly provided with seats and not obliged to lean up against trees or on one another to rest themselves. A walk through a portion of the grounds revealed some fine floral designs, similar to those we had seen at Del Monte, but without the rich coloring. One was a huge sun-dial which marked the time to the minute. There were enclosures containing bears, elks and other wild Western animals. There was a circular canal with boats propelled by steam power, a casino, a children's play ground and house, with many other attractions which were all in full enjoyment by the multitude there assembled. We took a share in them likewise until nearly evening and then made a rush for the cars with the rest of the populace, finally securing footing thereon and enjoying the down stairs run home again. It struck our ladies as very curious to see the San Francisco ladies out in full force with their sealskin coats on the last day of July. It seemed as incongruous as the sight of some of our party had on the ferry boat this morning, in straw hats, with their overcoats buttoned to the chin.

Dinner was being served when we returned and the electric lights in the ceiling of the dining room were partly lighted. The fried oysters, which were on the menu and were generally ordered, proved to be quite a curiosity, if they were oysters. From their size they might be barnacles off some old wharf log or the bottom of a ship, and so far as the taste was concerned, might be anything.

After dinner there was quite a rush to see the sights of Chinatown by night, although many remained at home ready to rest from the exertions of the day. The theatres were all open, as well as the churches, and the Salvation Army paraded in strong force, with drums, cornets and tamborines. With Chinatown in full blast, there was no lack of amusement for Sunday evening. A very pleasant call was had at the hotel from Sir Knight Baldwin, of Golden Gate, and his wife, who were at the Laclede, in St. Louis, for the triennial of 1886. They had many pleasant memories of their intercourse with the pilgrims of Mary at that time, when the two commanderies occupied adjoining parlors as their respective headquarters.

ROMEO AND JULIET.

CLIFF HOUSE AND SEAL ROCKS

Monday, August 1st, 1892.

EARLY everybody got up late this morning, some extending their morning naps so far as to lose their breakfast by coming down after 10 A. M. But we have performed such feats in the eating line for the past two weeks, that it is getting to be a burden to keep up in the procession of meals. Many of us feel the better of dropping a meal occasionally, although we are generally ready for the morning one. Still most of the party were afoot long before that hour, intent upon learning the ins and outs of the Golden Gate city. One jaunt taken was by the cable cars, which climbed the Haight street stairs to the park entrance. Connecting there with a steam road, you were whisked out to the beach in short order, and found yourself only a short distance from the Cliff House. The sidewalk from the depot on was lined with cheap restaurants and curio shops, while the dusty road echoed with the cries of fakirs, graduating from the peanut vender to a fellow with several cages of performing birds. The walk along shore was dusty and steep, and the Cliff House, when reached, rather a disappointment in appearance. The seal rocks were there all right, with the seals lying around on them in large numbers. Most of them were of a dirty yellow color and looked like big old sows lying in the sun. One immense old fellow, who was said to be called Ben Butler, was black, as were some of the smaller ones. The aid of a good pair of glasses brought them and their actions well into view, and it was curious to see them scratch themselves with their flippers, or work themselves onto the rocks out of the green water, by the aid of the same handy tools. They were quiet as a general thing, but would bark hoarsely when crowded too hard by a newcomer or jostled by the movements of a neighbor. These animals are also of the hair seal species and valueless for fur, or they might not lead so quiet a life as they are allowed to here. When tired of watching the seals a short but steep walk up the cliff, will bring you to Sutro Heights and the gate of Mr. Adolph Sutro's garden. After obeying the painted injunctions to leave your packages, canes and other weapons at the gate, in charge of the attendant, you

MAIN AVENUE, SUTRO GARDEN

are welcome to enter and feast your eyes upon the flowers, plants and statuary with which the taste and wealth of the owner have embellished the place for your especial benefit. The statues, large and small, with which the entire grounds are adorned, must have cost an immense amount of money, while the beautiful effects in landscape gardening to be seen on every hand, are adding to the expense of keeping up such a place all the time, yet it is without price to any who may desire to enter. The house itself is quite a commonplace affair to be surrounded by the park-like garden. Back of and above it is quite an eminence, paved with asphalt and surrounded by a stone balustrade. From this point of vantage you get a good view of the seal rocks, and afar off the Golden Gate. A succession of terraces, connected by stone steps, lead down the steep hill in the rear to a road below, which is supplied with iron toad-stool seats. Upon these you can sit and admire other statues, which are placed at every footing place on the rocks in front of you.

When you desire to leave the beauties of the garden, from a point near the front gates you take another steam road which runs you past the sand lots of Dennis Kearney fame, and within sight of the Presidio or military reservation to another depot. If you are in want of opportunities to invest your spare funds, there are innumerable chances to buy lots in staked off suburbs on the line of this road. At the depot you take the California Street cable road and go down more hills and still more. Down past the locality known as Nob Hill, where you find some of the finest residences of the city and about the only place you will find them built of stone. When you get down by the Vigilante Square, where the Vigilantes used to be called to assemble in the good old times when that organization saved much money to the county, you can slip off and walk to the hotel, through the busy crowds of brokers and other business men that line the sidewalks of that section. By the time you have made this round, you will discover that luncheon has been on the carpet for some time and you can go directly in for your share.

At 3 P. M. the ladies of California and Golden Gate Commanderies had assembled in one of the parlors on the ground floor of the Palace to receive the ladies of Mary Commandery. The attendance was large and the social intercourse a pleasant sight. Mary's traveling register was opened up and the San Franciscans availed themselves freely of the opportunity to sign their names and receive the geranium leaf souvenir. Outside the door of the parlor, before you looked in, you might have thought a mill wheel was clattering, but a peep within the door revealed the fact that it was only the ladies and Sir Field of Golden Gate talking. It was 5 P. M. before the visitors began to drift away.

Meanwhile Chinatown was getting done by relays all day long. This is the one attraction of Frisco that every one feels called upon to visit at least once while in the city. We felt it our duty to see it at least once a day and oftener if possible. It is but a short distance from the Palace and is really a city of another nationality within a city of English speaking inhabitants. In a space covered by from six to seven blocks long, varying from three to four in width, swarms a population of 35,000 souls of a distinct race, with entirely different habits, customs, dress and religion from any of those who surround them. To see the district in its entirety, it is a good plan to get one of the guides who make a business of showing the place to take you through. We were indebted to Mr. Robert Byrne, of 741 Sacramento Street for his thorough knowledge of the town and general fund of information, during most of our visits to its purlieus.

The stores of the Chinese quarter are also a distinctive feature. On Dupont Street they have quite large ones for the sale of fancy articles and silk goods. One of the latter was said to carry silk handkerchiefs to the amount of thirty thousand dollars and some of them have stocks to the value of from fifty to one hundred thousand dollars. The store of Sing Fat & Co. did a land-office business with the pilgrims during our stay, that was only equalled by the Yokohama store of Long Sing Quong across the way. If you confined yourself to the purchase of Chinese or Japanese nicknacks as curios or mementoes of the trip, you could load yourself up pretty well at small expense. But if you were not satisfied short of silk shawls or fine ivory carvings you could get rid of cash as quickly as you could on Chestnut Street. One of the Chinese drug stores of which there are several, was well patronized, one of its attendants being kept busily engaged in putting up prescription Number One. This was a sort of cure-all like some of our patent medicines, which contained a select assortment of black beetles, seven year locust shells, a dried horned toad and various sliced roots and herbs, the whole to be concocted into a tea and taken cold. Numbers of these packages were brought home, no doubt as mementoes, as it was generally thought it would require a pretty severe case of sickness to warrant the swallowing of the dose. If you stood in the store a few minutes, you would see a Chinaman come in with his prescription, written up and down on a slip of red shooting-cracker paper, and hand it over to one of the compounders. He would look it over sagely, in regular drug store style, open various drawers, and spreading out a sheet of paper, proceed to fill the bill. He would lift out a handful of cockroaches and drop into the mess, just as coolly as he laid in the slippery elm, and fire in a snail or a toad with as much imperturbability as he added a few pepper berries. The patient walked off with the whole as if it were no more nauseous than the concoctions the doctors delight to shoot into us. Probably it did not taste as bad as some of them. In front of the counter were two pots of elegant tea, nestling in boxes covered over with felt. In these nests it keeps warm or rather hot for several hours at a stretch and is free for all comers. The barber shops are very numerous and their operations open to the public gaze. The operator not only shaves the face but the head as well, that being a part of their religious observances. If a man has no money, the barber has to shave his head as comfortably as the one who pays cash, and trust to fate for his reward hereafter. The inside of the nostrils and the cavities of the ears are all shaved clean with a long narrow-bladed knife and the unfortunate who is being operated upon in the chair always holds a basin in his hands, in which the hair shaved or cut off is dropped.

The almond-eyed youngsters, who play Chinese tag or some other game under your feet in the streets, are shaved in exact imitation of their fathers and the diminutive pigtail which they wear seems to be sacred even in their rough play. You never see one grasp another by what the average American lad would consider a "daisy" handle, with which to swing an opponent around his head. The pawn brokers keep shop in the cellars and make little display of their accumulated pledges, but pass them in and out of a little square hole in the partition, behind which they sit. They are fully up to the tricks of their modern Eastern brethren however. One of them sold the writer a high-binder's sheath knife, in a carved bone case for a dollar. This was afterward duplicated by a new one, out of Sing Fat's store, for seventy cents He never even smiled as he took the dollar. The jeweler had his men working in dark and dingy cellar rooms and would not expose his wares for sale, because he was under contract to sell only by wholesale. The Baldwin and Palace Hotels of Chinatown were visited this afternoon and found literally swarming with in-habitants, more so than the ordinary habitations. How the dwellers therein could ever exist if the weather got warm, was a mystery. Few of the rooms had windows or ventilation of any other kind. Around each room on three sides, leaving an opening for the door only, would be tiers of bunks extend-ing from floor to ceiling, not over five feet long and maybe two and a half ·feet wide. In each of these sleep two Chinamen and between them reposes the opium lay-out with a pipe for each. In a room, twelve by fifteen feet, would thus be condensed from thirty to forty men and this was repeated story upon story from the sub-cellar to the roof.

The Palace was so called because it had a court-yard in the middle, with balconies on every side. You had to be careful in going through that you did not receive some drippings or slops from the upper galleries which ran around each story and afforded access to the rooms and had ladders from floor to floor. On the stone pavement of the court yard, numerous cooks were at work, over fires built principally of broken boxes, making stews in several cases in old tins that had held crackers or coal oil. Everything came useful to John. The Palace was said to harbor 1000 Chinese, to say nothing of its lesser inhabitants. In a club house on Dupont street, Milligan and Allen made several attempts to learn the art of "hitting the pipe" as smoking opium is called. The janitor in attendance finally took it from them with the remark that they were "no good." A visit to the Chinese theatre, in which the performance begins at 5.30 P. M., is a treat not to be missed. Four bits, or half-a-dollar, secures you a seat on the stage, to reach which you are conducted through various underground passages to the back of the curtain. There you find many performers in various stages of preparation for their parts. For the men the chief disguise was immense horse hair mustachios and beard, of which the Chinese face is altogether guiltless. For those who undertook the female characters, paint, eyebrows, a parasol and a falsetto voice answered every requirement. No women are allowed to take any part on the Chinese stage or to mix with the male portion of the audience, there being a gallery reserved for their especial use. A falling curtain over a doorway on either side gave admission to or egress from the stage. The stage itself was innocent of any scenery except the orchestra, which sat at the back of it between the two doors. The ear-splitting noise, which they made for music, never ceased while the play was in progress. Whether the actors declaimed or sung, fought or made love, died or got married made no difference, except perhaps a change of instruments. The leader of the band alternately played upon a two-stringed Chinese fiddle or banged two large gongs together. A sub-director, who appeared to give the cue for the changes, hammered with two little wooden mallets on a round block of hard wood, shifting occasionally to a drum made of a brass basin with parchment stretched over it. There were six of them and neither was capable of learning any of the others how to make more noise. We were furnished chairs upon one side of the stage and the properties needed for the night's performance were stood on the opposite side, while the property man stood by the orchestra smoking cigarettes continually. When a banner, an imitation tree or an umbrella was to be introduced into the act, he coolly picked it up, walked forward and deposited it in its appointed place and resumed his station.

The stage strides and attitudes of the actors, and the Boston glide of the female impersonators were great. Some of the costumes were apparently very rich, and one fellow was got up in excellent imitation of Joe Wright as Illustrious Potentate. After we had got enough of the infernal din on the stage, we were taken down through more underground and narrow passages to the living room of one of the actors. Here we found his wife and children, one of whom, a little girl four years old, sang for us several Sunday school hymns in very good English. She is an attendant at some of the mission schools and adds very materially to the family exchequer by exhibiting her proficiency in her lessons at the school.

After the theatre refreshments are always in order, and these we undertook to procure at a neighboring Chinese restaurant. It was a large and stylish institution, and we were ushered to the second floor. Some of the party tasted the tea, but could not stomach the eating. Most of us went through the entire course of tea, cakes, Chinese candy, preserved ginger and watermelon rinds. Sweet things seemed to predominate and all were first class. At the wind-up the waiter set a box of cigars on the table and the men each bought one. The sale of the cigar is the waiter's tip or perquisite, and all that he expects. The pay-counter is down stairs, and when you start down the waiter at the top will bawl out something in the Chinese lingo, which will be repeated by relays at each landing of the stairway, loudly enough for the Chinamen in the next block to know how much you have to pay. There is no sneaking by the cashier or pocketing of checks to be done here. By the time you get out of here you will find it very near the limit time for dinner, and can make your way through the now crowded thoroughfares to the street cars, which will take you more quickly to the Palace doors.

Our invitation from our fraters of Golden Gate is for to-night, and has been likewise extended to the members of the Denver Club. The ladies of our party have been invited to attend the theatre by Gorman, and depart under his escort at the appointed time. Then the members of Mary and the Denverites gather in the office and corridors to await their summons to the asylum of our hosts. At 8 P. M. the drill corps of Golden Gate Commandery marched into the court-yard, preceded by a band, and lined up on one side of the asphalt drive. Mary fell in, under the command of Capt. Gen. Munch, and took the right of the line, followed by the Denver Club, under E. Sir Joseph S. Wright, with the drill corps in the rear. In this order we marched to the asylum of Golden Gate and, after sending Emmerling up in the elevator which refused to be elevated with any additional weight, took to the stairs, reaching the top pretty well blown. After speeches of welcome to each of the visiting delegations, which were responded to by the respective commanding officers, the ranks were broken and a general exchange of fraternal greetings ensued. The card exchange business took a boom and Golden Gate made a vain attempt to match our baby's avoirdupois with a member of their own, Sir Frazer. He fell short sixty pounds and they gave up the contest gracefully. The march to the banquet table ensued and for an hour or more the business at the table superseded all else. Then began the toasts and responses. The flow of wine, wit and sentiment made a memorable night. We might say that wine flowed like water, but there was no water there for a comparison. Col. Edwards, who was chairman of the reception committee, put it very tersely when he said, "if California wine was not good enough for any one, he might choke." P. E. Sir Frank W. Sumner presided as toast master, by request of E. Com. von Wefelsburg, and was the right man in the right place and kept things moving. After a neat introductory speech, he called on the Knights of his own command for the Commandery yell, which they gave with a vim that shook the windows. The first toast to "the memory of those gone before" was drunk in silence. P. Com. A. G. Booth then made a welcoming address. Grand Junior Warden V. C. Metcalfe responded to the toast, "The Grand Commandery of California" and P. G. Com. Wright performed a like service for "The Commonwealth of Pennsylvania." "California Commandery No. 1" had its dignity upheld by its present Em. Commander W. G. Winter. Two of the members of the Golden Gate sang several duets. Past Com. W.

H. L. Barnes of California No. 1, responded to the toast of "Old Glory" or the American flag, in a speech that stirred the blood of young and old alike and aroused the patriotic feelings of the assemblage to a pitch that we have seldom seen equalled. The Star Spangled Banner was then sung by all present. Several poems were then read, Sir Knight W. F. Smith acting as substitute Commandery poet, the regular holder of that position being absent from the city. Sir Fred. Staude gave us a baritone solo and Capt. Woodruff, U. S. A. delivered a humorous address on the subject of "Truth," which contained many telling hits and abounded in sarcasm, which hit about equally the effete East and the wild and woolly West. Harmon Johnson was called upon to stand up for his favorites, "The Ladies" and Capt. Gen. Munch testified to the general excellence of "Mary" above all others. Some one had disclosed the secret of our train song and Munch was compelled to sing the verses so far as they had been indited, the whole room joining in the chorus of Ta-ra-ra-boom. P. E. Com. Duprez of No. 1, also gave us a very fine address, although totally unprepared until called up. The fun was fast and furious, and the time slipped away so rapidly that it was nearly 1 A. M. before our hosts would listen to any talk of departure. Col. Edwards and several more had serious designs on Capt. Gen. Munch and wanted badly to fill him up with wine, but Munch was too wary for them. Edwards had tried his hand on Emmerling earlier in the evening, but gave up the contract as being too expensive. They had printed a large placard, which was affixed to the back of Harry's chair, bearing the legend "Mary's Baby" and thought him literally the "greatest" Sir Knight that had ever visited California. We were finally allowed to depart with cheers for Golden Gate Commandery, which were responded to by the Commandery cry of G-O-L-D-E-N Gate, Gate, Gate, and very soon reached our quarters at the hotel.

Tuesday, August 2nd, 1892.

HE ASPECT of the skies this morning betokened another fine day. Our hosts have been fearful that we would strike a section of their foggy weather which is said to penetrate summer clothing instanter and to cut like a knife. So far we have not had a sample of it, except when we crossed from Oakland on Sunday. Even then it was not heavy enough for us to see, but we felt it instantly when we came through it. It is here as at other places along the coast, apt to be hazy in the mornings and look as though it would rain before many hours, but it generally clears by 9 or 10 A. M. About 4 P. M. every day, the trade winds begin to blow and attend to their duty pretty lively until evening sets in. The consequence is naturally a cool evening and comfortable sleeping weather. There was earlier rising this morning, in spite of the late hour at which we reached home, because some of the party did not care to lose two breakfasts running. After the meal was over, shopping seemed to be considered a great necessity. Everybody was more or less anxious to take home plenty of souvenirs of the Golden Gate, even if they neglected mementoes of other places. Many were again attracted to Chinatown, where they found plenty of material to instruct and amuse them. It was a remarkable fact that all the men soon learned that the shortest road from the Palace to the Chinese settlement, ran through the classic regions of St. Mary and Dupont streets. The hotel was practically deserted this morning until nearly noon and when the pilgrims began to straggle in, the numerous packages and bundles made it look a little like Christmas time at home. Some of the party were hunting up many other points of interest about the city. The old Mission building on Dolores street, the view from Telegraph Hill, the wharves and shipping in the harbor, Woodward's gardens and even the cemeteries came in for a share of admirers. A trip to Oakland and its attendant view of the harbor, with the outlying settlements nestled in the shadow of the mountain ranges, was much talked of by the participants. But nearly everybody seemed to gravitate again toward Chinatown after paying a visit to any of the other points. Milligan began to be a dangerous competitor in business for the regular guides, he having become as well or better posted than those who first introduced him to the locality. Luncheon was consumed in its regular order and, after that meal the court yard began to assume a business appearance. The Denver Club was to leave this afternoon, and the piles of luggage assumed huge proportions before the arrival of the teams that were to haul it away. Before departing for our usual runs about the city, farewells were bade to our fellow travellers, who were to precede us one day over the same route.

One of the parties in Chinatown this afternoon were lucky enough to stumble upon the ceremonies incident to a Chinese wedding, and after a little persuasion, were admitted to the presence of the bride and her female attendants. She was a pretty little China girl of about nineteen, and received the congratulations of the party with a sweeping little courtesy and a sweet smile. She looked to be worth all the happy bridegroom had paid for her, even if it was five hundred dollars. The bargain was that if she did not come up to all the specifications in the deed of warranty and he returned her, as he was at liberty to do, he lost his money.

The wedding celebration was going on in the third stories of two large buildings thrown together by a wide archway. Another Chinese orchestra was doing its level best to imitate the sounds in a boiler-making shop and a smiling heathen added to the din every few minutes by lighting a dozen packs of fire-crackers at once and throwing them on the floor of one of the rooms. His smile enlarged ten-fold when he threw one bunch under Mrs. Regester's feet and caused her to jump several feet in the air to escape being set on fire. In the other room were set out large tables covered with all kinds of Chinese sweetmeats and the inevitable tea-pots. Around these tables were grouped the invited guests in large numbers, endeavoring to do justice to the feed, while on the opposite sidewalks, were gathered greater numbers of the uninvited, gazing at the doors and windows for a glimpse of the fun within, pretty much the same as their Christian brethren in more favored localities. The decoration of the bride and her female companions with a Mary leaf left them all smiling and happy.

A visit was also paid to one of the largest Joss houses in the district, which is located on Dupont street. The abode of Joss and his attendant priests is on the third floor and all the way up to that point, the walls of the stairway and passages are papered with slips of red paper covered with Chinese hiereglyphics similiar to those on a tea-chest. These represent the subscriptions to the building fund as well as for the support of old Joss, who sits enthroned in the back of the large upper room in all the splendor of barbaric lacquer and gilt work. He is supported by lesser devils on the right and left

CHINATOWN STREET

and sits in the centre of a large screen or scene, which is again shut off from the daylight, that comes in at the front of the room, by a couple of other finely carved and gilded partitions.

This scheme of posting subscriptions in the hallway of the building might be a good one for some of our Christian churches to adopt, and would doubtless enable some of them to be supported without so many appeals for their winter coal and other necessaries. After the posting of two or three names, there would be an inevitable rush by succeeding subscribers to straddle their predecessor's blind, if they knew the fact would stare them and everybody else in the face every time they came to meeting. The attendant priests make a little spare cash by telling fortunes between prayers. At each of our visits we took time to have the horoscope of one of our number cast, for the delectation of the party. The priest first banged on a large drum, suspended to the right of the rear screen in a frame work of wood, to let Joss know that he was wanted in the shop. Then a number of Joss sticks or incense were lighted and stuck in different receptacles in front of the god and his deputies, in addition to the spiral coil of incense that burns always directly facing him. He then secures the name of the anxious inquirer and writes it on a piece of paper in Chinese characters. Then, prostrating himself before the altar, he bangs his shaven head against the floor several times and repeats a prayer to invoke the aid of Joss to give him the desired information, at the same time dropping two large blocks of wood on the floor so suddenly as to startle the lookers-on. Then taking a large box of thin flat sticks he kneels again and, by a peculiar motion in shaking the box, finally causes a single one to fly out of the box. Carefully making a note of the number thereon, he repeats the operation and secures another number. The paper with the name and numbers written on is then wrapped in a large sheet of paper which is set on fire and carried out on the balcony in front of the building, to be deposited in a furnace set in the wall for the purpose and allowed to consume. The book of fortunes is then opened and the secrets of the future exposed. No matter who was the seeker after knowledge, good luck or heap good luck, much money and happiness unlimited were in store for him or her. Thirty cents was a cheap rate for such pleasant information and was cheerfully paid.

The Chinese grocery and provision stores contained, in addition to the regular meats and vegetables of the Melican man, many other viands more curious to our sight. Some of these were huge baskets of dried clams, the shells wide apart and the contents looking like leather. The same shell-fish had been opened in some cases and the contents dried and strung on strings. Smoked ducks, picked, split open and kept stretched flat by wooden skewers. Duck's feet, smoked and dried were a separate dish. Duck eggs, encased in a sort of black loam. Razor backed hams and dried sausage. Oysters, dried and strung, various kinds of dried fish, apparently unopened and as hard as a section of paving stone, all go to help the Chinaman to keep in remembrance his native land from which most of them are imported. Bamboo baskets, with lids of the same material, contained live eels in sea-grass. One lot of these looked suspiciously like water snakes, of which the attendant John opposed any handling or too close inspection. Pigs, roasted whole and nicely browned, lent variety to the scene and were cut off in slices as required by the exigencies of trade.

Chinese cobblers sat out on the sidewalks in nearly every square, busy with the implements of their trade and surrounded by specimens of foot gear more or less dilapidated. One owner of a fruit stand had built a box, up in the iron frame-work of the awning over the sidewalk of the store in front of which he had his stand located. It extended from the straight iron chord up to the slanting bars which supported the awning, probably four feet high at the highest part and six by five feet on the ground plan. In this he lived and moved, cooked, existed and smoked his "dope" as comfortably as a snail in its shell. In one of the rookeries was shown us what is known as the "happy family." In a room six and a half feet high and not over six by eight feet on the floor, lived an old Chinaman and his wife with eight or ten cats and a couple of dogs, as well as a choice assortment of smells. The old lady was a habitual beggar for ten cents and lied about her age just like any ordinary female, giving a different age at every visit paid to her domicile. The China-man with the wooden yoke across his shoulders, bearing burdens of various kinds dependent from either end, was a common sight and manœuvred his apparently clumsy apparatus so as to steer clear of all collisions.

This evening had been set apart to respond to the invitation from Cali-fornia Commandery No. 1 to visit them at their asylum. Little was accord-ingly done after dinner until the time should arrive for us to depart in that direction, except to see the ladies off on their way to spend the evening at the residence of Sir Knight A. D. Baldwin, in response to an invitation from the estimable consort of that gentleman. When the escort from our fraters arrived, headed by a band, the lines were formed and a short march taken through several blocks to the asylum of No. 1. The spectators on the street seemed puzzled to account for the unusual spectacle of a body in citizen's dress, with white slouch hats, escorted by a large turn-out of Knights in uni-form. The march ended only with the third floor of the Masonic Temple and we were pretty well winded upon our arrival at that point. The band had the best of it, as they stood at the foot of the stairs and blew us up to the top. We were warmly received and fraternally welcomed by E. Com. Winter col-lectively and, after the lines were broken, individually by a large number of the Sir Knights of No. 1, in addition to those who had formed our escort. After considerable time spent in fraternal greeting, the lines were formed to enter the banquet room by placing a member of the home commandery beside each visitor, thus ensuring alternate seats at the tables. A peculiar and to us very interesting feature of the furnishings of the banquet room, was the number of banners of visiting commanderies hanging around the walls. Prominent among these we were happy to see that of Mary displayed, a relic of the Conclave of 1883. After the business of demolishing the toothsome viands, provided for our entertainment, had been got through with, the speech makers were called upon to do their share.

We thought we had listened to a toast-master last night whose equal would be hard to find, but were forced to yield the palm to-night to Sir Duprez, who occupied that position at the head of California's table. His polished phrases, and the happy manner in which he added the climax to the peroration of one speaker and led up to the introduction of the next, were a revelation to our members. Many happy remarks were made by members of each command. Dr. J. Beverly Cole made the welcoming address, in which he took occasion to compliment Mary Commandery very highly. Rev. Dr. W. E. Smith, who is pastor of the Central Presbyterian Tabernacle, spoke in a happy vein and his remarks were interspersed with considerable badinage between himself and Dr. Cole, in which the reverend gentleman did not always come off second best. We have endeavored to condense some of his talk, as follows.

Eminent Commander:

The distinguished Sir Knights we greet this evening seemed to be somewhat dazed, by the monumental lies which have been eloquently unfolded at this banquet by our silver-tongued orators, as well as some they have heard at other points in this state. I feel somewhat like calling a halt ; but, on reflection, I believe it will do these saints from the City of Brotherly Love some good to feed on the marvellous. It is a different kind of diet from the one they are accustomed to in the city from which they hail. Gentlemen, swallow these California stories about our fruits, flowers and climate without mastication ! Bolt them ! Even though they may give you dyspepsia. It will be a new experience to you. Some of us have been wondering why this visiting Commandery is named "Mary." Does the "Saint" properly belong as a prefix before that name Mary? I think not, judging from the appearance of our guests of this evening. Sir Knights, I am free to confess that you are not very saintly looking, save with one exception. Your " Baby " personifies a saint with credit to himself and with honor to you. You cannot help but love him for his angelic form : for he is, like myself, the embodiment of the beautiful and the incarnation of the lovely. How he succeeded in mounting the three steep flights of stairs to this asylum is more than I can understand, unless the music of our band inspired him to spread his soul wings to flit this way. Sir Knights, we are glad to see you, and we trust your Denver experiences will fittingly supplement the pleasure of this evening and your return to Philadelphia be as joyous as are our benedictions.

Sir Asa R. Wells of No. 1, also gave us a good impression by a series of quiet remarks, some of which tendered to touch up the fraters of San José a little. A Sir Knight from Santa Rosa gave a glowing account of the delights

123

of that locality and offered us great inducements for a visit there at some future
time. Milligan gave a resumé of our journey thus far through the Golden
State while Munch stood up to acknowledge in fitting terms our appreciation
of our reception. Harmon Johnson was interesting as usual upon his favorite
theme of "the Ladies." While the festivities of the evening had not so much
of the "hurrah" about them, the time was spent in a manner calculated to
impress upon our minds the deep fraternal feeling of California toward Mary
and, when we bade her fraters farewell at midnight, it was with the assured
feeling that, though far from our own homes, we were not altogether strangers
in a strange land. The magnificent floral decorations of the table were turned
over to our hands at our departure for presentation to the ladies. It was not
quite as late an hour as upon last night when the massive doors of the Palace
opened to afford us shelter for one more night.

Wednesday, August 3rd, 1892.

OLD SOL ushered in another bright day for our benefit and had been attending to the duties of his position for a good spell before many of us were aware of the fact. The morning air was very cool and it looked unseasonable to us, out on Market Street, to see the people hurrying along to their business with light overcoats buttoned to the chin. Soon after breakfast the members of Mary's family were on the alert and dispersed to various quarters to make good use of their last day in "Frisco." The boat rides on the bay, out to the Golden Gate, were much in vogue and heartily enjoyed. The bay is a grand harbor, which contains many picturesque islands and is backed up by the coast ranges of mountains, under whose shadows lie the many surrounding residence places of the San Francisco business men. The islands in the bay are not mere level patches of ground always, but great masses of rock rising boldly and precipitously from the waves. Goat Island attains to a height of more than three hundred feet. Alcatraz Island commands the Golden Gate and is heavily fortified with a view to that object. On the highest point of the island a light-house sends forth its warning rays. Angel Island is the largest in the bay and is also fortified by Uncle Sam for the defence of the harbor. Permits to land at the fortified points must be secured from the military authorities.

The branch U. S. Mint, Court House, Merchants' Exchange and Stock Exchange, in which the wild chase of the members after boodle differs little from the scenes in our own Exchange, were all visited by members of the party. The dry goods, fur and jewelry stores were all ransacked again for tokens of the journey to the Pacific, and the packages and bundles, as well as packing cases that poured into the hotel, made the committee feel nervous lest the baggage car would prove too small to carry the accumulations. But they found before reaching home, that a baggage car, like a horse car, always has room for more. Cantlin left us during the morning to pay a short visit to an uncle at Sacramento, and rejoin us when we passed through that city. Chinatown was again invaded and carried by storm, as it probably would have been every day if we remained here for a week or two. The number of flower peddlers on the streets here is remarkable. The open street at the junction of Market and Annie streets, at the upper corner of the hotel, was a regular flower mart, forming a bright picture in the midst of a busy thoroughfare. Charlie Patton turned up at the hotel just before luncheon, and was given a red-light cigar to work off on Rev. Dr. Smith, with whom he expected to lunch. In the afternoon, our jovial and reverend frater came around and requested the loan of a couple of the same brand, with which to initiate some of his clerical brethren who were to take dinner with him this evening. Sir Knight and Mrs. Baldwin also continued their attentions toward the ladies of the party. Mr. and Mrs. Blackwood, of our party, had found friends here who had almost monopolized them since our first advent. Mrs. Fairlamb had secured a government permit to take a party this afternoon on board the tug which carries the convict laborers to and from their prison, and the points at which they are put to labor around the harbor. Misses Haldeman, Chapin and McAlpine, with Master Edgar Allen accompanied her on the trip, and watched the transfer of the tough-looking gangs under military escort, back to their prison quarters from various points where their labor had been utilized through the day. Dr. J. Beverly Cole called at the hotel and took Munch and Kessler for a drive to the Cliff House and Sutro Heights, behind a spanking team of horses.

The propriety of changing the time of leaving San Francisco to 11 P. M. had been discussed to-day, with a view of bringing our train over the Sierra Nevada by daylight. It was finally determined to adhere to the schedule time 9 P. M., as it was very doubtful, if we lost two hours, whether the time could be made up again. Baggage had been ordered in readiness by 3 P. M., and from that time until the dinner hour, the porters were engaged in transferring it to the court yard. Dinner once disposed of, everybody was more or less anxious to be on the way to the train. A number of our San Francisco friends were at the hotel to bid us good-bye, among whom were the Baldwins. At 8.30 P. M. the carriages were in waiting, and soon transferred us to the foot of Market street, where we had to wait some time for the ferry boat. The ride across the bay in the bright moonlight would have been quite romantic, but for the fact that a very heavy prosaic dew drove all hands into the comfortable cabins. The train was awaiting our advent on the Oakland side, and we were installed into our old quarters with many expressions of deep satisfaction at being once more "at home."

At 9.30 P. M. we had started on our homeward journey. All hands remained up until Port Costa was reached. This station is on the far side of the Straits of Carquinez, which are really a part of the Bay of San Francisco. The trip from here to Benicia, the station on the opposite side of the Straits, is made on the Solano, the largest ferry boat in the world. The steamer is 480 feet long, and can carry four trains of cars abreast. No sooner was the train on the boat than we were all out to examine her and admire her length, breadth, with the immense boilers and powerful engines, polished to a strange contrast with their grimy surroundings. To walk from one end of the Solano to the other and return, took about as long as it did for the steamer to cross the Straits. Once secured to the Benicia side, the train ran again on to terra-firma, and started off on its eastward bound trip. All soon after turned into their berths for the night thoroughly tired. The four days at San Francisco had been inserted in the itinerary with the idea that they would constitute a rest from the fatigues of the previous journey across the continent and up the coast, as well as a chance to recruit for the one about to be commenced. But we left there worse tired than at any point on the trip. It was such a constant go that there was little chance to secure any rest.

Thursday, August 4th, 1892.

E managed to lose time during the night by some mischance, and in consequence were only rounding Cape Horn, in the Sierras, at 5.30 A. M. Those who were up had the privilege of enjoying a memorable view, the train being stopped for a few minutes to enjoy the same. The bed of the road was cut from the solid mountain side, workmen having been suspended from the top by ropes until they had blasted away sufficient rock to gain a foothold. The rocks rise straight up on the one side and you can drop a stone down on the other, a distance of more than half a mile into the rocky bed of the river, which tumbles through the gorge below. We had been climbing up all night, and just before rea hing Cape Horn had crossed a trestle work one thousand feet long and one hundred and twenty-five feet in the air.

From this point we ran through a succession of mountain gorges and ravines of the most rugged and romantic character. Ten pairs of eyes would see as many different points of interest or beauty at the same moment, and endeavor to call the attention of all to their own particular portion of the view at once. At Gold Run, the first placer mines were seen, with the pipes through which the operation of hydraulic mining had been carried on, together with the effects of the same where whole sides of the surrounding hills had been washed away and carried down into the neighboring valleys. These mines are now idle. the work having been discontinued for a time, on account of injunctions granted by the courts, on the prayer of those who were seriously incommoded by the dirt carried down the streams. The fight in the courts is still in progress.

Ordinary mines were plentiful, and the way in which they are stuck into the sides of the mountains in every direction is truly wonderful. A mile in the air you can see the miners' shanties built out into space, and supported by scantling, in places where a step from the front platform would mean a descent of five hundred feet at one jump. Prospect holes were bored into the face of the rocks almost as plentifully as the prairie dog homes in the desert. Once in a while, a well traveled trail from a hole to the bottom of the cañon would tell a story without words, of how some one had struck luck.

At 8 A. M. we saw the first stretch of snow-sheds, and were soon flitting in and out of any number of short reaches of them. Several times we laid over for trains coming in the opposite direction, and at Blue Cañon station, made a stop of thirty minutes to lay in ice and water, of both which commodities our train consumed a powerful sight. On the station platform the natives had put up a large packing box with one side slatted and a canvas cover over it, labelled Great American Red Bat. There were no suckers until Pop Millick came along and took the cork clean under. He was followed by Blackwood, and both were satisfied with the appearance of the brick within. Just below the station stood a small house, back of which a path led up a little hill, on whose summit were some blackberry bushes. Enochs, Sr., strolled up the path, picked what berries he could find, and came leisurely down again. Before he reached the foot of the hill, a snake came over the brow of the hill and descended the path as leisurely as had Enochs. He was soon espied by McIntyre and Edgar Allen, who began to throw stones at him. He came on down and coiled up in a small hollow in the path, filled with rubbish. His enemies rushed upon him until a cry from young Allen, of "look out, he's rattling," called a halt. McIntyre secured an old shovel, and by a fortunate blow, stunned the snake and cut off his head with the remnant of the blade. Sure enough he had been rattling, and Mac cut the five rattles from his tail for a keepsake.

The edge of the iron shield on the handle of the shovel cut Mac's finger so that it bled freely, and some one told Mrs. McIntyre that he had been bitten by a rattlesnake, in proof of which he held up the bleeding hand. Now Mrs. Mac was the custodian of a bottle of fine "Old Scotch," to be used for medicinal purposes only, and the way she hustled for that bottle and poured its contents into Mac was a caution to the whole generation of snakes. Her repeated injunctions to take plenty did not pass unheeded either.

Invitations had been already issued this morning for a three o'clock tea in stateroom B, by Mrs. McIntyre, and also for another smoker in the cat's car by McIntyre himself. The latter was to be held for the purpose of exchanging experiences in San Francisco. Soon after leaving Blue Cañon and its sociably disposed rattlers behind, the line of snow-sheds became almost continuous over an extent of forty-nine miles. Once in a while, where a section of the boards covering the sides were off, and all the time through the cracks thereof, could be seen tantalizing glimpses of the magnificent scenery without. It seemed as though we never wanted to look at it so badly as at this time, when you could not see it. We had an indistinct idea, before we saw them, that the snow sheds were a sort of fence or barrier put up on one side to keep the snow from drifting onto the track, and the reality somewhat surprised us. Imagine fifty miles of a solid timber structure, with an octagonal roof, completely shutting in the tracks, except for the cracks between the boards at the sides and top to let out smoke. The timbers are about ten by ten inches, and millions of feet have been consumed in building the structures. So far as seeing the country is concerned you might just as well be in a tunnel.

A ride at the glass door of the baggage car revealed a weird scene. The flame and sulphur laden atmosphere, emitted by each respiration of the iron horse ahead, with the rays of sunlight filtering through the cracks above and bisecting the clouds of smoke at all angles, was a sight not soon to be forgotten. The centre of the roof was but a little distance above the smoke stack, and the bevelled angles between that and the sides just seemed to leave room for the roofs of the cars to pass.

In this dry part of the season, fires on the sheds are frequent, and at Red Mountain, a station in the sheds where we made a halt, a house is built away up on the side of a neighboring mountain, where watchmen are stationed to look out for fires on the roof of the timber tunnel. A telephone wire connects them with this station, where a locomotive is kept, hooked up to a flat car with a fire engine on it, ready for service, to be instantly dispatched to the scene of the fire when word came across the wire. Soon after entering the sheds our engine set off a torpedo on the track. Our speed was slackened and the whistle kept going, like a gigantic screech-owl with its whoo-whoo, until we found a gang of trackmen, who had set the alarm for their own safety, and had now lifted their car from the track and turned it up against the timber walls to let us pass. At Butte Canon bridge a new and substantial iron bridge was being set in place without removing the old wooden structure, over which we ran very slowly and were saluted by the numerous working gangs on the bridge. Lafferty and Dill had branched out this morning in a desperate attempt to become cigarette smokers, a practice which has been set down upon in the train ever since we started on this pilgrimage. When due representations were made to them of the invariable tendencies of cigarette smokers in this section of the country, they soon desisted from the nefarious habit. We thought, for a few minutes, at 10.15 A. M., that we had got through the snow sheds, but soon struck more of them, running through many more stretches of them until we reached Summit at 11 A. M. This station formerly enjoyed the reputation of being the highest railroad point in the country, it being at an elevation of 7,000 feet, but it has had to knuckle under to more modern railway engineering which has attained to much greater heights.

This range of the Sierra Nevadas is one of the great back-bones or continental divides from which the waters flow in different directions and wind up many hundreds of miles apart, although starting perhaps from the same snow bank. The surrounding scenery is of the grandest description, mountains towering all around, lakes shimmering in the summer sun, pine and hemlock trees with their evergreen tufts at the top and a deep valley, into which we are about to descend, ahead and to one side of us. At 11.15 we got an aggravating view or series of disjointed views of Donner Lake. This is a beautiful and placid sheet of blue water, imprisoned by mountain walls on every side, but with a clean gravelly beach surrounding it. It has no outlet and, our conductor asserts, has never been fathomed. It takes its name from the leader of a party of emigrants, of whom thirty-four are said to have starved to death on its shores in 1846. The mountain sides here are covered with a heavy growth of timber up to the vegetation line. We would clear a snow shed, get a striking view of the blue lake, lying peaceably at the bottom of the deep valley and, at the next instant would be peeping at it through the cracks of the next shed or maybe get a little better passing glance at it where a board or two had been blown off. We wound around and down the mountain for some time before losing sight of it altogether. Huge patches of snow are visible on all the high peaks around us, even extending sometimes far below the line of timber growths. Truckee was our next stop at 11.45 A. M. and we put in a half hour there. A long line of straggling stores, across a wide thoroughfare in front of the station, constituted the business portion of the town. Some of the store signs revealed odd combinations, one of which we thought worth copying. The owner professed to deal in dry goods, groceries, banking, insurance, lumber and wood. · Saloons were plentiful and a solitary buck Indian sat on a backless chair outside one of them, evidently awaiting the advent of an angel. Lumber seemed to be the leading industry and scarcely a sign was without the name of that staple on it, as well as its twin brother wood. We had now come down to the elevation of 5,800 feet. We left Truckee at 12.15 P. M. and followed down the course of the Truckee River, a swiftly running but shallow stream. Dams and saw-mills lined its banks at every convenient location. Plenty of the former could have been found up around the top of the mountain, where we were endeavoring to secure a good view of Donner Lake.

Soon we entered into Truckee Canon, through which the river finds its outlet. The railroad is compelled frequently to shift from side to side and the varying scenery of mountain, river and forest calls for constant admiration. Along the mountain sides are immense V-shaped flumes, leading down to the level of the valley, propped in the air and used to bring down lumber and cord-wood, which are turned off or shot out at any desired point. Donkeys, laden with a bale of hay on either side, tramped stolidly along, bearing their burdens to the mountains, along paths up which no vehicle but a mule can travel. At Verdi station we entered the Commonwealth of Nevada which we traverse in its entirety. At 1.15 P. M. the bold and rocky mountain formations on either hand began to change into lower elevations, with wider valleys between, then to detached groups or scattered single buttes. The sage brush, with its jack-rabbit tenants haunted the sides of the track and other unerring signs denoted the near approach to the great Humboldt Desert. Reno at 1.30 P. M. began to make us think that different weather was in store for us, from that to which our constitutions had become acclimated. The mercury in the

PIUTE INDIANS

smoker shot up to 89° and we did not relish it much. Wadsworth at 2.30 P. M. showed no improvement and we would have offered no opposition if the train had been turned about and struck out Westward again. From this station we turned right into the desert and its unvarying prospect of sage brush and alkali dirt. At Wadsworth were a number of Piute Indians, who were more or less habited in store clothes. These were probably some of the good Indians of romance, none of whom we had yet become acquainted with on this trip. The noble red man, if he ever existed outside of Cooper's imagination, has become extinct and there has sprung up a dirty, lazy, stunted and dwarfed species that will inevitably soon become extinguished likewise. At 3 P. M. McIntyre's smoker convened in the rear car. Mac made the introductory remarks, in the course of which he presented each one with a souvenir cane of orange-wood and stated the object for which the smoker was held. Munch responded for the crowd generally and all hands joined in the chorus of "Mac's a jolly good fellow." "Comrades" was then sung with great gusto and efforts ensued to bring about the swapping of experiences in "Frisco," but they were comparative failures. The experiences that we could judge pretty well beforehand came freely enough, but those we were anxious to get at, remained a sealed book. In the midst of our efforts to get details from the reluctant ones, we were surprised by the entrance into the car of the entire body of ladies, evidently intent upon business of their own. They called Milligan aside and, after a short conference, he proceeded, according to their request, to present to Gorman, a diamond locket as a testimonial on the part of the ladies of their appreciation of his many acts of kindness and courtesy towards them on the pilgrimage. The recipient was at first pretty well knocked out, but soon recovered sufficiently to return his thanks for the unexpected token, drifting as usual into poetry before he reached the peroration of his speech.

The ladies were then requested to remain as interested parties in a trial which was to take place at once. Complaint had been duly entered before Judge Milligan and a warrant issued in regular form for the arrest of one Jimmy Baird, alias Jim Crow, for feloniously disturbing the peace and breaking the morning rest of the residents of Mary's Denver train. The Judge took his seat, after an ineffectual attempt to don one of the ladies' silk duster as a robe of office. He only desisted when it was found that a split up the back would be the inevitable result of getting the garment on. He was supported on the right by Bickel as Prosecuting Attorney, while Munch acted as Clerk of the Court. Emmerling was sworn in and mounted a blue cap to act as Copper to the Court. The proceedings were opened by Clerk Munch with the regulation proclamation and the indictment of the Common-poverty vs. Jas. W. Baird, alias Jim Crow, was duly read. It set forth that the said Baird, alias Crow did, on the 34th day of July in the year of the 400th anniversary of the discovery of the glorious climate of California, enter into a certain passenger car, known as the Cats' car, at the unseemly hour of 3.56 A. M.;

and did then and there wilfully and maliciously make, produce and emit certain diabolical sounds or noises which disturbed the beauty sleep of Pop Millick, et al.; and did then and there wickedly, unlawfully, and with malice intent, conspire with one Flattery, alias Plucks, and one Slenderson, a member of the Big Four combination and now a fugitive from justice, to make and produce certain unearthly sounds by the aid of tin horns and other wind instruments, to disturb the peace of said Pop Millick, et al., contrary to the peace and dignity of this dishonorable Court.

At the conclusion of the reading of this formidable document, the defendant fled in dismay and the copper was sent in pursuit. Meanwhile a jury was impanelled, and the spectators were surprised to see in answer to the names of Grover Cleveland, Benjamin Harrison, Andy Carnegie, Ben Butler, Jay Gould and Sing Fat, the well-known forms of Register, Christ, Foster, Zeitz, Phillips and Keen enter the box. Clerk Munch then obligated the jury to convict the prisoner, no matter what the evidence might be. By this time the copper had returned, perspiring and puffing, with the prisoner whom he had captured up at the refrigerator in the baggage car. He had compelled his captor to squeeze through all the narrow passages around the staterooms, toilet rooms and kitchen, going and coming the whole length of the train.

Upon being arraigned before the court. the prisoner pleaded not guilty to the indictment. When asked by the court if he had any counsel or any money to hire one, he answered in the negative. The court then assigned Sobernheimer as counsel to defend him, whereupon the prisoner exclaimed, " Good Lord ! if he is to be my counsel I will plead guilty." The court then decided that he could only be cleared in this court on the ground of insanity, and the prisoner said he would gladly admit the insanity to escape the counsel, but the judge ruled that insanity must be proven. Bickel then opened the trial with a speech for the prosecution, gave a Mexican dollar to the foreman of the jury, and called as witnesses, Millick, McIntyre, Emmerling and Johnson, who, after being sworn by the clerk to tell the truth, the whole truth and more than the truth, testified to the malicious acts of the culprit and his aiders and abettors. All cross-examinations by the counsel for the prisoner failed to elicit one word in the prisoner's favor.

Sobernheimer then made the opening speech for the defense, and stated that he would endeavor to prove his client insane, but called the attention of the jury to the vacant stare of the prisoner as evidence in itself of the fact. His witnesses, Hemphill, Blackwood and Axford did their best to prove the counsel's assertion, and cited the instance of his having paid a dollar for three drinks and a cigar at Del Monte as proof positive. Upon cross-examination, Bickel elicited the fact that the dollar was unwillingly paid, which somewhat reduced the value of the evidence.

The judge said that his charge to the jury was generally five dollars each, but that it would be remitted this time on account of the distinguished character of the gentlemen composing the jury, and then proceeded to score the defendant as feelingly as if he too had been one of the sufferers by the invasion of the sleeping car. The jury shouted "guilty," with one voice, without leaving the box, and the judge then sentenced the down-cast prisoner to go without shoes or stockings every morning until 7 A. M.

Mrs. McIntyre had been assisted in receiving at the tea in her stateroom by the Misses Graham, and Brooks supplied a colored door-tender for the occasion. The cars were not swinging so violently to-day as on the occasion of the last tea, and drinking the beverage was not so difficult. The souvenirs distributed to the ladies were little albums of pressed natural flowers from California, which were received with many manifestations of pleasure. The final act of the occasion was the raid upon the "smoker," as detailed heretofore.

At 3.30 P. M. we passed the Humboldt sink. This is another of the numerous lakes of this remarkable region, which receive the fall of waters and have no visible outlet, except to communicate occasionally with one another. The Humboldt River runs into this lake, and its overflow runs into Carson Lake, which retains all that it receives. At Lovelace, at 4.15 P. M. more Piutes were on hand, fit inhabitants for the desert which environs them. By this time the heat was worse than ever, and the mercury had climbed to the century mark, as had been the case on the southern desert at the Needles. The heat did not make one perspire, but the alkali dust which we stirred up here was an added aggravation that we did not encounter in our southern experience. At 5 P. M. we reached Humboldt, and everybody was out of the train in a twinkling, while it was being watered up. This was the first time we could truly understand the meaning of the time-honored expression, "an oasis in the desert." To come so suddenly upon such a green spot with its cool platform shaded by large trees, its emerald green carpet of grass and its variegated plateaus of flowers, after our hot and dusty ride of the afternoon, caused a revulsion of feeling that gave us a slight taste of what the foot-traveler in the Sahara of Africa might feel when coming suddenly upon a spring of water beneath shady trees, after nearly perishing of thirst and heat. The station is only an example of what irrigation can do even in this desert land, for this is truly a desert, and we miss the luxuriant growth of cacti and other wild plants that characterized the lower so-called deserts. We left the acre or two of Humboldt station with as much regret as any place on the trip, although its only attraction was the brightness of its appearance as compared with its surroundings, like unto an emerald set in a leaden ring. Black rocks are scattered in various places along the plains, which are said to be lava or something of that kind, the supposed results of volcanic action. Star Peak was visible from the train in the range of Humboldt mountains. Its top was covered with snow or its appearance, which gave rise to a discussion as to whether it was really snow or only alkali-covered rocks. Lee inclined strongly to the latter opinion, and he is an authority in these parts.

As evening came on and the sun set, it got much cooler, but the feeling of discomfort produced by the alkali was more aggravated. At Winnemucca we were an hour and a half behind time. The concert in the "smoker" lacked its usual spirit to-night, and there was a marked disposition to lie around and keep cool. Battle Mountain was about the last station at which we slowed up before seeking rest for the night and leaving the train crew to enjoy the pleasures of the desert ride.

SETTLING THE DUST

Friday, August 5th, 1892.

E HAD turned in last night in Nevada. This morning we awoke in Utah. Awoke with a strange feeling of the skin, as though all the oil had been tried out of it and left it hard and leathery. We had been traveling across the desert or around the edges of it all night and knew little of its discomforts during that time, but could feel the results. We passed Promontory this morning in the land of the sage brush. The place is unimportant, but is noticeable from the fact that here the two Pacific railroads were finished, and the junction made of one from the East, and the other from the West. All this morning we have been skirting the shore of the Great Salt Lake. The shore for a long distance from the shining lake itself, looks like the bottom of a former lake, the mud being encrusted with a white deposit, and cracked by the heat of the sun into innumerable crevices. Outside of this line the grass grows abundantly, and large herds of cattle are grazing.

Fireworks had been played on a new brakeman this morning as usual, and he begged another cigar for the engineer, clambering over the coal in the tender to present it to him, and waiting to have a chat with him and the fireman until it went off. The engineer was leaning out of the side of the cab when it did go off, and nearly fell off the engine in his astonishment. The brakeman came back on the heaped up coal like a cat (and in a big hurry) as one lump of coal followed another in his direction till he was safe in the baggage car door.

At Brigham at 8 A. M., cattle getting very plentiful and all looking sleek and fat. We arrived at Ogden at 8.30 A. M. When we alighted and took a look at the cars, we thought they might have run through a lime-kiln in the night. This is the termination of the Southern Pacific line, and the beginning of the Denver and Rio Grande broad gauge system over which we continue our journey. Major Lauck, the Southern's traveling passenger agent, had expected to come this far with us, but had not showed up when we left San Francisco. This point appears to be a railroad centre of some magnitude, and trains were shifting backward and forward in all directions. The mountain scenery in the

137

immediate neighborhood was very grand, the Wahsatch range being in very
close proximity. What we could see of the city showed some very solid and
substantial buildings with wide thoroughfares. The water supply of which we
took a share, is brought down from the mountains which furnish a pure and inexhaustible supply. This is the first point at which our time changes on the
East bound route, and the time between breakfast and luncheon was cut one
hour in consequence. Going West, we sometimes left a station an hour before
we arrived at it, as at Dodge City, Kansas, but we cannot perform that feat any
more. Although not expecting any mail here, we received a letter for Harmon

A SALT LAKE COACH

Johnson that put him in rare good humor for the day. The inspector, whose
duty it is to ring the anvil chorus on the car wheels at every stop, at this point
found a slight flattening on one of the wheels of our smoking car and promptly
condemned the same, ordering the car off the train. Now our smoker was one
of our pets, and had attracted much attention throughout the far West as the
first of its kind to make its appearance there. We considered it indispensable
to our comfort, and the result was quite a considerable kick on our part. A
master mechanic was sent for who, after some hesitation, decided to allow the
wheel to go as far as Salt Lake City. It must have worn round again before we
reached that place, as we never heard of it again.

We left Ogden at 10.05 A. M. by the new or Mountain time, following out the regular Pacific train. Our way lay between the shore of the Salt Lake on our right and the Wahsatch Mountains on the left. The intermediate land was a fine farming country, on which harvesting was still being carried on, the farms all appearing to be under thrifty management. Oats and the alfalfa were plentiful, and there seemed to be a necessity in this part of the country for barns in which to stow them. Orchards were also numerous but the fruit was not yet ripe.

Salt beds, from which that staple is produced by evaporation, were plentiful along the shores of the lake, and 178,000 tons of the article were manufactured here in 1891. At 11.05 A. M. we pulled into Salt Lake City. We had telegraphed ahead for teams with which to get a view of the capital of Mormondom. These were now in waiting, and included the celebrated coach Raymond, a sort of magnified band wagon that carried forty people comfortably. The rest of the party occupied carriages of smaller size. A committee of Utah Commandery No. 1, headed by Sir L. B. Smith, was also in waiting to welcome us to Salt Lake, and accompany us on our round of sightseeing. The streets of the city are 128 feet in width, with a deep ditch on each side through which the clear mountain water is sent flowing at certain hours every day. Fine shade trees line the sidewalks on all the streets, but the roadway itself is not paved. One of them is said to extend for twenty miles and all are laid out at right angles. Our first stop was at the immense Tabernacle or building constructed for the conferences of the Mormon church. It resembles the upper half of one of the new turtle-back steamers set on columns. Its dimensions are 250 feet long by 150 feet wide, and 80 feet high. The roof is 10 feet thick, and conceals a series of lattice trusses. The seating capacity is for 8,000 persons, all of whom can get a good view and hear everything that is said on the platform. Our party were stationed in the far end of the gallery, while the man who has charge of exhibiting the building explained its uses and dimensions in a low tone of voice from the platform, every word of which was audible to the listeners. He wound up by securing silence and then dropping an ordinary pin on the chancel rail in front of him. The noise of the pin striking the rail was plainly heard at the far extremity of the building. The Tabernacle is not much for beauty, although an oddity, but its acoustic properties are certainly unrivalled. It has a grand organ with nearly 3,000 pipes. The organist could not be found, so we were forced to leave without hearing the instrument.

The new Mormon Temple, on the same block of ground as the Tabernacle, is not finished but the time of completion is set for next year. The outside work is about done and the building presents an imposing appearance. The central tower rises to a height of 220 feet and is surmounted by an angel of heroic size, blowing a trumpet. ("Looked like Fred. Munch on the Mariposa coach," somebody remarked.) The work on the Temple has been in progress

TABERNACLE, SALT LAKE CITY

for forty years. The Assembly Hall, another place of meeting for the Saints, is also located on this block, which goes by the name of Temple Block. The whole square is surrounded by a stone wall fifteen feet high and five feet in thickness.

The Lion House is one of the residences erected by the late Brigham for some of his numerous families. It is so called from the stone effigy of a lion on it, which might pass for a calf. Another house used for the same purpose, adjoins this and is called the Bee Hive House from the carving of that article which adorns it. Brigham knew enough of women's ways to put a good fence between them. The Gardo House or Amelia Palace, in which his favorite and nineteenth wife was ensconced, was off on the opposite side of the street and now bears the signboard of a branch Keeley Institute Cure over the front door.

The Eagle Gate, which spans the street adjoining the Bee Hive House, was in process of repair and the Eagle was down. The White House was another of Brigham's numerous nests which was built for his first helpmate and adjoins the special school-house erected to accommodate his seventy-eight children. A little farther down First Street is the iron rail fence which encloses the Young family cemetery. Brigham's grave is at the end farthest from the street and enclosed in another iron fence. Our driver said that a chunk of stone weighing twenty tons was planted on top of the coffin, to prevent any one from hiving the old Mormon's remains.

The Tithing House is close to the Temple and Tabernacle. This is the place where the pure and unadulterated Mormon blows in one-tenth of all his produce of whatever kind, except children. From the same point, the jack-pot is distributed to those entitled to receive the same, after the deacons have sweated the pile. An immense store, fitted with as great a variety of goods as Our John's, occupies a prominent location on Main Street and is labeled the Zion Co-operative Mercantile Institution. It is said to do an immense business annually and has numerous branches. Wherever you see the letters Z. C. M. I. on the front of a building, you may know that it is subordinate to the Co-op. as the institution is called for short.

The Utah Exposition grounds occupy a block of ten acres. The buildings erected so far are quite ornamental. The Templeton and Knutsford hotels are both large and of striking architecture. The ride along Brigham Street revealed many good residences on either side, but the appearance of the street generally was detracted from by the number of houses of lesser pretensions. Many of these were of Mormon origin, which fact was revealed by the numerous one room additions and ells planted against the original edifice, whenever the captain made a new splice. You could tell within one or two, by counting the additions, just how many rocking chairs and looking glasses the owner had to buy to keep peace in the family. The streets running past the four sides of the Temple Block are named North, South, East and West Temple Streets. Beyond in each direction they are numbered First, Second and Third Streets,

North, South, East or West as the case may be. East Temple is also called Main Street and South Temple rejoices in the cognomen of Brigham Street. Want of time prevented us from taking the drive to Fort Douglass, the U. S. military post, but the souvenir spoon fiends found time to indulge their curiosity, as well as to get a chance at the agate, carnelian, topaz, opal and other native gem stones.

The weather had been getting pretty warm since we started. This, coupled with the fact that few of the dirt roads over which we rode were sprinkled, did not add anything to the pleasure of the ride. Many of our party were disappointed with Salt Lake City, having generally heard it spoken of as a Paradise. Probably without the attendant heat and dust they would have had a somewhat better opinion of it, even with the cursory glance we were obliged to take. We can imagine how such a spot seemed like a heaven to a party of weary Mormons, who might have years ago toiled across the plains in emigrant wagons and landed here. But we had been much nearer to Paradise in several localities in Southern California, and perhaps expected too much from hearing a title hastily given.

We were finally landed at the narrow gauge depot, whence the road takes you to Garfield Beach, in time to take the 1 P. M. train, on which two special cars had been reserved for our use. To save time, Brooks had promised to have luncheon sent to this train for us. True to his word, he came up smiling promptly to time with the needed cold bite. To say that the meal was much enjoyed is stating the case very mildly, though Brooks was kept busy keeping track of the Pullman forks and spoons.

The ride to the beach is almost level, but mountains encircle us in every direction except on the lake side. When we got close to the beach we were skirting right along the base of one range, although the greater part of the run resembled that across the meadows to Atlantic City. The cars were open ones and the wind blew so strongly as to necessitate putting down the curtains on the near side, making it very cool and pleasant after our warm ride through the city. A run of forty-five minutes brought us to the front of the watering place. Amid all the wonderful sights we have witnessed in the West, the Great Salt Lake is one of the most remarkable. Here was a lake with an area of about three thousand square miles, more than a thousand miles from one ocean and two thousand from another, and perched up in the air over four thousand feet higher than either. Imagine the waters of this inland sea being six times as salt as those of the oceans, notwithstanding the fact that four large rivers pour immense volumes of fresh water into it at all times, without raising the level of its waters one inch, or diminishing its intensely saline qualities a tenth of a degree. One can only wonder and inquire how such a thing can be, but science, which is ready to account for almost everything on the face of the globe, is dumb so far as any response can be made.

The similarity of the map of the Salt Lake Valley and that of Palestine, with the two Dead Seas, the parallel mountain ranges, the two Jordan Rivers flowing from similar fresh water lakes, and the large mountains overlooking the end of each valley, is so remarkable that we reproduce it here, believing it to be not so generally known in this section of the country.

In addition to the immense quantities of salt held in solution in these waters, and commercially extracted with great profit by evaporation, they con-

tain large quantities of soda, which, in one spot near Salt Lake City, is piled up on the shore on windy nights by the hundred tons. Upon the occasion of our visit no lovelier looking body of water ever rippled in the sunshine. Near shore the water was of a pale green color, and as clear as crystal, showing every inch of the pure white sand of the bottom. Farther out the water was of a deep blue tint, becoming almost purple in the distance. Numerous islands are visible on the face of the lake. Not the flat banks we are usually in the habit of associating with the name island, but bold elevations of rock, rising to the height of three or four thousand feet. The largest and nearest is Antelope Island, which is sixteen miles long and five miles wide. It attains the elevation of four thousand feet and is said to abound in exquisite natural scenery.

Notwithstanding all the ingredients of this Dead Sea, which had been drilled into us by word of mouth and guide books as well, the rush to get tickets and bathing suits was a wild one. Emmerling alone was sad. There were no suits that would even fit him by splicing two together. After hopelessly wrecking one in an attempt to install his ample form therein, he took revenge out of the shower-bath, by letting it run on himself for a half hour, and dressed again. Meanwhile the crowd all waded out in front of the pavilion, which is itself built far out in the lake, and connected with the shore by a bridge.

The water deepened so very gradually, that at the distance of a half mile out you could still wade. The depth made no difference, however, as when once you lifted your feet off the bottom you floated, and only by extraordinary exertions could you regain your footing. It was equal to a half dozen circuses, and every bather was a star performer. You simply could not and would not sink but one end at a time. You can sit down, hug your knees and float around like a rotten apple. You had only to lie over on your back, smoke a cigar, clasp your hands back of your head and float in dreamy content, or paddle with your hands to move slowly along. There are no shells to cut your feet, no sharks, no crabs to nip your toes. No snakes to swim across your path nor bull frogs to jump in and scare the nervous. There is no living thing in all the vast expanse of this Dead Sea except the bather. Even his nether extremities under the pale green water take on the hue peculiar to a "stiff." When twenty-five of the crowd got into line, floating on their backs, with each one's feet hooked under his successor's arms, and the whole procession paddling with their hands, it looked like the sea-serpent or a gigantic centipede trying to swim across the lake. More ridiculous sights were to be enjoyed from the vantage ground of the pavilion than we had seen for some time. When you get the water splashed into your eyes you cannot open them, and if you rub them with your fingers you make them worse. If you are up to the proper caper, you first suck the salt off your finger and then wipe out your eye. Each bath house has a shower-bath in it to wash off the salt water when you come out, or you would find yourself covered with white crystals when you dried off.

Our cars did not go back until 5 P. M., which gave us ample time to enjoy all the peculiarities of the lake, the music and dancing in the pavilion, and the view of the mountain, which rose to a great height not two hundred yards back from the shore. From a pier a short distance above the bathing houses, a little steamboat made hourly trips out on the waters of the lake, over toward one of the large islands in view.

Our ride back to the city was uneventful and we took the electric cars at
the station direct for the Knutsford, at which we were booked for dinner.
Here were found numerous letters and telegrams for our pilgrims and all hands
were soon deeply immersed in news from home. One of the telegrams was of
the kind that cast a gloom over the entire party. Cantlin's father was so very
ill that the message was sent to call him home as quickly as possible. It was
not made known to him until after dinner, when arrangements were made by
Purdy and Milligan to send him back to Ogden in the morning. From that
point he could take a more direct line for home than the route we were on and
would save a day or two in time on the road. We were more than sorry to
lose the company of any of the party for the rest of the trip and especially of
Cantlin, whose sprightliness and unassuming manners had won the esteem of
all. After dinner, which was served in the grand dining room of the Knutsford
and enjoyed the more on account of having made a rather lighter luncheon
than is customary with us, many sought the reading rooms to answer their
letters. The hotel had large books, descriptive of the house and to some
extent of the city, already done up in wrappers, which you could have for the
asking. Most of the party availed themselves of the chance to mail one to
their homes. A number strolled out into the city highways again, although
our time was limited. We were scheduled to leave at 8 P. M. and the Rio
Grande station was a good mile away. The electric cars ran from the corner
above us to the station and the majority took advantage of their convenience.
Some few walked, arriving at the eleventh hour, and a half-dozen stragglers
headed by the Captain General, were only saved from following on a later
train by the good nature of an accommodating conductor, who held the train
until 8.10 P. M. A few miles out we passed a number of silver smelting
furnaces, strung along the tracks on either side. We could only tell they were
there by the aid of the light from their own furnaces. All hands were tired
with the picnic to-day and the porters soon had more orders to make up berths
than they could fill. A number waited up for a sight of the Spanish Fork
Canon and were well rewarded for the time spent. Entering abruptly between
solid rock walls four thousand feet high, with the track winding in and out
through its circuitous and picturesque recesses, a fine effect was given to the
scenery by the semi-darkness of the gathering night. The whirling and tumbling stream, down the centre of the canon, did not detract any from the
beauty of the scene. At 10 P. M. we stopped for a little while in front of the
water cure establishment at Castillo Springs, in the heart of the Canon, at
which the hotel was still ablaze with lights. There is a great swimming pool
here, with baths of all sorts of water and every degree of heat, which cure all
the ills that the human body is heir to. A tramp who dropped off from under
one of our cars as we stopped here and started off limping out into the darkness, replied to McIntyre's query, as to the name of the place, that "he did
not know."

GRAND RIVER CANON

Saturday, August 6th, 1892.

WOKE this morning and found the train going through one of the canons of the Grand River, which lasted from five until seven A. M. We had crossed over a summit of 8,000 feet during the night, and were now getting down to the level of this part of the country again. About 6 A. M. we passed the dividing line between Utah and Colorado. It was marked with a broad band of white paint down the yellow rock of the canon, with the name of the silver state lettered on one side and that of the Mormon paradise on the other. We had long since exhausted the English adjectives usually made use of, in the endeavor to express our feelings about the matter of scenery and could now only sit and gaze our fill of the great and stupendous work that has been piled up around us by nature.

We are told that we passed some very fine effects during the night. We are almost half glad that we have had a night's rest from it, but we should have liked a view of what is called Castle Gate at the end of Price River Canon. The walls of the Canon we entered first this morning were of a hard yellowish stone, with hardly a seam visible in them and towered far above our heads. On the opposite side of the Grand River was pointed out to us a formation in the rocks that looked like a gigantic son of the desert, with a white stone turban and cloak and a red sandstone face. Behind him stood a dromedary more than a hundred feet high, awaiting the pleasure of his Arab master, as he had doubtless been doing patiently for more than a few years. A few hundred yards farther on was a procession apparently of priests of immense stature, the smallest of the party being nearly as high as the camel we had just passed. With the aid of very little imagination, many figures can be made apparent to the mind's eye among the vagaries that Mother Nature has been guilty of in these mountains. The Canon soon opened out into the desert again, as the country through which we had been flying all night is called, but we are still shut in all around by mountain ranges. At Fruita or Fruitvale, irrigation has made a change in the face of the country, and we see immense orchards of different kinds of fruit as the result.

We drew into Grand Junction at 7.30 A. M., having picked up a half-hour on the schedule. The train of Mecca Temple, of New York City, was lying here in charge of the train hands. The pilgrims who had come out in it, preliminary to the meeting of the Imperial Council at Omaha, were in on the Narrow Gauge Denver and Rio Grande R. R. taking in the scenic wonders of that road. Our dining car crew and those of the Mecca train had a general jubilee over the encounter. One conductor had been killed on their train and another injured since they had left home. This is not only a railroad junction, but the point of juncture of the Grand and Gunnison Rivers and the chief city of the Grand River valley. Irrigation has also been the making of this place and, with the more than plentiful supply of water obtainable, the fruit and grape culture, which has proven a success in a very short time, will doubtless be indefinitely prolonged. The streets are lined with shade trees which give the town a cool and pleasant appearance. The inhabitants speak of the situation of the town as low, because its altitude above the sea is only 4,450 feet.

We left the Junction at 8.15 A. M., following the course of the Grand River, soon entering between the high rocky walls again and clearing one canon or gorge only to enter into another of similar character. At one point in one of the numerous gorges, on the opposite side from that on which the track ran, a natural explosion, of some unknown character, had hurled hundreds of tons of rock down into the river and the fresh face of the rock left standing showed the lines of fracture. We were going steadily up grade all the morning and always along the turbulent waters of the Grand. De Beque was reached at 9.15 A. M. At this point a rope ferry was in use as a means of crossing the river, but a bridge was in process of construction. Strong guys were necessary to make the boat stem the swift current of the river as it was pulled back and forth. Many cowboys were congregated around the town, betokening the presence of cattle at no great distance. One of them tried to push his horse into keeping up with the train, but was soon distanced. The Big Four were on the stool of repentance this morning, Zeitz being unusually quiet and thoughtful. All of them were apparently meditating over the early morning disturbances in the cats' car or else studying fresh deviltry or it might be, in a regretful mood over the memories of Chinatown. 10.05 A. M. found us at Rifle Creek. More cow-punchers enlivened the scenery here and the place seemed to be a sort of head-quarters for them. The houses were mainly log huts with the chinks plastered up with mud. There were also shelters for stock, built of small tree trunks for frame work and covered in with thatched roofs. Borings for coal were frequent and our local conductor claimed that sufficient area of coal beds had been located in one county to last the entire country for a century to come.

Our next halt was at Newcastle at 10.35 A. M. A large deer head with a fine pair of antlers, lying on the station platform, attracted general attention as soon as we stopped. It was immediately discovered that more of the same articles could be bought from the station hands. We only stopped a matter of some ten or 'twelve minutes at the platform, but in that time we had become the possessors of five deer heads and one of a large elk, together with various wild-cat and deer skins. The baggage car was taxed sorely to provide accommodations for the elk-head, but the deers' antlers were more easily provided for. At 11.10 A. M. we ran into Glenwood Springs nearly an hour ahead of time. Another delegation of Sir Knights waited upon us, immediately upon our arrival, and tendered us the hospitality of the Springs and an invite to a head-quarters they had opened. The train was halted at the end of a new iron foot bridge which has been built across the river to reach the grounds surrounding the Springs, which are located on the opposite side from the town. As soon as we vacated the train, it was backed down to the outskirts of the town, to await our departure.

The entire body of pilgrims was soon at the grand bathing establishment, which has been erected as an adjunct to the Springs, where they were immediately supplied with the suits necessary for a swim in the big pool. The surrounding hills soon re-echoed with the loud noise made by the bathers. Even the waters of the pool were loud and in the slang of the period, "rotten eggs were not in it" with them. The main swimming pool is about 600 feet long by 110 feet wide, the depth being graded from three to six feet. It is walled around with stone, the bottom being paved with brick, on which any article can be plainly seen in the deepest part, owing to the clearness of the water. Much amusement was afforded by the determined efforts of the bathers to bring up nickels and dimes from the bottom. The appearance of the bare skin of the human body, under the surface of the water, was a great deal worse than in Salt Lake and can only be described as "ghastly." The volume of water that flows into the swimming pool is simply marvellous. The statement that the springs which supply it furnish two and a half millions of gallons per day, does not give half the idea of the volume that you receive when you stand at the walled rim of the largest spring and see the water boil up out of the ground in twenty different places and rush through the aqueduct built for its conveyance to the pool. In the spring itself, the water is about as hot as you want to dip your hands into and the pool is kept at a temperature of 90°. Bathing therein goes on in winter, just as in summer, even when snow is on the ground around, while the water loses none of its fragrance as well as retains its heat. Some of the large springs are led directly into the river, through an underground conduit, the waters thereof not being used, except to be drunk by invalids whose insides are so far gone as to render it immaterial what is put into them. The springs are said to have formerly bubbled up in the midst of the river, but the enterprise of the present proprietors has turned what was part of the river bed into a garden-covered island. The whole valley was part of an Indian reservation and the red man had to be bought off for transplanting. The government now has charge of the sale of the land and the cash secured

GLENWOOD SULPHUR SPRINGS

for it goes into the pockets of the Indians, if it does not stick on the road. The island is laid out with walks, well shaded with trees, and elegant grass sward between.

A menagerie had been started at the upper end of the island only a day or two before our arrival, by making a wire enclosure around some of the tree trunks. Its contents at present were three young elks and a spotted fawn. They were very tame and did not mind being handled in the least. The bath house is built of red sandstone, lined inside with pressed brick and is of pleasing architecture. The private bath rooms are fitted up in gorgeous style, and each one has a room attached as a dressing room, which is also fitted with every convenience if you desire to lie down and rest after the bath.

Our party had not long been in possession of the pool before the whistle of an engine denoted a fresh arrival. It was only a little while after when a rush into the waters announced the presence of the pilgrims of California No. 1, who were escorting the Grand Commandery of their state to the conclave at Denver. We recognized many of our entertainers of the Pacific Coast and were glad of a further opportunity to fraternize with them. They had come in over the Colorado Midland road, which parallels the Rio Grande a greater part of the way to Denver. What little noise was needed to fill the balance of the crevices in the mountains was supplied by No. 1, and we left them still whooping it up, to go to the train for luncheon. We found Brooks there, ready as usual, feeding all comers as they dropped in. After dinner several of our party walked over to the California train and inspected their accommodations. The path led us through several very extensive brickyards, in which they seemed to be handling a very fine grade of clay and turning out a superior article of brick. Adjoining the floor of one yard was a regular plantation of dwarf sun-flowers, of which generous bunches were gathered for the ladies. We had expected to leave here at 2.30 P. M., but the press of business on the single track road prevented our departure. We were forced to wait here until five empty trains were brought through, passing this point to go on to Grand Junction. One of these had contained a Boston Commandery, while all the others belonged to our Pennsylvania fraters, who had gone in over the Marshall Pass on the Narrow Gauge, and would only get back to their own trains after reaching Grand Junction.

A committee of Sir Knights had been sent down from Leadville to escort us to that city. Finding California here also, they had divided their forces and detailed three of their number to go with that command. Sirs Kellogg, Godbow and Reef elected to act as our division of the escort, and right worthy traveling companions they proved. It was 3.20 P. M. before we were able to pull out of the Springs, and the engineer had orders to make up for lost time as far as possible. We dived right into another canon of the Grand which was thirteen miles in length. This was the noblest Roman of them all in the canon line that we had yet seen, and its bewildering succession of ever-changing scenery was devoured with eager eyes. You could not call your next neigh-bor's attention to a peculiar formation before it had assumed an entirely different shape by a turn in the road. Castles, turrets, bastions, pyramids and statues turned and whirled in the air apparently, on the opposite side of the canon, while on the near side, the rocks towered straight up above the train, until it twisted your neck in an effort to get a sight of the top. It was a good plan to put a cushion on the floor of the smoker, kneel upon it at the open window and look ahead or back at the transformations in the kaleidoscopic picture on every hand. At the same time you ran a big risk of getting cross-eyed in the endeavor at times to look both ways at once.

The river was foaming down in a succession of falls and cascades, its pro-gress being impeded by sections of black rock, which had evidently been water worn through many ages. Vistas of deep gorges or clefts in the walls opened up in rapid succession, reaching far back into the country. Now green with verdure to the very top and again bare of any vestige of vegetable life, and show-ing only the bleak prospect of rocks. The different colored strata of stone and earth lent a new charm to the scene, and we were filled with wonder that such things could be, as well as with gratitude that it had fallen to our lot to behold them. The black rocks in the bed of the river and many more masses of the same kind scattered along the shores are evidently the results of volcanic action. At the end of this canon the road emerged into a wider valley, which was still hemmed in with lofty mountains on each side. We left behind us the muddy torrent of the Grand and started up the valley of the Eagle River. The waters of the latter were as clear as those of the Grand had been muddy, and the bottom covered with gravel, although enough rocks had lodged in the bed of the stream to give it a wild look in some parts. At times it would run into quiet pools, overshaded by bushes and trees. At such spots you are very likely to see a fisherman throwing his line out over the calm surface. If the fish are in proportion to the number of fishermen we sighted along the banks this afternoon, there must be a good supply of trout in the Eagle River.

At Gypsum station at 4.20 P. M. the snow patches on the high peaks of the adjacent mountain ranges stand out in bold relief. There is a thunder-storm in progress of rehearsal away up in the hills somewhere, of which the ac-companying thunder rolled and reverberated down the valley, but we received none of the down-pour. We are running through Brush valley, where most of the ranches possess comfortable looking dwellings. The crops which are still being harvested, show the fertility of the lands of the valley, and the many herds of fat cattle offer additional testimony to the fact. A little shack house, with a small farm surrounding it, gained all the sympathy of the train load for the loss it was shown to have sustained by the solitary little tombstone near by, enclosed with a rough picket fence.

EAGLE RIVER CAÑON

At 5.45 P. M. we entered Eagle Canon, in which the grandeur of the scenery of the other canon is repeated and enhanced. Two engines were hooked on to take us up the steeper grade which we encounter here. The canon was at first very narrow, and we popped in and out of an occasional tunnel. The lofty and seemingly inaccessible crags were as parti-colored, and consequently as picturesque as those through which we had passed in the Grand, calling forth all the enthusiasm of the party. Presently the canon opened out a little wider as we entered into the Battle Mountain mining district. Here our veneration for the sublime work of nature was forced to give way somewhat to admiration of the pluck of man, who had overcome the difficulties and dangers consequent to the ascent of such elevations in his search after the precious metals. Beginning right down at the water's edge, the borings into the sides of the mountains ran up their faces almost as thickly as the holes made by a flock of swallows in a sand-bank. Some were timbered at the sides and top where they entered, while others were encased only by the rocky wall into which they had been pierced. Away up near the extreme top were perched whole villages of frame houses, similar to those we had seen a few days ago, but in larger numbers, and still more hazardous situations. It was a poor place in which to raise a family where there was but one step 2,000 feet deep from the front door down to the level of the yard. The walking for moonlight strolls was also very limited and equally rough. In many places, vast sections of the face of the cliffs had been thrown down by the miners and made the scene seem still more rugged and ragged. The railroad had run in sidings in many places, some of which had apparently been abandoned and left to decay. Most of them were still in use and labor saving machinery, in the shape of endless wire ropes with bucket attachments were run to all heights of the mountain faces to bring down to the cars the result of the miner's toil and risk. There was nothing so well calculated to impress upon our minds the daring and skill, as well as the greed after the almighty dollar, of the average American, as these crow's nests perched, not on anything, but simply against the almost perpendicular face of these rocks, from which to bore into their granite cased veins on the mere suspicion that there is boodle in them. At Red Cliff, at 6 P. M., we were greeted by the bulk of the population, principally female, with much waving of handkerchiefs. Just beyond we were shown the fort or earthwork, behind which the primitive settlers fought a battle with the Ute Indians, Battle Mountain having taken its name from that incident. Red Cliff Canon, a little further ahead, was short but quite as beautiful as any of its peers of larger extent. Crane's Park was the cognomen given to the valley, up which we passed before reaching Tennessee Pass, and it furnished us another grand view of mountain and valley combination, with a more practical addition of a great row of charcoal ovens. They do not make charcoal here, as in the East, by banking up the tree trunks and covering with dirt, but have large kilns built of brick, very similar to the coke-ovens around Pittsburg.

Through a break in the mountains, our escorting committee made a desperate effort to show us the well-known figure of the Cross, on the side of a
peak of one of the lateral ranges, which is renowned of guide books and
immortalized by numerous poets and gives its name to the Commandery in
Leadville. We were too obtuse or passed the opening too quickly to discern
the Cross or more probably did not have time to draw on our imagination
sufficiently to line up a cross. At 6.45 P. M. we entered the tunnel under
Tennessee Pass from which we soon emerged on the Eastern slope of the Great
Divide. We have passed under, or over or around so many divides or back-
bones of the American continent, that we are at a loss to know just where the
true division of the East from the West is located. This is called the Great
Divide anyhow and we will accept it as such. We do know of this point that
the water that falls and the snow that melts on one side, enters into the Grand
and finally finds its way, via the Colorado, into the Gulf of California; while
that on the Eastern slope travels down with the Arkansas, to mingle with the
muddy Mississippi and drift along to the Gulf of Mexico. We are also
reminded that they travel downward 10,418 feet, while in transit, just as we
have ascended that distance to look upon their starting points. Snow was
lying around in great profusion up in the gullies and hollows of the mountain
peaks which surround us and rear their heads proudly even higher than the
level of the Pass. The road onward from the mouth of the tunnel did not
descend much, but wound around a crooked trail. Plenty of timber had
covered the mountain sides all this afternoon, but great inroads had been made
into it. Piles of railroad ties line the track and more charcoal ovens are
visible. Presently great clouds of smoke, rolling across the plateau, locate the
smelting furnaces of Leadville and at 7.25 P. M. the train drew up beside the
station at that point. Efforts had been made to have dinner over before the
time of the arrival, but they were not wholly successful. Mount of the Holy
Cross Commandery No. 5 of Colorado was in line at the station, with sixty
Sir Knights and a band of music, to escort us to their asylum. Carriages were
provided for the use of the ladies and the Baby. Capt. Gen. Munch formed
the column of Mary and followed the escort as promptly as possible, because
they expected California in over the Midland at the same hour of our arrival and
went after them as soon as they had brought us to the hall.

We found the asylum well filled with Knights and their ladies from Leadville, as well as our own who reached there before us. Our traveling register
was brought along and was soon in great demand for its aid in securing a Mary
souvenir. In the adjoining banquet room a set-out of eatables and drinkables
was ready for all comers. Mary was hardly equal to the occasion, until a later
hour of the evening, at which time they were able to do justice to the profuse
hospitality of the Holy Cross. After a short season spent in introductions and
fraternal greetings, the Leadville Committee announced that conveyances were
at the door for the use of any of their visitors who desired to visit, either one

of the silver mines where the precious ores were dug out or the smelting furnaces in which they were reduced to a marketable shape. These were soon filled with our party after they had made their election as to choice between the sights to be enjoyed. Those who went underground had a rough and hilly ride, after leaving the main street, up to the Maid of Erin mine. Here a busy enough scene was being enacted on top of the ground, no matter what was going on beneath. There were numerous boiler and engine rooms as well as hoisting apparatus rooms containing huge cylinders, filled with wire rope. The director thereof stood by with a lever in his hand, constantly obeying the signals of the gong to raise or lower. Three or four shafts were in steady operation, over the mouths of which the automatic doors would fly up, heralding the advent above ground of a small square platform, entirely unenclosed, upon which a tub of the silver carbonates would be located, ready to be wheeled off and dumped into the immense timber receptacle built outside for its storage. If you descended into the mine, that platform was the conveyance by which you were carried 700 feet straight down into the bowels of the mountain. You were provided with a miner's tarpaulin coat and hat, together with a candle, as your outfit for the journey. Four or five could stand on the platform at once, cling to one another in the absence of anything else to put faith in, commend their souls to God, and slide quickly down the square shaft, black as night save for the flickering light of the candles, to the bottom. It was a short trip and did not consume the time it takes to tell of it. Once down the investigations were conducted by the aid of the candles you carried, assisted by those of the miners and laborers in the different drifts, who were hard at it with pick and shovel. Several ladies of the party made the descent, including Mrs. Lowry, Mrs. Regester, Miss Haldeman and Miss McAlpine. The latter three penetrated to the farthest recesses of one of the drifts, to reach which they even climbed a perpendicular ladder which some of the rest declined. Emmerling roamed around down there, until he came to a fat man's misery in a side drift, through which his corporosity could not be forced and he returned to the main shaft. It was not the most comfortable promenade in the country, even for the smaller ones. Fine specimens of the ore could be had from the miners for a small gratuity, although Holy Cross Commandery had a large boxful, sitting in its ante-room, at the service of any one who chose to carry specimens with them. When the return trip up the shaft was made, the first rush of air put out every candle and the ascent was made in total darkness. A huge sigh of relief was the first salute accorded the upper air by each individual as the trap opened.

Each carriage was driven off as its complement returned from the lower regions and went the round of the streets of the city. Seeing a large gilded sign, upon the plate glass window in front of a goodly sized building on the main street, bearing the name "Board of Trade," all ablaze with light and surrounded by people, we wondered what such an institution found to occupy its attention on Saturday night. Plenty of other folks were passing in and out,

so we followed the stream in. Once inside, we found that " trade " was boom-
ing or being boomed by two or three hundred members of the " board " who
were indulging in Keno, Roulette, Rouge et Noir or any other form of the
peculiar trade to which this board was addicted. Many other institutions of
the same ilk were found in full blast in the course of our peregrinations, there
being one attached to most of the saloons in the place. The typical " bad
man," who used to be a prominent ornament of this city and would bore a
hole in you for looking cross-eyed at him, has evidently been gotten under
legal control. In his stead, the bad woman flourishes openly like the green
bay tree. The visitors to the smelter were driven to the opposite quarter of
the city, where they drew up at one of the dark gloomy looking buildings. A
plank inclined plane led up the outside of the house, which demanded a steady
head for its ascent, there being no protection on either side. When admission
was gained to the second floor thereby, workmen were found busily engaged in
feeding the tops of the furnaces with a mixture of silver ore, wood and coke.
The place was full of smoke and dust, the latter alone being sufficient to choke
all hands. The path down the incline was cautiously retraced and an entrance
effected to the first floor. Here a half-dozen large furnaces were in active
operation and the showers of sparks flying through the air in all directions from
the molten metal as it was drawn off at the bottom of the furnaces, bore a
family resemblance to a Fourth of July celebration. The metal was run into a
basin on wheels and rolled outside to cool off. This first result is said to be
smelted over again and run into pigs or bars. The precious metal, or what
pas ed for it, looked more like lead than silver.

All parties returned to the asylum of Holy Cross and found California
No. 1 also in possession. St. John No. 4 of Philadelphia had also been
expected this evening, but did not make its appearnce. California had turned
out in fatigue uniform, they having their traps with them on the train. They
retired early, but we remained at the asylum until 11 P. M. Before departing,
Sir Munch drew up the pilgrims in line and returned thanks for the kind reception, knightly courtesy and fraternal care that had been extended to Mary by
the Sir Knights and ladies of Mount of the Holy Cross Commandery and the
citizens of Leadville.

The high altitude of this city and its consequent rarefied air caused some
unpleasant feelings to a few of the party, but nothing of serious import.
10,200 feet was a little above their ordinary standing in the East, and gave
some of them headache or palpitation of the heart, or a sick feeling in the
stomach. Going up stairs was an especially severe exertion, and one of the
California ladies fainted when partly up the stairs of the asylum. The Knights
of Leadville deserve more than passing mention for their share of attention to
visiting fraters during this Triennial. Numerous commanderies, which did
not visit the Pacific Coast, extended their trips westward to Grand Junction,
and all paid a flying visit to Leadville. All were received and entertained in

true knightly fashion, and assisted in their efforts to see what might be of interest in the city. They had received or expected to receive twenty-four commanderies, and none but those interested in such affairs can appreciate the amount of labor and expense involved in 'such a series of receptions. The stores and dwellings of the city were decorated as if the conclave itself were to be held here, and no trouble was spared to make your visit a pleasant one, if only lasting a few hours.

The career of Leadville has been a most remarkable one, and a few of the facts in relation thereto may not be out of place in these pages. First brought into notice in 1859 as California Gulch, it became celebrated as a gold field, and five millions of dollars of that desirable commodity were washed out of the ground before 1864. The gold got scarce and the camp was almost abandoned until 1876, when the carbonate beds containing silver were discovered. Another rush ensued for the site, which was then named Leadville, and the population rose rapidly to 30,000 souls. In ten years the product of its mines in gold, silver, lead and copper, amounted to 160,000,000 dollars. Overcoats were in demand in the course of our rambles around town, and still more so as the hour grew later. Carriages were in waiting to take all hands back to the train, to which the committee accompanied us upon our return. We found a caller there in the person of Sir Franklin L. Hall, of St. John No. 4, who was out this way on business. Everybody was at home on time, and most of the pilgrims had retired, when the train pulled out at 11.30 P. M. for Salida, only a couple of hours away, except a wagon load of smokers, who waited to finish their butts before going to their berths.

VOICES OF THE NIGHT.

Sunday, August 7th, 1892.

OUR engine left us on the track, directly in front of the station at Salida, at 2 A. M. There was such a scurrying past of trains and shrieking of locomotive whistles from that time forward, that our sleep was disturbed and our rest much broken. We could have been run onto a convenient siding, a few hundred yards in our rear, and it would have been pleasant sleeping, but no one knew where we were until daylight. It got quieter towards morning, and all hands were loath to get up, not more than ten being abroad when Brooks made his " first call." The consequence was that some of the tail-enders had to hurry their eating to be in readiness for the trip over the Marshall Pass on the Denver and and Rio Grande narrow gauge. The morning wrestle was with the following :

········**BREAKFAST**········

FRUITS IN SEASON   BERRIES AND CREAM

OAT MEAL AND CREAM

BROILED SALMON   CODFISH BALLS

CALF'S LIVER AND BACON

SIRLOIN STEAK, PLAIN, WITH MUSHROOMS OR TOMATO SAUCE

HAM   BREAKFAST BACON   MUTTON CHOPS, PLAIN OR WITH TOMATO SAUCE
TENDERLOIN STEAK

EGGS, BOILED, FRIED, SHIRRED OR SCRAMBLED
OMELETS, PLAIN, WITH HAM, PARSLEY, JELLY OR RUM

POTATOES, BAKED, FRIED, STEWED IN CREAM

GREEN TEA   ENGLISH BREAKFAST TEA
COFFEE   MILK   COCOA

VIENNA, GRAHAM AND BROWN BREAD
CORN BREAD   DIPPED AND CREAM TOAST   HOT ROLLS
DRY TOAST   BUTTERED TOAST

The broad gauge road over which we have been traveling, we find equipped with a third rail throughout, so that the narrow gauge trains can make use of it at will. The same system is carried out all the way to Denver. Salida is a distributing and receiving point for a number of mining camps which surround it. It is a good sized town, with wide streets and the mountain water running through ditches on either side of them. The climate is claimed to be as nearly perfect as at any point in the West, the sun shining brightly, on an average, 320 days in the year, and to-day was one of them. It is not as high up as Leadville, being only 7,050 feet above the sea-level. The air is the same rarefied brand which we find all through this section. The first thing to strike the eye upon emerging from the train this morning was an immense red cross, which had been planted on top of one of the high hills opposite the station. It was visible for a long distance, and had been placed in position by the Knights of Salida. The views of the mountain ranges from the station were particularly fine, there being several of them in sight, with the higher peaks streaked with snow.

The train we were to take was only a few feet distant from our location and we got away on it at 8.15 A. M. in three cars, with two engines attached. The series of curves and twists, by which we overcame the grade up the mountains, made the ride simply bewildering. Horse-shoe, grape vine, corkscrew and base ball curves were all in it. We could see so many sections of track at times that we were hardly able to tell in which direction we were bound. As we ascended in the air, the view became more unobstructed and we could see mountain peaks by the dozen. The Sangre de Cristo range towered away above the others, but did not seem to be wooded like those we were ascending. They looked liked yellow clay, except where the white patches of snow lay in profusion near their tops. All of the mountains got more or less bare above a certain height, the line of vegetation being clearly marked. The most remarkable thing in our immediate neighborhood was the variety and great plenty of the wild flowers along both sides of the track. Some of them were familiar to us, but the majority were new and the brightness of their colors was a source of wonder to all of us. Some of the grades which were visible ahead of us, before we reached them, seemed really insurmountable to a railroad train, but our two engines walked us up with apparent ease. An occasional snow shed would be passed. Not the massive timber construction of the Sierra Nevadas, but something much lighter in character and of but short extent, to protect the track in some of the clefts of the mountains. Down in the gulches, around which the road winds, clear mountain streams leap and dash over the stones in wild attempts to reach the bottom.

We reached the Summit at 9.35 A. M. and stopped to reconnoitre creation from the height of 10,852 feet. Some ascended to the top of the observatory and gained enough altitude to make it up to 11,000. The scene was an impressive one; made so more by the far-reaching silence than by the views of rocks or trees.

The Pass is over a shoulder of Mt. Ouray, whose main peak towers still 3,000 feet above us. There was a dwelling at the top, in front of which a pleasant old lady had bunches of the mountain wild flowers made up for sale and kept fresh in old tin cans full of water. Silver specimens were also on sale, together with photographic views of the scenery hereabouts. The tracks and switches at the Summit were covered in with a large enclosed frame building, with a corrugated iron roof. This narrowed off to a snow shed on the down starting side. Outside of this was a level space from which the view could be enjoyed and prominent in the front of the elevated plateau were the arches of a croquet

SUMMIT MARSHALL PASS

ground. St. John had been here ahead of us and had chalked the name of the Commandery high up on the side of the snow shed. Philadelphia No. 2 had left her mark likewise. Sam Thomson was boosted up and left the name of Mary high above all. Headaches were frequent in the party this morning, presumably from the rarefied air of the mountain tops and not, as might be supposed, relics of Leadville. Brown got a shot at some of the party with his camera and Blackwood snapped his kodak right and left.

At 9.53 A. M. a start was made down the opposite side of the range for Sargeant. The snow sheds on this slope were much more numerous and of greater length, often interfering with the view from the train. Great windfalls

MARSHALL PASS

of trees laid in serried ranks along the mountain sides. They scarcely ever seemed to get beyond a certain height, before they were leveled to the ground and laid there to rot. They did not attain to much of a diameter, but grew tall and straight, with flattened out roots that apparently laid on top and had little hold of the ground. Shack houses and burrows, made of saplings and plastered with mud, were so frequent along the line as to excite comment. The query was as to what anybody could want to live on these mountains sides for, unless it was to make charcoal. The mystery was solved when we found that they were relics of the people who labored at the building of the railroad and made themselves fresh habitations as they moved along the grade. There was less variety of wild flowers on this side of the mountains, although still enough to appear remarkable in such a situation. Enochs busied himself at every opportunity in making a collection of such as he could get at and had quite a large bunch when he got back. Sargeant was reached at 10.45 A. M. and all turned out to view the situation, while the cars were run around on a Y to get them reversed for the trip back. Wild flowers and grasses were in demand, but the former were not near so plentiful as on the slopes of the mountains. A little stream, called the Tomatchie, ran along in a field facing the station, which looked as thought it might be the home of a trout or two and several fishermen started to examine the little pools where its banks overhung the water. McIntyre pretended to see one and aroused Pop Millick's curiosity until he got him close to the bank, when he struck the surface of the water with the flat of a shovel and nearly drowned the old man, protesting that he had aimed at a fish.

The neighboring valley is pretty well cultivated, but the ranches and houses are small. A nice little stone station is built on one side of the track, whose freshly painted wood-work left a lasting impression on most all members of the party, who leaned up against it at one time or another of our stop. Promenading on the two platforms on either side of the track, was taken advantage of as a means of keeping warm in the cool air. Also to excite jealousy in the breasts of some by hooking on to other people's property in plain sight of the owners thereof. But these efforts seemed to be flat failures. We started on our return trip at 11.15 A. M. and generally changed seats to the opposite side of the car, from that on which we had ridden down, so as to see both sides of the question. The ascent of the far side grew rather monotonous and did not excite as much comment as had the Northern side. It was generally remarked that all would have been as well satisfied to return to Salida from the Summit instead of going on to Sargeant. The latter point is only seventeen miles distant from the Summit, but in that distance an elevation of nearly 2,400 feet has to be overcome. 1,900 feet of this is climbed in nine miles of the distance, being a continuous rise of over 211 feet to the mile. The two engines puffed and snorted over the job, but went up with a steady pull and no halts until the top of the pass was again reached. Here another rest was taken to view the Sangre de Cristo range, from outside the shed again. Boys must be amused and a stone throwing contest was inaugurated, to try and hit a post down the slope of the mountain. Some of the crowd nearly threw their shoulders out of joint in their attempts to emulate their feats of that kind forty years ago. Milligan suggested that here would be an appropriate place for all to join in singing " Praise God from whom all blessings flow," in consideration of the number of miles we had traversed without accident or mishap of any kind to mar the pleasure of the journey. Also of the fact that probably many of the party were now nearer the heavenly regions than they were ever likely to be again. The idea took root at once and all hands were invited into the ladies' car with that object in view. Charley Shaw was requested to lead the singing and started off with some Choctaw Methodist tune, that nobody else had ever heard before and sang a solo to the end of the Doxology. Disappointment was visible on every countenance until Munch started up the old familiar tune, which even the car-wheels knew, when the vast train shed was made to echo and re-echo the grand old strain. Another excursion train had come up from Salida, while we were down the Southern slope, and the people thereon gazed in wonder at the volume of sound which issued from the car. Once started, the service of song was kept up all the way down the mountain. The turns and twists of the road on this side looked more dangerous in the descent than they had while climbing up and the speed was certainly much greater. But we pulled into Salida again at 1.45 P. M. sharp set for luncheon, which Brooks quickly announced. We were to have departed at that hour, but the press of business on the road again delayed our starting time. It was 2.35 P. M. before we could make a start for Manitou, which was to be our next stopping place. Another thunder storm was being hatched in the mountains around us. The thunder reverberated among their recesses in a startling manner and black clouds hung in heavy masses around the higher peaks, but no rain reached the station.

Soon after we left we ran into another prairie dog country, where we saw many of their habitations and not a few of the occupants. The little stream which we followed was one of the sources of the Arkansas River. At 3.30 P. M. we ran into Arkansas Canon, in which were many very curious formations of rock. All the lower part of the rocks showed the action of rushing waters at some primeval date. Emerging from the canon, we struck a little level country again, with more charcoal ovens alongside the tracks. The sides of the mountains had been almost denuded of timber to supply the demand for the fuel. At 3.45 P. M. we ran into a heavy shower of rain, the first we had seen since leaving Sante Fé. Following the course of the Arkansas River, which has now grown to a pretty respectable stream, we passed a placer gold mine, worked by hydraulic machinery, which was taking out from 300 to 400 dollars weekly of the precious metal, when stopped by an injunction of court,

ARKANSAS CAÑON

procured by the owner of the ranch upon which it stands. Until some legal point is settled, that amount of weekly profit is being lamented by the miners.

Upon the siding at Texas Creek we were held up again until 4.15 P. M. This was the scene of the exploits of the notorious McCoy gang of train robbers and, just below us, the gorge opens through which they escaped and were trailed into the Indian Territory and captured. The Arkansas here is a swiftly flowing and turbulent stream and the canon is subject to cloud-bursts. At such times the river gets its back up to such an extent that it carries down huge boulders, washes out the railroad tracks and sweeps everything before it. We saw at one point, a long section of track that had been washed away two weeks ago, still lying on its side in mid-stream, with the 72 pounds steel rails bent almost double by the force of the current. At 4.35 P. M. the rain, which had been following us up along the canon, slackened up and the sun began to break through the clouds. So much has been written of the Grand Canon of the Arkansas that it is like attempting to gild refined gold to add anything to the already published descriptions of the marvellous scenery contained within its rocky walls. For nearly one hundred miles, the railroad and river run in close proximity within its embrace. This is necessarily the case, because the shore of the river affords the only practicable route for the railroad. But how any mind should be daring enough to first conceive the idea of building a road over such a route surpasses our understanding. It is like the old chestnut of Columbus and the egg. Once accomplished, the smallest mind can see just how it has been done, but, unlike that feat, not one among a hundred thousand could see this contract successfully carried through.

The towering rock walls hem us in for the entire length of the canon, except where an occasional wedgelike rift, in the Sangre de Cristo range on our right, gives us a passing glance at the tree-clad cross ranges running back into the country. The shapes the mountains assume are countless and indescribable. Nowhere, except perhaps at Niagara, can man get so perfect an idea of his insignificance beside the stupendous works of nature as in one of the canons. When you step off your train and look up at the amount of rock overhanging it, you cannot help but feel that a very small slice of 8,000 or 10,000 tons of it dropped down would make short work of a whole train load of very self-important humanity, and the costly handiwork of his skill to boot.

At Parkdale station, at 4.40 P. M., we halted long enough to put a torpedo on the track behind us, to prevent another train from attacking us in the rear while stopping in the Royal Gorge, which we enter a mile further on. This section of the Grand Canon of the Arkansas, about ten miles in length, contains the *ne plus ultra* of canon scenery, and is known throughout the civilized world. The way gets narrow as we penetrate the gorge, and, at every moment, the further progress of both railroad and brawling river seems about to be blocked by solid walls. But another turn reveals another short stretch of roadbed, partly robbed from the already circumscribed bed of the

IN THE ROYAL GORGE

river and partly blasted out of the solid mountain wall on our left, until we halt in the narrowest part of the gorge, where a bridge shows ahead of the train. The entire party left the cars and walked across the hanging bridge, as it is called, which will probably only hang in case of a washout beneath it. The outer girder, which supports the outward ends of the railroad ties, is attached to two angular iron arches which span the chasm and abut on the rocks on either side, apparently holding the bridge up. But a solid stone wall under the bridge, built up from the river bed, does its share of the work so long as the river shall be content to let it remain there. The rocks tower above and over us to the height of a half mile, and the thunder rolling above and echoing through the rocky defile, was by no means reassuring to nervous people. Brown got out one of his cameras and took several pictures of the scenery and its pigmy like adjuncts of train, passengers and bridges. Some of the party had to climb up a cleft in the rocks to break off fresh pieces of stone as mementoes, as though the thousands lying on the ground were not of a good enough stratum. When we had gazed our fill, or rather when our time was up, for it would take a long while to satiate one's appetite for such a scene, the train was brought slowly across the bridge, and we reluctantly stowed ourselves away in it once more. For the remainder of the distance through the canon we had to be content to get on our knees at the open window and watch the ever-varying landscape, with the turbulent and now muddy waters of the river, until the narrow defile gradually opened out, and we were at no loss to discern a pathway ahead for the train.

Just beyond the outlet of the canon, on the opposite side of the river, was a picturesque little building which is known as the Royal Gorge Hotel, built as an adjunct to another series of hot springs, with which the state seems to abound. A little further down, on our own side of the river, was a free hotel surrounded by a fine stone wall. At intervals, on the top of the wall were little turrets, and in front of each stood a man with a rifle on his shoulder, whose duty it was to see that none of the guests should leave without having paid his board bill in full. This is the Colorado State Penitentiary, which seemed to·be made up of some remarkably fine buildings. Back of it, and away up on the mountain side, we could see the line of an immense irrigating canal which is being constructed, and is designed to penetrate the wall of mountains to the opposite side. The labor of the convicts is now being utilized to further the operation. The prison is situated on the outskirts of Canon City, at whose station we drew up at 5.25 P. M.

The city looked as though it might be a very pleasant place to live in, the houses being neat, and well shaded and each having a plentiful share of garden and orchard around it. After leaving here, we emerge into the broad and fertile Valley of the Arkansas. Fruits and berries seem to particularly engage the attention of the ranchers here. The orchards particularly are very extensive, although the ripe fields of grain, still being harvested, also attest the fruitfulness of the valley. Irrigating ditches are also in use here and water wheels in the river are a new feature of the business to us. The current of the river drives them and raises the water, by means of buckets, into a trough, which carries 'a continuous stream over the bank into the ditch at a higher elevation.

High buttes of red sandstone hem in the sides of the valley and are worn into many odd shapes. We can see various black clouds discharging their cargoes of moisture, up in the mountains beyond them, but none of them are engaged in the business in our immediate vicinity. At 5.45 P. M. we came upon the coal-oil fields surrounding the town of Florence. At first sight we could imagine ourselves on the line of the Erie road in the oil belt of Pennsyl-vania. The derricks, pumps and tanks looked like ancient friends and were a revelation to most of us, who had never heard of coal-oil finds in this section. As we passed through the town, flaring torches of natural gas made the scene still more homelike, and some of the old stagers, like McIntyre and Tom Henderson, inquired of the conductor if Pig Island was anywhere near the town? Oil is largely produced and as much as 150 carloads per day are shipped from this point in addition to what is carried by a pipe line to Pueblo, twenty-one miles away. Many cars of coal were also lying on the tracks at this point. These came from Coal Creek, six miles distant, to which a branch road runs. The mines are said to be very extensive and the coal of excellent quality. We did not reach Pueblo until 7 P. M., when we found Washington and Potomac Commanderies just preparing to pull out. A committee from Pueblo Commandery No. 3 waited upon us at the train and regretted that our schedule did not include any stop at their city. We have since been sorry also that this was the case, as we should like to have visited their Mineral Palace, if nothing else. This is a building they have erected here to show the mineral resources of the State of Colorado. The building itself cost 200,000 dollars and is reputed to contain mineral specimens to the value of 5,000,000 dollars. A large Bessemer steel plant is also operated at Pueblo, or a suburb thereof called Bessemer, at which all the materials used are of native extraction and we were given some small Maltese Crosses, made of the steel, in commemoration of the fact.

The building, in front of which our train stood, known as the Union Depot was a model of its kind and of vast extent. The city was handsomely decorated out of compliment to the Knights who did make it one of the stopping places of their pilgrimages. A fine mist was beginning to fall, as we got orders to go ahead and pulled out from in front of the station, which made the inside of the cars a pleasant place to be. Not far from Pueblo, at the end of the double tracks, we were again held for orders until 8 P. M. The moon popped up out of a cloud bank in the East, and a lunar bow of great brilliancy was thrown on a mass of black clouds in the far West, out of which rain was falling in torrents. It was a very fine and unusual spectacle and we enjoyed it amazingly. We got along on our road by hitches and jumps and were subject to numerous delays to-night, the Knights Templar trains along the railroads being as plentiful as clothing stores on South street. We did not sight the lights of Colorado Springs until 9.20 P. M. and it was 10 P. M. before we were safely tracked in our berth at Manitou. The lateness of our arrival did not prevent the cats' from sallying forth to fraternize with those of like tendencies from the numerous trains around us, as well as to investigate the attractions of Manitou.

NO PLACE LIKE HOME.

MANITOU ARCH

Monday, August 8th, 1892.

ANITOU, the blest! is the fanciful name given to this place by the poetic red man; the one who has passed away and left his prosaic and dirty successor as his sole representative. All the springs which give the name to the City of Colorado Springs are located here, although this is six miles away from that point, on a branch road, with another settlement intervening, called Colorado City. When we turned out this morning, we found plenty of neighbors, quartered on Knights Templar trains beside and behind us. St. John No. 4, Reading No. 42, the Denver Club of Philadelphia, the Denver Club of Central Pennsylvania, were all on hand and Philadelphia No. 2 came in during the morning. Jimmy Baird, in the course of his nocturnal rambles, had attempted to climb on the rear of St. John's train. The brass gate came open and dropped him back against a stone wall which supported the embankment on which our train stood. His head was hard enough to ensure that from any damage, but the scalp was too thin for the sharp edge of the stone and was badly cut. When dressed by one of the medical staff of the Denver Club, with cross patches of adhesive plaster, it formed quite a decoration. When assured by his fellow pilgrims that he sported the only genuine cross and crown in the party, Jimmy was quite proud of his badge. The morning broke clear and pleasant, the bald head of Pike's Peak being plainly visible, between the two smaller elevations which flanked it right and left, beyond the city of Manitou. The latter consisted principally of the main street, but that contained many very pretty buildings which were handsomely decorated, while an arch of extensive proportions and elaborate design spanned the width of the avenue. Our first visitor this morning was P. Com. Chas. W. Packer of Mary, who had come out with St. John's, being unable to spare the time for our extended trip. Our folks could not help contrasting their circumstances this morning, as they sat at the tables in the dining car, with those of the Denver Club, whose people walked past on their road to the Mansions Hotel, nearly a half-mile away, to procure their breakfasts.

At 9 A. M. carriages were on hand for a trip to the Garden of the Gods, which lies East of Manitou about a mile, over a rather dusty and hilly road. At the immediate entrance to the Garden is the Balanced Rock. This is an

immense boulder, delicately balanced on a small portion of its little end which is downward, and looks as though a not very hard push would bring down its tons of weight with a crash. The road winds through a sort of red clay soil, whose surroundings bear little semblance to a garden, except in the odd statuary of natural formations that adorn it. In these a great many were disappointed very much, no doubt through their expectations having been raised to a high pitch by the grandiloquent name bestowed upon the locality. The different formations were very curious, although the imagination had to be strongly drawn upon in some cases, to detect the fancied resemblance. A bed of mushrooms was very apparent as were the camel and the seals. The lion would have made just as good a calf and the cathedral spires were only gigantic skewers of stone. The bear and seal formed so small a portion of the immense rock, over the top of which they appeared to be climbing. as to require to be minutely pointed out. Castles, towers, pinnacles, facial resemblances, flocks of stone sheep and other designs are detected by the curious or shown to them by the driver. What is known as the Gateway of the Garden, at the far end, consists of two lofty blocks of the stone formation rising to a height of over 300 feet, with a space of about sixty feet between. When you get on the far side of them and look back, you get a good view of Pike's Peak framed between them. The most curious part of the Garden is the existence of these weather worn sandstone formations, in a park of comparatively level ground, out of which they rise without any connection with one another or with any other stone formations. The stone is a soft sandstone, of an intense red color, which has evidently been worn by the elements into the fanciful shapes they are found in. After a stop at a shop near the Gateway, which is open for the sale of photographs and curios, a further drive was taken, to see Glen Eyrie, the residence of Gen. Palmer which lies in Queen's Canon. The same character of stone formations is found here, though less in numbers. The principal one was the Major Domo, an elongated shaft which was larger in diameter near the top than at its base. It stood up very straight to the height of 300 feet. An eagle's nest, on the inaccessible side of one of the rocks, gave the name to the estate. The Glen is pretty much shrubbery and trees, with a small mountain stream flowing here and there through them. It is backed up by a high mountain, and altogether it struck us as a place where a man might want to hide himself from the world, after having become disgusted with his fellow-man or gone back on his best friend.

The ride back to the train was rather warm. The sun had come out in all his strength and there was little air stirring in the valley, so that the shelter of the cars was very welcome when we reached them. Shortly after arriving there, the sky became overcast and at noon there was a shower of rain, which was repeated at intervals all through the afternoon. Our calculations had been made to go up on the Peak after luncheon, but Purdy met us with the information that we could not be furnished with a train until 7.30 P. M. so great was the

GARDEN OF THE GODS

rush to ascend the mountain. That would bring us down later than the time set for our departure and few of the party cared to go up after dark. That part of our programme was therefore abandoned, although Sheeler, Wells and Phillips, by persistent waiting at the station, were able to secure places on one of the trains and gratify their ambition of ascending the Peak by rail.

After taking luncheon on the train, the party started out in sections to do the country independent of Pike's Peak. The springs lie along the main street of the town, which follows the course of a creek called the Fontaine-qui-bouillé, which in turn is created by the waters of the springs. The station, just ahead of our train, was a tasty little building of a pinkish white stone. The grounds in front of it were embellished with flower beds, one of which bore the name of the station. Nearly opposite, and down a cross road a short distance, stood the Hiawatha Club House, into which no ladies are ever admitted. It is a handsome building and, besides a finely decorated bar, contains rooms in which are facilities for all known games of chance. After 1 P. M. roulette, rouge et noir, faro, crap or anything you wanted to invest in, was at your command from one dollar upwards. Fine pictures are on the walls, curious carvings on the cabinets and mantels and an extremely courteous proprietor to welcome and explain anything you want to inquire into. Further up the street, you find all the saloons with annexes devoted to the same business and all as open to the world as the drug or jewelry stores, their neighbors. On the porch of the Hiawatha was a fine telescope, mounted on a tripod and trained upon the landing place of the railroad at the top of the Peak. This was at the service of any gentleman caller and was the next best thing to going up yourself. Those who had been successful in making the ascent could be seen walking around over the rugged top, as well as the locomotive and cars which had carried them.

A number of large hotels offer accommodations to the visitor, among which the Manitou, Mansions and Barker are conspicuous for their size, fine grounds and extensive porches. Opposite the latter is a very fine bath house, supplied with the soda water from the Navajo Spring. The water of this spring is also bottled and shipped over the country by the Manitou Spring Water Co. It finds an extensive patronage and several cases of it, done up as ginger ale under the name of ginger champagne, which found its way to our baggage car, did not last long enough to judge of its merits. The soda baths were greatly enjoyed by our party.

The Shoshone, Manitou and other springs are also located along the creek. The Iron Ute Spring is up in Engleman's Canon, from which the railroad starts up the peak. At one time this morning nearly a thousand people were clamoring around the little station for tickets to go up the mountain. It was broadly hinted that by paying a bonus to outside holders, tickets could be secured in short order. The railroad is nine miles long and overcomes an ascent of 8100 feet above the town. In addition to the usual rails it has a double cog rail in the centre, into which the three driving wheels of the engine fit, the outside wheels merely turning upon their axles to carry the weight. The road-bed is on solid ground nearly all the way up, the only exceptions being four short iron bridges. The engines bore the honored name of Baldwin, like many more in this Western country. Williams' Canon is but a few minutes walk from the northwest corner of the town. In it is located the Cave of the Winds, which is in a small way a rival of the Mammoth Cave and Luray Caverns, and contains many curious formations from the drippings through the limestone roof which covers it. Many of its halls and chambers are of large size, but the formations, as usual, draw largely upon the imagination to recognize their likeness to the names bestowed upon them. In the Ute Pass, another short drive from the town, we find the Rainbow Falls, so called because when the sunlight strikes them at the proper angle you can see the rainbow. This afternoon being void of sunshine, the rainbow was not on duty. Higher up the pass are the Manitou Grand Caverns, with more of an assortment of stalagmitic and stalactitic formations. Of these the opera house is remarkable for size and similarity to its namesake. The bridal chamber, grand organ, coral beds, flocks of sheep and some others compare favorably with their prototypes in other cases of this kind.

The showers of rain, which came at regular intervals through the afternoon, did not deter some of the party from visiting these curiosities in Manitou, nor from seeking similar resorts at Colorado Springs. The electric cars for that point started just across the road from our station, and nearly every one went out loaded to its utmost capacity. It was about a half hour's ride and the conductor collected a nickel at the start for your fare to Colorado City. About the time we had reached that point he had got around his load of passengers, and started over again to gather in another nickel for the balance of the ride. At Colorado Springs the side tracks were filled with more Knights Templar trains from all sections of the country. When we saw their number we were at no loss to account for the rush on the Pike's Peak road, or the crowds on the electric cars. Colorado Springs lies upon a comparatively level plain, although surrounded on all sides by mountain peaks. It has very broad streets, well shaded with trees, and many beautiful hotels and other buildings. The Childs-Drexel Home for Printers shows up well on a slight elevation down one of the main streets. It rained as regularly there during the afternoon as at Manitou, and the streets, which are not paved, were a little sticky to the feet. Electric cars were plentiful and took you in almost any direction. One branch ran out five miles to the Cheyenne Canon, which is a narrow gorge, between rocks rising 1,000 feet in the air, with regular canon scenery for about a half mile. At the far end it rises abruptly, and the stream of water, which has been running down the centre all the way, comes tumbling from the top of the rocks in a series of romantic cascades, known as Seven Falls. A Jacob's ladder or series of them enabled you to climb to the top of the falls, if you had ambition enough left in you, and enjoy another fine view. A trail from the top also leads further up the mountain, to the grave of H. H., or Helen Hunt Jackson, the Southern authoress and poet. Not far from the entrance to the canons, of which there are two, the South and the North, is a very fine building, called the Broadmoor Casino, which is a popular resort, where you can row or sail upon a lake, listen to an afternoon concert, join in the dance, or get anything you want to eat, for cash of course. The afternoon rain had brought very chilly weather with it, and on the ride back to Manitou in the grey evening, overcoats were at a premium. The summit of the Peak had been invisible this afternoon, more often than it had been visible, while at times the clouds floated below the top of the Peak, hiding the lower part of the mountain and leaving the top exposed. The reports of those who came down showed that it had been snowing or sleeting up on the Peak several times. Up the face of the mountain flanking the Peak on the left, the Sir Knights of Manitou had fastened down on its slope a large white muslin cross. It was a favorite scheme to get a new visitor to guess the size of the cross, which was probably distant from the station about three miles. The arms of the cross were apparently about two feet wide ; taking that for a basis, it would be about 80 feet long and 60 feet wide. When the glasses were brought to bear upon it, they showed that eight widths of muslin or 24 feet was the width of each arm, and the cross extended 320 feet one way and 240 feet the other. Another instance of the deceptive and delusive atmosphere of Colorado.

Quite a number got in late to dinner to-night, but we had ample time to spare here. McIntyre took the register through the Reading train, to allow their pilgrims to sign it, and we had several callers through the evening, from other trains, to procure a souvenir leaf from Mary. The most of our party were drifting through the town or up to Colorado Springs until late in the evening, but all hands were on deck before 11 P. M., the hour at which we pulled out for Denver. Our train was the last to leave Manitou to-night.

Tuesday, August 9th, 1892.

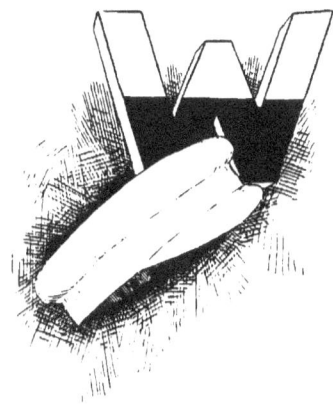

E WERE due here at 3 A. M., but, after much backing and filling were finally drilled into our resting place for the next three days, at 4.30 A. M. The railroads around Denver had been very much blockaded for several days back and it was reported on Sunday night that fifteen miles was as close as a train could get to the city. We were side-tracked in an excellent location, one block above the Union Depot and immediately in the rear of St. John's train. The committee started out before 6 A. M. to look up our headquarters and open the sword chest and banner case. The cable cars, right at the end of the train, ran directly to the house, which was opposite the pointed end of the Brown Palace Hotel. Our frater H. Chester Rockey had been in the city for a week previous and had all our cases hauled from the depot and opened, so that everything was ready to our hands. Our landlord, Mr. James Costello, was on hand and rendered us all assistance in his power, as he continued to do during all of our stay. The manner in which he had decorated the front of his building for us gave us great satisfaction, the more so as it was totally unexpected. On our way up town, we saw a number of visitors who looked as though they had not been in bed, leaning against walls or posts with their gripsacks in their hands. They had evidently arrived too late and too early to find quarters or secure attention from the committees.

The quarters being found perfect, passage back to the train over the cable road was again secured. In the dining car, breakfast was being served first to those who intended to take part in the parade. All of these were soon on their way to the headquarters, where they were joined by Past Commanders Packer of our own Commandery and Wm. A. Foster of Kadosh No. 29, as well as Sir Knight Matthias Ziegler of Kensington No. 54, all of whom participated in the parade with us. The Band of the Second Battalion Infantry of Colorado reported for duty, with twenty-five pieces, at 9 A. M. Captain General Munch soon had his command of 31 men in line and headed for their position in the 5th or Pennsylvania division. The head of the line moved promptly on time and we did not have long to wait until our turn came. P. G. C. Jos. S. Wright was in command of our division and P. G. C. Geo. W. Kendrick acted as one of his staff. St. John No. 4 did not parade in the line, having been selected to act as escort to Grand Commander J. P. S. Gobin of our State, who was the head of the Grand Encampment.

Mary was received with many demonstrations of friendship along the line, and her banners brought forth liberal expressions of admiration from the assembled multitudes. Out of all the commanderies in the division, the Denver papers eulogized "Mary" alone as "marching like veterans." The route of the parade was past our headquarters and the only appearance of a fault in our wheelings, was when the corner at that point was turned and every fellow cocked his eye up to the balcony to see if the ladies were particularly looking at him. When California No. 1 came past, and were cheered by our representatives, they wheeled out of the column and gave three cheers for Mary, before resuming the march.

It was well we had secured a band, as the only other one in the division was the one placed at its head by the parade committee. St. John had the celebrated Cow Boy Band of Pueblo but, as we mentioned before, they merely escorted the Grand Commander to the reviewing stand and back to his hotel. The parade was a very creditable one and occupied about two hours in passing a given point. There were few halts, after once starting, and we got over the route in an hour and a half. We had got back to the headquarters, doffed our uniforms, put them away and started back to the train for luncheon, long before the end of the line passed our corner.

The headquarters were opened for callers, immediately after the parade. A constant stream poured in and out during all the afternoon and evening. At nearly midnight it was found necessary to close the doors, or the reception would have had to be kept up all night. It was impossible at times for all our visitors to sign the register, but all were supplied with the souvenir leaf. John was kept busily engaged in replenishing the bowls of claret punch and lemonade until his arms ached, while the members of Mary, assisted by the ladies did their best to see that all of our guests were entertained. The band was provided with seats in the front yard, where they gave us a fine concert throughout the afternoon and up to 9.30 P. M.

At that hour, Capt. Gen. Munch formed the lines, in which most of the ladies were included, and, headed by the band, started out for a call at St. John's and other headquarters. The ladies enjoyed the, to them, novel experience of parading the middle of the street behind the band very much, but were glad they were away from home. Bands and commanderies were marching and countermarching all the evening, calling upon their fraters, giving a tune or two and passing the loving cup. With us, the officer in charge would sign our register for himself and as many men as he had in line.

HEADQUARTERS IN DENVER

The immense masses of humanity on the streets of Denver to-night were a sight long to be remembered. Sidewalk and street were alike filled and the Mayor had requested all street traffic, except that of the cable cars and necessary carriages, to cease in order to lessen the chance of accidents. The illumination of the city, by means of colored incandescent globes and the electric light, was one of the greatest sights that has been witnessed on this continent. The grand arches that had been built across the main streets blazed with the lights. The fronts of public and private buildings were studded with them and both sides of the streets for miles were lined with globes of all colors. Strings of them crossed the streets at intervals, suspended from the centre of which were designs of various forms and wonderfully rich in colors. All this was not merely on two or three streets, but on dozens of them. We had thought the illuminations of St. Louis in 1886 a hard thing to surpass, but have concluded that we must yield the palm to Denver.

The decorations of store and dwelling, outside of the illuminations, were almost universal and were made up into unique and costly designs of bunting or other colored cloth, in which of course the Templar cross and Beauseant predominated. Night was turned into day, at least two thirds of it was this night, with the exception that no business was done. Everything was given over to the fraternal greetings of the hour and those who were not receiving, were being received. The easiest and most generally accepted path for locomotion was down the middle of the street.

The hour was late when all of Mary's lambs had been gathered into the fold and little time was lost in seeking rest from the labors of a busy day.

Wednesday, August 10th, 1892.

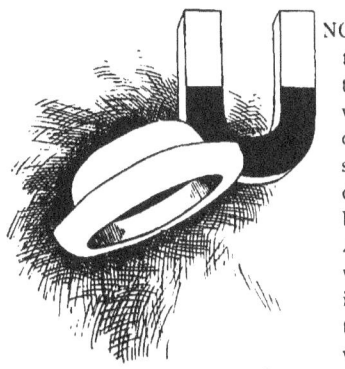

NCLOUDED skies greeted our opening eyes this morning, after drawing up the curtains of our berths. The hour was not very early and there was a continuous line of pedestrians passing down on the opposite side of Wynkoop Street toward the depot. Grips, baskets, boxes and bundles betokened the traveller, homeward bound. A half dozen other avenues to the station were similarly or even more thronged, independent of the crowds that came on the cars or in carriages. Inside the station was a seething mass of humanity, bound for the ticket offices or awaiting a chance for a train. It was with a great feeling of relief that we congratulated ourselves upon not being obliged to make up any fractional proportion of such a crowd.

Denver had undertaken a contract which had enlarged on her hands to an extent that no one had dreamed of. For a city of less than 150,000 inhabitants to take to its bosom more than 100,000 guests, invited and uninvited, was a feat that would probably have alarmed the projectors if they had received any previous intimation of the stream that would flow in. As it was, the railroad facilities for getting away were probably the worst feature in the shape of a drawback to the success of the Conclave. But that lasted only for a few hours and could but be expected in a temporary rush like this. The feeding, lodging and entertainment of the multitude was apparently perfect. There was no excuse for anybody going hungry or dry, at least. The number of headquarters that kept open house, with all that was needed to eat and much more than was needed to drink, precluded the possibility of any one suffering in either direction.

One of the greatest features in that respect was a large double tent, just opposite our quarters and adjoining those of Hanselmann Commandery of Cincinnati, on Seventeenth Street. Each tent was about 75 feet in diameter, set all around with tables and counters, loaded with anything you might want to eat, from sandwiches to ice cream, with from twenty to thirty people in constant attendance to minister to your wants. Lemonade was made in puncheons, so that you could drink a bucketful if you wished and other drinks were in profusion. Although this sort of thing was going on in a hundred or more other places in the city, the beautiful part of this particular episode was that it was the work of the Odd Fellows of Denver. Odd Fellows performed the labor and footed the bills, and did it right royally too.

It mattered little whether the act was done in requital of former kindnesses or why it was done. The grand scene was there and we were glad to look upon it as one of the greatest sights we had witnessed during our pilgrimage. We even pretended to be hungry, that we might be able to say we had partaken of their hospitality.

There were also other headquarters outside of the Templars' own. The former residents of our own State had organized a Pennsylvania Club, which kept open house and the same was true of other States. All day long the visiting, serenading, marching and countermarching continued. St. John's, with their cowboy band, occupied a goodly share of attention, at least the band did. They were togged out so as to look real devilish, with their six shooters stuck in their hip pockets. The drum major carried a pistol that was encrusted all over the handle with precious stones of all kinds. It did us no good to see him pull out his gun and fire a blank cartridge over the top of the steer horn prizes, carried in front of the band on poles, when he wanted them to blow. What we ached for was to see him draw his shooter and plunk a coon standing around, or even a stray Chinaman or two, just to make the thing look real. We thought perhaps he might forget himself after awhile and do something of the kind, and so followed him to a headquarters or two, but it was time wasted. He was just as mild, except in the make-up, as the rest of us.

Mary's quarters were opened again early in the day and the scenes enacted there were but a repetition of those of yesterday. Many visitors came expressly for a view of the banners and admired them to their hearts' content, thus filling the measure of our vanity at the same time. Some of them thought well enough of the grand banner to gouge three of the pearls out of the embroidery on the back to preserve as mementoes of the Conclave and Mary. The Sir Knights and ladies were in constant attendance throughout the day and far into the night, only going to their meals in relays, that none of our visitors might be neglected.

Upon returning to the train for luncheon, we found that one of our colored cooks, Smith by name, had cut his hand so badly by a plate breaking therein, that he had nearly bled to death before the aid of a physician could be secured. He had cut an artery and the doctor thought it advisable to send him to a hospital for better treatment than he was prepared to give. The surgeon there insisted upon his remaining at the hospital for a couple of weeks, but Smith had no notion of being left so far from home and turned up before our departure to occupy a berth in the baggage car for the trip home.

Meanwhile we found time to take a few rides and drives to see what manner of place Denver might be.

There are many fine structures to attract the attention of visitors. Prominent among these are the Masonic Temple, on Sixteenth Street, where the Grand Commandery of Colorado was doing itself proud, Tabor Opera House, High School, Broadway Theatre, Equitable Building, People's Bank, Stock Exchange, Court House, Brown Hotel, Hotel Metropole and Union Depot, each and every one of which is a model architecturally. The Denver Club building is a distinctive feature and the churches are both numerous and costly. The stores and business blocks have a strong tendency to sprout upwards, like those of Chicago, but only in isolated cases. The fact that everything is built of stone or brick, and frame buildings prohibited, gives Denver a substantial and permanent look, that few of the Western cities we have struck seem to possess.

A drive through the residence localities of Grant, Sherman and Lincoln Avenues and Broadway, revealed as handsome residences as could well be constructed, far beyond the expectations in a new city. The fact, which our queries brought out, that many of the finest were occupied by real estate operators, indicated one of the bonanzas of the Silver City for a few years past. The new Capitol building, which is still unfinished, will be a central and prominent ornament of the city. The care that has been taken to secure wide avenues everywhere and large plots of ground around the public buildings, will be appreciated in the future. The one thing that is giving trouble at present was the want of grade lines when building was rife a few years ago in the business section. Six months ago there were no paved streets in the city. Yesterday we marched over a number of miles of asphalt pavement and more is being rushed down in various directions. But as grades are established and curbs set, the inattention to building lines becomes wofully apparent. On one side of the street the buildings will be away above grade, while the opposite corner is level with or even below the curb line.

The cable car system here is very extensive and like more of the Western systems, can give great points to the so-called cable lines in our own city. If our conductors had to wait on street corners for passengers as they do in Denver, the Norristown Asylum would not be large enough to contain them in a month's time. Yet the cars make better time than ours, because between the streets they run like a streak and swing corners in the same style, without any of the snatch-em-along tricks in vogue at home.

Other thousands of people were leaving the city to-day and the jam at the depot was as great as ever, but you could not miss them as yet on the streets or cable cars or at the headquarters. Mary's callers were still quite as numerous as on yesterday and many of those who secured a souvenir took much pleasure in relating to us with what care they had preserved a similar token from the Triennial at Washington. The Denver Club paid us a visit in a body in the afternoon.

In the evening, Mary went out calling again. At the quarters of California Commandery, the entrance was found packed with those struggling to gain admittance. We succeeded in getting through at last and met with an enthusiastic reception. Our California friends had been in the competitive drill to-day and were going to take a silver brick back to the Golden State as their share of the prizes. Dr. Cole and E. Com. Winter were justly proud of their following and stirred up our boys to share in their enthusiasm. When we were able to get away finally, the two bodies parted with mutual cheers and the Pacific Coast Knights were obliged to acknowledge that the limited number of representatives from Mary could at least make more noise than the large party California had present. A number of other quarters were drummed up, among which was that of Ascalon of St. Louis. Our fraters of that command were mostly absent, having made an excursion to the Loop and not having returned yet.

Our frater Lafferty had run afoul of an old West Philadelphia chum, H. S. Bailey by name, who had been in business here for twenty years, in all which time they had not met until Bailey hunted up our quarters. He has taken Lafferty and Billy Dill in charge and is showing them the town, bringing them back to the headquarters occasionally to show us that he keeps them in proper trim. He has also been very kind and generous in his treatment of the commandery while here and remembered them on their departure.

The flour and feed warehouse, to which belongs a portion of the platform against which our train is lying, belongs to a gentleman named Hinkson. We had been here since yesterday morning before Billy Dill found out he was a cousin of his, also resident here for a number of years.

A bicycle parade was one of the features of entertainment for this evening and, as the route passed our quarters twice, we had a good opportunity to view it. There were many novel and handsome decorations on the wheels, as well as some ingenious imitations of arbors, boats, swans, and a whole menagerie of animals in the line. The weather had warmed up considerably through the middle of the day, but it got quite cool again as soon as the sun went down. The illumination of the city continued to-night as heretofore and the crowds never seemed weary of gazing upon it, as if determined to impress the scene indelibly upon their minds. Our own quarters were kept open again until nearly midnight and it was long after that hour when we reached home, as everybody has learned to call the train.

Thursday, August 11th, 1892.

HE SAME streams of people, flowing towards the depot, were the first sights to greet our eyes when we turned out this morning to the sound of Brooks' first call. The crush at the station this morning was as bad as it had been on either of the preceding days, but the streets began to show plainly the effect of the exodus. Many of the Sir Knights, as well as the other visitors, had taken advantage of the opportunity to visit some of the scenic wonders within hail of Denver before returning to their homes. The location of this city seems to have been well chosen as a centre, from which to make any number of short excursions, in which the traveller can see the greatest possible variety of things that can be seen in no other single State in the country.

Gold, silver, copper, lead, and coal mines, oil wells, natural gas wells, mountains and hills of all heights, valleys of corresponding depths, springs hot, cold or lukewarm, impregnated with salts, soda, sulphur and other evil smelling luxuries of the pharmacopiae, three tracked railways, loops and tunnels, gemstones and granite, trains running up mountains or diving into the ground, canons and gorges, cascades and falls, snow in August, game of all kinds, two legged and four, horses, cattle, sheep, Indians, Chinese, Cowboys, train-robbers maybe and, above all, big hearted men and women, are but a tithe of the attractions offered the visitor to Colorado.

Calling and receiving was still in progress to-day, but the blare of the brass bands was thinning out and you could make respectable progress on the sidewalk. The weather was perceptibly hotter and the shady side of the street was in demand. We thanked the lucky star, that has hovered over Mary throughout this pilgrimage, that we had been enabled to parade on Tuesday rather than to-day. Our quarters were again opened at an early hour. Visitors came in steadily, but not such a rush as we had on the previous days. There was another attraction on the street this morning in the shape of a parade of the Denver Fire Department. The showing it made proved it to be in first-class condition and equal to any emergency that might arise. Crowds of people lined the streets along which the turnout passed and freely expressed their admiration of the excellent condition of men, horses, harness and apparatus.

Steamers, hose carts, a hook and ladder truck and a big water tower were in the line. We had been discussing the question of leaving here as soon after night-fall as possible, in order to gain two or three hours in Chicago and it was finally resolved to make the attempt if we could secure an engine to pull us out. Preparations were accordingly begun, in the middle of the afternoon, by gathering in all bills and settling them, packing the banners in their cases and making everything ready for Chester Rockey to ship back by freight after our departure. At 5 P. M. we closed our register and turned Mr. Costello's rooms over to him, after thanking him cordially for all his efforts to make our stay on his premises the pleasant one it had been. Callers were coming in up to the last moment and, more than likely, some of them had to be entertained by our quondam landlord after our departure.

Some of our party had been continuing their investigations of Denver and vicinity to-day. Elitch's Gardens and Manhattan Beach were taken in, and several who went out to see the Loop on yesterday had not turned up since, but at the dinner hour all stragglers showed up for that meal, as well as to learn the hour of departure. Upon hearing that it was fixed for 8 P. M., there was no leaving the train after dinner, but the time intervening between that meal and our leaving was spent in promenading the long platform beside our train, in order to get as much exercise as possible before the thirty-six hours ride ahead of us. At 8 P. M. our engine was hooked on, but we did not move until 8.30 P. M. We then backed gracefully out of Denver for four or five miles and came in on another track, which brought us into the Union Depot, where there was another little hitch. It was 9.30 P. M. before we were off for good. Our last view of Denver was the sight of the glare in the sky from the grand illuminations that were still kept up. We were informed that $35,000 were spent for illuminations alone, and the electric light for each night cost $2,000. As we passed the streets running at right angles to the road, we caught glimpses of the strings of many colored lights, with a gorgeous cross and crown pendant to the last one.

The Kazoo Band blossomed out in full force in the ladies' car to-night, and blew itself hoarse and dry until 10.45 P. M., after which hour things quieted down pretty well. It was a fine moonlight night and the smoker was occupied until a much later hour by some of the cats, who were exchanging experiences of Denver. Speaking of cats, we were informed that the air of Colorado is not conducive to the well-being of that animal, and that they do not live long when brought here. While it did not have any bad effect on those that we had brought with us, we noticed that few of the felines were to be seen in the course of our rambles. It may be as was asserted, that there are few cats in Colorado. We are not sufficiently well posted to argue that point, but the one thing we are prepared to prove to the satisfaction of any-body is that "there are no flies on Denver."

Friday, August 12th, 1892.

AWAKENED in Nebraska this A. M. to the well authenticated fact that it was a clear and pleasant morning. The mountains had collapsed and dwindled into hills, and the foot-hills had been flattened out into rolling prairie, while the country through which we are passing is an eminently agricultural one. The crops were still being harvested, as they had been all along our route since we had left Santa Fé, outward bound. At McCook, at 7 A. M., we suddenly dropped another hour of our time and made it 8 A. M., Mountain time changing to Central time. This made it seem as if the first relay had been consuming an unconscionable big breakfast, and brought the luncheon hour uncomfortably close upon its heels.

Invitations were out for another progressive euchre party this afternoon, in the names of Mrs. Branson and Mrs. Johnson, in the dining car, at 3 P. M. The rolling farm land and the low hills which bounded the view were a most striking contrast to the lofty mountains and narrow valleys to which we had been accustomed for days past, and few remarks were brought forth by the scenery. The thousands of grazing cattle, however, called forth general admiration, as well as the plentiful grain crops on every hand. Blackwood varied the general monotony by getting hold of one of the firework cigars and smoking it with great gusto until it blazed forth. It is queer when one of these articles is handed any one, how the wink goes quietly around and all are on the *qui vive* for the expected blaze, except the unfortunate smoker himself. That Blackwood may have a record of time and place, we state for his benefit that it came off at Kenesaw station, at 11.20 A. M.

At 11.50 A. M. we stopped at the city of Hastings for ice and water. The city appeared to be of considerable size, but our time was too short for any critical examination. After leaving Hastings we ran into a corn country. Immense fields of that cereal were passed, which, if you gazed steadily upon them, gave you the impression that the corn-stalks were learning to waltz. Large stock farms also occupy this section of the state, on which many horses were grazing. The greater number had been bred from Percheron stock, as was evidenced by the size of their Chicago feet.

Lincoln, the capital of Nebraska, brought us to a sudden halt at 2.25 P. M. Orders to hold us were received here, as we found, owing to the fact that the train of Reading No. 42, which had been sent ahead of us, in order to run first into any obstructions that might be on the road, had turned its engine upside down and ditched the baggage car. This had happened two miles out of town, and we were compelled to wait until the track could be cleared. The regular train soon came in behind us and was also halted. On it we found Dr. Winter, the Eminent Commander of California No. 1, who was making a trip to St. Paul before going back to his home. We were glad to take him in for a time to relieve the monotony of the wait for both parties. The sun had come out pretty hot and both trains stood right out in its full blaze. Several of the party took advantage of the halt to send telegrams to their homes. We had received one from Cantlin, in Denver, containing the sad news that his father had departed this life one day before he had been able to reach home. A dispatch was sent to him, on behalf of the party, expressive of their sympathy with him in his sad bereavement.

The euchre party began business as soon after 3 P. M. as some of the delinquents, who were hunting shady spots outside, could be drummed into the dining car. They had hardly finished a game before Milligan called a halt and requested Conductor Brooks to stand up. Brooks, who was one of the competitors in the game, innocently complied with the request, and was thereupon presented by Milligan, in an expressive and complimentary manner, with a testimonial from the pilgrims on the train, in acknowledgment of his kindness and care on this trip. It was only the beginning of the game, but Brooks was euchred. He managed, after a time, to return his thanks and express his appreciation of the gift, but it was a knock-out in one round.

The committee having run out of lemons, thought this would be a good place and time to secure a supply. They accordingly skirmished around the city, close to the station, to find some. The entire stock in town was found to consist of one box in a wholesale fruit store, which was gratefully purchased and taken to the train over the pavements of round cedar blocks set on end and filled in with gravel, with which the whole town seemed to be paved. The train was waiting for them, and it left as soon as the fruit was on board, at 4.25 P. M. When the scene of the accident was reached, the train was halted to give a view of the overturned engine, which laid with its wheels in the air, completely on its back. Emmerling had been given a ride in the cab of the engine from Lincoln out, until we halted at the upset, the engineer evidently thinking that his weight would prevent any repetition of the accident in our case. The euchre game lasted well on to dinner time, before it was called and the prize winners announced. At 6.15 P. M., just as the first call was made for dinner, we passed into Pacific Junction, ahead of the train of

Philadelphia Commandery No. 2, which had been to Omaha and arrived at the short cut in time to be cut out. They soon came in beside us at the station and laid there for some time exchanging left-handed compliments with us. We tried hard to buy chairman John Baker's cowboy hat, but he was afraid that his official position would not be recognized if he parted with that emblem of his authority. At 6.35 P. M. we crossed the Missouri River into Iowa, and had made a stepping stone of another state on our homeward route.

All day long an immense watermelon had been freezing in Baird's ice cream tub, which had followed our fortunes throughout the trip. It was intended for the watermelon party and concert announced for 9 P. M. in the smoking car. The concert began long before the hour named and was wound up by cutting the melon. It was then found that the melon had been plugged and charged with a bottle or two of wine. The general opinion seemed to be that some wine had been wasted and a first-class melon spoiled. Several new verses were brought out when Munch sang the Ta-ra-ra-boom to-night and one on Purdy especially brought down the house, while Purdy grew red with apprehension. The song being now complete, we insert it in our pages that it may be preserved for future reference.

July fifteenth we sped away,
With spirits high and feelings gay;
Our friends were there to squeeze our hands,
And God-speed us to those distant lands.

CHORUS—Zing-ta-ra-ra-Boom ! Etc.

Next morning at the earliest dawn,
An invite came from Ascalon
To banquet with them on that night.
And our boys know they did it right !—*Cho.*

Then came another invitation,
From one in quite a lofty station ;
So we spent an eventful day
As the Governor's guests, in Santa Fe.—*Cho.*

Governor and charming Mrs. Prince,
We've thought of you quite often since ;
But I must also make a confession,
Your lovely niece made a deep impression.—*Cho.*

There's Sir Knight Harry Emmerling,
He's an awful big fat thing ;
The mud bath he took at Montezume,
Lost him ten pounds that afternoon.—*Cho.*

There's our Captain General Munch.
The only officer in the bunch ;
At Santa Fe he spoke his piece,
With one eye on the Governor's niece.—*Cho.*

And Harmon Johnson you all know
A dandy masher, never slow ;
He loves the ladies all the while,
Old maids and widows suit his style.—*Cho.*

George Lafferty, who's known as Plucks,
Eats everything from pork to ducks;
He eats all day, with all his might,
But never goes to bed at night.—*Cho.*

Then there's our friend Sir Billy Dill,
For thirty years he's run a mill;
In the baggage car you'll always find him,
With Plucks and his gang right close behind him.—*Cho.*

From Norristown there's old John Bickel,
On Monday he was in a pickle;
He thought the smoke would make him sick,
When he saw the fun, he thought he'd stick.—*Cho.*

And his side partner, Sobernheimer,
Whose name would rattle any rhymer,
When he happens to have nothing to say,
He's thinking of that fee from Emilay.—*Cho.*

Our worthy chairman, Clifford P.,
There are few things which he don't see;
He's always cheerful, always true,
The success of our trip to him is due.—*Cho.*

Then Milligan, our six-foot judge,
From the path of duty he don't budge;
He's glad we're having a good time,
And that's what makes his bald head shine.—*Cho.*

And Kessler, who's so painfully quiet,
Careful even in his diet;
After each meal he takes a pill,
Lest railroad riding should make him ill.—*Cho.*

We have from Baltimore, M. D.,
A knight you cannot fail to see;
We never knew he was so gay,
Till he changed his pants three times one day.—*Cho.*

There's Billy McIntyre the bold,
We've known him all of us of old;
For his good points we love him dearly,
"And the mune was shaining cleerly."—*Cho.*

Now there's the Ladies we all love,
Seem like a blessing from above;
They've added much to our "plaisir,"
And made themselves to us quite dear.—*Cho.*

From the Twentieth Ward there's Mrs. D.,
The most youthful matron I ever see;
She won but two games the other day,
But luck does sometimes go that way.—*Cho.*

You've doubtless heard of our Three Graces,
They're charming without silks or laces;
They joined this party to have some fun,
If they don't get it I'm a son of a gun!—*Cho.*

Then Mrs. J. from Diamond Street,
And Mr. J., who is always neat;
He and his Dollie have reason to brag
Of the stuff packed in that "little black bag."—*Cho.*

Jimmy Gorman is quite a beau,
He flatters all the ladies so;
With his palaver he takes them in,
It's a toss whether he or Brown will win.—*Cho.*

And Jimmy Baird, the noisy cuss,
At four A. M. he raises a fuss;
Comes in our car with yell and shout,
Ain't satisfied till we get out.—*Cho.*

There's Blackwood and Brown, with their kodaks,
Chasing "Injuns" around the tracks;
They'll no doubt have a fine collection,
Even if they're not perfection.—*Cho.*

One morning we determined to go,
To Tia Juana, in Mexico;
Cigars were bought and other trash,
How those greasers did hive our cash!—*Cho.*

We had hardly started from the train,
When I laughed until I had a pain;
To see Sir Dill from the wagon slip,
And his pant's broad bosom get an awful rip.—*Cho.*

One beautiful morn, in wonder I stood,
With raptured soul and fevered blood;
Of the garden spots in this world wide
I yielded the palm to Riverside.—*Cho.*

At Redondo, Schuehler on sport was bent,
So he took a pole and fishing went;
He hadn't a bite for one whole hour,
And his humor made our milk turn sour.—*Cho.*

When Pop Millick missed that train,
How it happened he wouldn't explain;
We learned the attraction was a girl in the surf,
We had thought the old buck was "off the turf."—*Cho.*

Fresno gave a reception most hearty,
A drive and banquet were tendered our party;
The banquet was graced by wife and daughter,
And they gave us everything but water.—*Cho.*

In the swimming pool at Del Monte,
We floated and kicked the water to spray;
Charley Shaw dived the waves beneath,
But opened his mouth and lost his teeth.—*Cho.*

There's one man for whom we all should pray,
Neddy McDowell, once young, now grey;
It's really a wonder he's still alive,
For instead of one woman, he looks after five.—*Cho.*

In 'Frisco there's the "Golden Gate,"
With them we smoked, we drank, we ate;
Their knights are of the proper stuff,
And I'm not giving you any bluff.—*Cho.*

And "California, Number One,"
A great Commandery from the setting sun;
May our acquaintance always be,
Marked with love and chivalry.—*Cho.*

At Denver, in the big parade,
Our Mary was not in the shade;
With martial tread behind our band,
We surprised them on the reviewing stand.—*Cho.*

Our agent, Purdy, who's been so attentive,
Although his memory's not retentive,
When exchanging badges with a lady
He made a mistake, and—keep it shady.—*Cho.*

One night Cas. Lowry, I'm sorry to say,
Endeavored in the wrong berth to lay;
He heard a sharp scream, and the mistake was found.
Since morning the car had been turned round.—*Cho.*

There's the Big Four aggregation.
The Knickerbocker Combination;
What they haven't seen the Lord only knows,
They've spent all their cash, but still own their clothes.—*Cho.*

On Mr. Brooks there have been no flies,
We've looked for him with eager eyes;
In our favor he's a winner,
When he shout's "first call for Dinner."—*Cho.*

We finally reached old Philly again,
And regretfully left our homelike train;
Glad to set foot on our own dear sod,
Although it meant a return to the "hod."—*Cho.*

Now one more verse before we part,
On a subject very near my heart;
It's not about love or politics,
But MARY, NUMBER THIRTY-SIX.—*Cho.*

F. M.

The Kazoo band rang in its notes on the chorus with great vim and
assisted likewise with some of the other songs, as well as coming in occasionally
on its own hook. Meanwhile we were travelling at full speed across the great
State of Iowa without seeing much of it, except the lights in the stations or
houses as we flash by. It was not much later than 11 P. M. when the crowd
in the smoker had thinned out to the regulars, who took their final smoke
always after the first instalment had retired.

Saturday, August 13th, 1892.

E DID not know at what time we crossed the Mississippi, but found this morning that we had straddled another whole State in the night and were now speeding across the flat prairies of the Sucker dominions. The weather had cooled off again, the temperature this morning being very pleasant. There was little to do on the train, except to prepare for our rambles around Chicago. An order had been issued by the conductor that everything should be packed up and transported to the baggage car, in order that the sleepers might have a thorough cleaning while at the yards in that city. This was countermanded by the Committee, who thought it useless to put everybody to that much trouble when we would only be out another day. Dirt had become our normal condition anyhow and forty-eight hours would find us at home, where our hands would stay clean for a couple of hours after being washed. Two minutes sufficed here as a recompense for the labor of cleaning them.

Our object, in starting ahead of time from Denver, had been well nigh defeated by the numerous stops we had been compelled to make. But our engineer of the past night had made up much of the lost time and put us into the Union Depot at 9.30 A. M., four and a half hours ahead of our schedule. This was quite an addition to our limited stop here and the pilgrims were quick to take advantage of it. The train was scarcely emptied before a raid had been made on the cab stand outside and the party was scattered in squads, anxious to see some special objective point.

One party made direct for the stock yards and packing houses of the Messrs. Armour, who showed them how a pig can be stuck, scalded, disembowelled and hung up on a railroad track in the ice-house before he has uttered the final squeal. What shopping the ladies wanted to do, had to be done before noon, as it was Saturday and the major part of the stores closed at that hour. They accordingly went into the business with their whole hearts, investing in all kinds of goods with a reckless abandon as to where they could be stowed away in already overflowing trunks.

We were recommended to see the new Masonic Temple. It was no trouble to find it on State Street, because it out-Heroded Herod in the matter of Chicago tallness. Buildings were all around which took a full grown man to look up to the top of their twelve to sixteen stories, but the new Temple requires a man and a boy to see to the top of its twenty-one floors without straining the eyesight. They shoot you up in an elevator a distance of nineteen stories. Then, if you want to get a view of the city from the top, you were mulcted two bits for allowing you to walk up the other two stories. You

IN LINCOLN PARK

can see as much smoke and fog over the city as you can remember in a year's time, but out on the lake you can see a long distance.

A glimpse from this point of the panorama of Lincoln Park, induced a drive in that direction. Crossing the black waters of the main ditch of the Chicago River, the business portion of the North Side was soon traversed and a charming ride ensued through a fine residence district and along the boulevard which skirts the shore of Lake Michigan. The ride along the lake was a grand one and the cool breezes off its surface very refreshing. The waterworks crib, away off shore, attracted attention, as well as the pumping station itself, with its polished and noiseless machinery and the huge stone-encased standpipe. The Park itself was worthy of a long journey to see, being now in the height of its floral beauty. The great number of fine statues and the monuments to Lincoln, Grant and other great figures in the history of our country have to be seen to be appreciated. A fine enclosed harbor for yachts is one of the features at the upper end of the Park. Another is a zoological garden with quite a show of animals. The designs of growing plants reminded us of California, but the bright colors of the Golden Shore were wanting.

The round of the Park having been made it was time to seek the Auditorium where luncheon and dinner were to be provided for us. It was a long ride back from the park to the hotel at one stretch, although Dearborn Street afforded a great variety of sights in its length. It was remarkable only on one point for us, in that it afforded us the first sight of a funeral we had seen since leaving home. At the hotel rooms had been secured as resting places both for the ladies and gentlemen. It is doubtful if the latter even saw theirs, the preference being for the washroom and the rotunda of the hotel afterward. Considerable mail had accumulated here, in advance of our advent, which was distributed to its rightful owners as they turned up, hungry and tired. Right facing the hotel, along the lake front, were numerous steamboats which run from landings there to the World's Fair grounds. Each has a barker or two out and a brass band, either on the boat or the pier adjacent, to entice passengers on board. If Ikey Solomon, of South Street, could watch the efforts of these barkers for a half hour he would turn green with envy. After luncheon was disposed of, the majority of the party turned their attention to means of attaining the exhibition grounds at Jackson Park. The boats, elevated road, cable cars and carriages were all made use of. The ride along the lake was very pleasant, but he who took a carriage and drove along the Boulevard and through Washington and Jackson Parks struck the right thing to do.

The designs formed with growing plants in Washington Park out-did any-thing in that line we had ever seen or heard of. The landscape gardener who designed and executed them is without a peer in that business, although we did not learn his name. We were about to say that he has done everything here with flowers except to make them talk, but he has even accomplished that. On the slope of one of the terraces is a calendar, in letters and figures about thirty inches high, which informs us that it is Saturday, August 13th, 1892, all in growing plants. Two life sized figures, seated in open boats, each pulling a pair of oars, are Harrison and Cleveland, racing for the Presidency. A figure of Atlas, bearing a globe not less than six feet in diameter on his shoulders, with the continents mapped out in darker colored plants than the oceans, is also formed of growing plants. Vases, urns and a huge sun-dial are formed by other growths. A flight of brown stone steps, about twelve feet wide, with a parapet on each flank, and a carpet of rich design and bright colors running down the centre and a large pair of gates at the top partly ajar, required a second look or more to convince you that stone steps, parapets, carpet and gates, were all living and blooming plants. A little further on, two rolls of carpet were lying on the ground. The rolls themselves were about two feet high, but five or six yards had been unrolled from each along the ground to show the pattern, a pattern that might do for the real article at any time. We were loath to leave the attraction of these wonderful flowers behind us, even to see the buildings of which we had set out in search. It was quite a long drive to the grounds of the Exposition, being some eight or nine miles from the Auditorium Hotel and the results attained hardly paid for the trip. While many of the buildings were in a forward state, the grounds were so encumbered with timbers, iron, plaster, broken stone or cement and other impediments, that it was as much as you wanted to do, to navigate either on foot or in carriages. The entrance fee to the grounds is twenty-five cents and, if you had a carriage, the same for your driver. The ticket taker looked long at the horses, in some doubt as to whether he ought not to collect fifty cents for them, because they had four legs, but finally concluded to wait until the show opened. The outside of the building was all that could be seen just now, except an occasional view through some door or window or the open end of an unfinished structure. The interiors were jealously guarded from intrusion, by a whole army of blue-coated gens d'armes who are probably all distant relatives rung in by the Commissioners of different States. From the number on duty, they must all have fruitful families, too. Quitting time came while we were inside and the army of workmen, that rolled towards the gates, gave ample evidence of the number of men at work on the place. Still the buildings were not in the advanced condition calculated to convince the looker-on that they will be finished in time for the Exposition, while the grounds are in almost a state of chaos. You cannot smoke within a quarter of a mile of the buildings, which is perhaps as well, because if a fire ever started among them, they would disappear in a whirlwind of flame. They are packed in so close together and the entire arrangement is simply a forest of dry hemlock with a thin coating of rough casting on the outside.

The drive back to the hotel took us again past the floral sights in Washington Park and through another section of the city, which seems to have been monopolized by our friends, the Hebrews. The houses all have basement stories, and the first floors are elevated from twelve to fifteen steps. It was a holiday afternoon for them, and the families generally were out front for an airing. In many cases the whole flight of steps were insufficient to contain the numerous progeny of the family, and they had overflowed onto the sidewalk. In the course of the afternoon we drove over Belgian blocks, wood blocks, asphalt, cobbles, vitrified bricks and dirt roads, showing that Chicago is not wedded to any particular style of paving. As an appetizer for dinner, we can recommend the Hebrew thoroughfares with the round wood blocks, but they are hard on the back. The dining hour found pretty much everybody on hand and sharp set for the really excellent dinner that was served by the Auditorium. The dining room is on the eleventh floor or top of the house, and has a beautifully arched ceiling, with windows opening above everything around, and giving plenty of air. The air to-night was a little too cool, and the windows had to be closed. The elevator which runs up from the first floor to the dining room, does not run for anything else, and has no communication with any other floor. The Auditorium also has an observation tower, which is claimed to be ten feet higher than the Masonic Temple. Many of the party availed themselves of the opportunity to go up in its elevator, still for two bits, and get a clearer view of the lake and city.

After dinner a party was made up to take in one of the theatres, and departed in search of that recreation. Another received information of a great natural curiosity, and departed, intent upon making a critical examination thereof. While the third section, feeling tired enough with the exertions of the day, were content to rest themselves at the hotel until it should be time to go to the train. At 10 P. M. they walked to the cable line on Adams Street and boarded a car, which after a short run in the cool night air, landed them again at the Union Depot. Here our train was found lying beside that of Reading Commandery, which was again designed to clear the track for us by starting ten minutes ahead of our time. The theatre and other parties came along in due time, with the exception of Lee, who found that some business he had to attend to at this point could not be finished up to-day, and had made up his mind to lay over for it.

When our train was shifted here, by some means the cars had been turned end for end. When Cas. Lowry, at a late hour, went to see after the welfare of Mrs. Lowry, before retiring to his seat in the arm chair, he pulled aside the curtains of her berth, as he thought, and saluted the occupant with "Well, old girl, how do you think you are making out?" A little feminine screech, coupled with repeated injunctions to "go away from here," soon convinced Lowry that he had struck the wrong berth. His bewilderment ended when his better half called to him from the other end of the car. When Reading pulled out at 2 A. M. and we followed suite at 2.10 A. M,, we were all oblivious to sights or sounds.

Sunday, August 14th, 1892.

NOTHER lovely morning broke upon the view of those who got up soon enough to see it break. Conscience sat lightly upon the minds of all the pilgrims this morning, as all were sound sleepers. There had been little rousing out in the early dawn since Jimmy Baird had cut his head open at Manitou. He said that he did not get up so soon now, because his head hurt him, and many fervent prayers had ascended that Jimmy's head would continue to hurt until we got home, but no longer. At 6.45 A.M. we were laid off to let the Limited go past us, in a whirlwind of dust and coal gas. We had crossed the dividing line between Illinois and Indiana before daylight, and reached Fort Wayne at 7.25 A. M. The first call for breakfast was made at that time and few of the cats were ready for it, although the cooks had caught the general infection and were also behind time. At 7.45 A. M. we skipped across the line into Ohio, and ran through the quietest country we had been in for many days. It was a peaceful country Sabbath outside our windows, and it seemed as if the entire population had no other thought than observing the day, while inside the train our party of pilgrims had just about enough ambition left in them, after their thirty days travel to join in with them.

We made a stop at Lima at 9.40 A. M. and another at Crestline at 11.40 A. M. Here we caught up again with the Reading train and walked forward to see how they were getting along. They appeared to be perfectly happy with the exception of one man who had lost two bottles of beer and made enough lament over them to have lost a barrel. The occupants of the rear car were engaged in singing hymns, while the forward car sinners were deep in a game of cards. Both trains were forced to wait here for a clear track.

Lakeville was passed at 1.05 and a short stop made at Orrville at 1.55 P. M. When the train came to a halt, the weather was tolerably hot, but so long as it kept in motion, a breeze was created that made it very comfortable. At Alliance at 3.30 P. M. and Salem at 4.05 P. M. large parties were assembled at the stations, apparently awaiting the return of their home commanderies.

At 4.40 P. M. we crossed the State line and were once more on the soil of the good old Keystone State. At this time all hands were assembled in the ladies' car in obedience to the summons of the Committee of Ways and Means, to witness one of the closing scenes of the pilgrimage. Tourist Agent Purdy was first called in and presented by Judge Milligan with an engrossed copy of a set of resolutions, setting forth our appreciation of his labors in our behalf and signed by all the participants in the pilgrimage. The Judge read the resolutions and followed them up with an additional eulogy that made the recipient blush. Purdy, although taken aback, fittingly signified his pleasure at the manner taken to show the value we set upon his services. Conductor Backus and Baggage-master Speakman were also brought to the front and presented with testimonals on behalf of the tourists, Milligan making the presentations.

Capt. Gen. Munch then made some remarks, in which he congratulated the party upon the unalloyed success of the pilgrimage and the extreme good-nature that had characterized all our intercourse during the month just passed. Sir Shaw then offered up a fervent prayer of thanksgiving for the Divine protection that had been vouchsafed to us during all our wanderings, our freedom from accidents or sickness and invoking a continuance of the same for the balance of our journey.

At Rochester at 5.30 P. M. Mrs. Branson left us for a stay with her sister, who lives at that place and was on hand to receive her. Her departure left a void in the party that would have been hard to fill, the brightness of her spirits having been a large acquisition to the pleasures of the month.

Of course a number of the inmates of the ladies' car, as well as a majority of the gentlemen, had to get off on the platform to take leave of their fellow traveler, although all of them had already gone through that ceremony inside the car. As the halt was necessarily short, it took considerable scrambling for all to secure a footing upon the steps of the cars which had begun to move after several unheeded calls and warning whistles.

A considerable number of the souvenir leaves had been left on hand after the closing of the head-quarters in Denver, and it was now suggested that they be distributed at the stations through which we passed this afternoon. They were accordingly brought forth and scattered in the air whenever we passed a station at which the people were gathered in any numbers. At times the onward rush of the train would whirl them high in the air, like a swarm of green butterflies. As they came down to the ground they were eagerly gathered in by the bystanders, to be preserved as mementoes of pilgrims from the far West.

As we drew nearer to Pittsburgh, there seemed to be more life infused into the general aspect of the country. More people were on the move, who had the appearance rather of holiday seekers than that of searchers after rest. Numerous boating parties on the river waved greetings to us, which were answered from the train.

We were eating dinner as our train ran through the suburbs of Pittsburg.
We had collared one of the menus of the Auditorium dinner last night and
turned the same over to Brooks. After inspecting the card, he had asserted
that the "Pullman" could get away with the Auditorium at any time and in
proof thereof, set us out the following substantial dinner.

⇆MENU⇄

DINNER OF MARY COMMANDERY

En Route August 14th, 1892.

SOUP
TURTLE SOUP, A LA REINE

BOILED
BOILED CHICKEN WITH SALT PORK

BOILED CALIFORNIA SALMON   FRENCH PEAS

POTATO CROQUETTES   SLICED CUCUMBERS

HOT JOINTS
PRIME ROAST BEEF   BONCHES A LA REINE

ROAST SPRING LAMB, MINT SAUCE

ENTREES
BROSCHETTE OF KIDNEY   BAKED BEANS A LA SHERWOOD

CURRY OF MUTTON, AUX CREOLE   CALF'S HEAD, A LA TOULOUSE

BELL FRITTERS, WINE SAUCE

VEGETABLES
MASHED POTATOES   NEW POTATOES IN CREAM

STUFFED EGG PLANT   BOILED RICE

MACARONI, ITALIAN   STEWED TOMATOES

RELISHES
GHERKINS   CHOW-CHOW   TOMATO SAUCE   WORCESTERSHIRE SAUCE

PLAIN BREAD   BROWN BREAD   GRAHAM BREAD

DESSERT
ORIENTAL PUDDING WITH BRANDY SAUCE   ICE CREAM

RUSSIAN CREAM PIES   FRUITS   WATERMELON   CAKE

COFFEE   TEA   COCOA

BENT'S CRACKERS AND CHEESE

When you got through with dinner you wanted to lie down and wait for a resurrection.

We pulled into the depot at Pittsburg at 7.40 P. M. Wells was to leave us here for his home in Wellsville, Ohio. The boys, and girls too, gave him a send-off in the depot that must have done his heart good. A grand chorus of "He's a jolly good fellow" and "So say we all of us," followed by three rousing cheers for Wells, set the timbers of the depot roof to ringing and made the travelling public look on in astonishment. Emmerling waved Field's duster around his head, in his enthusiasm, until it split into two parts and was hung up in the baggage room among the other trophies of deers' heads, palm leaves and orange branches that already decorated the walls. Wells had been through the ladies' car and had taken leave of all the female contingent before the first call was made for dinner. He probably thought that the worst portion of the farewells he would be obliged to attend to had been got through with, but the hand-wringing he had to undergo outside, with the attendant send-off, caused him to flee in dismay up the station platform with a ruddy tinge on his face which was a match for his auburn hair.

We were off again at 8.10 P. M. The shades of our last night upon the train had begun to gather around us and the street lamps and electric lights of the city flitted past us like fireflies. The talk in the smoker was mainly upon the near-by troubles on Homestead and speculation was rife as to how near we ran to that point. A bright lookout was also kept as we drew near to Johnstown for any evidence of the late disastrous flood, but the lights of some of the dwellings and smoke from the numerous cupolas of the iron works were about all that could be seen. The Committee took advantage of the quiet into which the party had subsided, as they began to realize the near approach of the termination of the trip, to make their way through the train and take a personal leave of each participant and receive any suggestions that might be for the advantage of future pilgrims. To the gratification of the Committee there seemed to be but one voice in the entire party as to their perfect satisfaction with every arrangement that had been made, either for the comfort, information or entertainment of the whole family. Spencer left us at Tyrone as the most convenient point from which to reach his home. Mr. and Mrs. Crist, accompanied by Brown, took their departure at Altoona for a like reason. The crowd generally had turned in before that time and they were allowed to depart quietly.

Monday, August 15th, 1892.

SUCH of the inmates of the cats' car as had imagined themselves sure of a good night's rest were destined to have their minds disabused of that idea for at least several hours. A conspiracy had been hatching out, chiefly by the machinations of the Big Four, to make the last hours of the pilgrimage memorable to the inhabitants of the rear car at least. Henderson, Zeitz and Hemphill had drawn to their aid in the scheme the services of Lafferty, Dill, Schuehler, Enochs, Jr., and conductor Backus. The latter extinguished the lights in the car, while his fellow-conspirators were up in the baggage car busily engaged in shaving ice into a bucket. When the utensil was filled and a fire-shovel secured from the cook's domain, a stealthy march was made through the train into the rear car. The first intimation of the raid the occupant of a berth received, would be the raising of his blanket and the swish of the ice as it left the shovel and came in contact with his bare skin. Hot iron was not more efficacious in disturbing a man's slumbers than the hydropathic treatment of the raiders. Several battles royal ensued in the course of the journey through the length of the car, in one of which Billy Dill was put hors-du-combat and the invaders temporarily routed. They returned to the field, however, leaving Dill in the hospital, and kept up the racket until after Altoona was passed, when the car was allowed to settle down to its normal condition, so far as it possibly could with the damp condition of the berths. Emmerling had been the recipient of a double or triple dose, and sought to exchange into some of the unoccupied berths, from which he was successively routed as the owners thereof turned up.

Several times during the night the violent lurching of the cars from side to side made it evident that our engineer was going to take us in on time or break something. This was still more evident when we looked out from behind the curtains at 5 A. M., and began to descry familiar features in the landscape, of towns surrounding the city. A scramble to get dressed and washed up ensued. In short order we were crossing the bridge over the Schuylkill and rumbled into Broad Street Station at 5.30 A. M., a half hour ahead of time. There was a rush out of those ready to depart, a less precipitate descent from the cars of those who still had their traps to gather together and the train was side-tracked to allow a few of those who had just arisen to finish their toilets and afford an opportunity to unload the baggage and send it to the lower story. The deers' heads were taken down, that of the elk carefully unloaded, the palm leaves and orange branches, from which the oranges had long since been shaken by the motion of the train, stripped from the sides of the baggage car. The refrigerator, like many other things that have served their turn, was cast forth as useless. Everybody's hands were full, and it became a necessity, at every yard or two of progress, to deposit the right hand load upon the floor in order to shake hands with some one.

Many friends and relatives were on hand to welcome the returning travellers, although a greater number were disappointed who fully expected the train to come in a little late, instead of ahead of time. Carriages and wagons were in waiting or soon arrived, and by the time the train was actually due, the last straggler had departed for home.

A delightful trip had come to a pleasant end, and the pilgrimage of Mary Commandery to the Twenty-fifth Triennial Conclave of Knights Templar had become a matter of history.

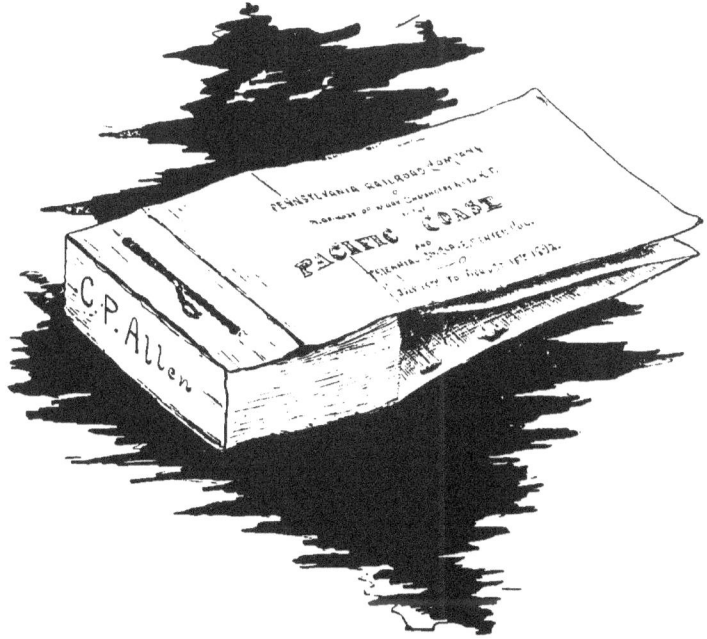

⤳ROSTER⤶

......OF......

DENVER PILGRIMAGE MARY COMMANDERY

〜〜〜〜〜〜〜〜〜

FRED MÜNCH, C. G. . . . . . Philadelphia
EDGAR S. McDOWELL . . .   "
MRS. E. S. McDOWELL. . .   "
WILLIAM McINTYRE . . .   "
MRS. WILLIAM McINTYRE .   "
WILLIAM McINTYRE, JR.. .   "
MRS. ISABELLA BRANSON . .   "
MISS SADIE BRANSON . . .   "
CLIFFORD P. ALLEN . . . .   "
MRS. CLIFFORD P. ALLEN .   "
J. EDGAR ALLEN . . . . .   "
ROBERT J. JOHNSON . . . .   "
MRS. ROBERT J. JOHNSON. .   "
JOHN K. KEEN . . . . . .   "
MRS. JOHN K. KEEN . . .   "
JAMES D. BLACKWOOD . . .   "
MRS. JAMES D. BLACKWOOD   "
JAMES W. BAIRD . . . . .   "
MRS. JAMES W. BAIRD . .   "
MRS. M. JENNIE FAIRLAMB .   "
MISS L. B. HALDEMAN . .   "
MISS MARION GRAHAM . .   "
MISS BERTHA GRAHAM . .   "
GEORGE KESSLER . . . . .   "
WILLIAM J. MILLIGAN . . .   "
LEWIS C. SCHUEHLER . . .   "
MISS PHILLIPA V. CHAPIN .   "
MISS MARTHA McALPINE .   "
CASPAR F. LOWRY . . .   "
MRS. C. F. LOWRY . . . .   "

JOHN D. PHILLIPS . . . . Philadelphia
FRED A. SOBERNHEIMER . .   "
HARMON JOHNSON . . . .   "
CHARLES SHAW . . . . .   "
CHARLES M. SHEELER . . .   "
WILLIAM T. MILLICK . . .   "
GEORGE W. LAFFERTY . .   "
HARRY EMMERLING . . . .   "
JOHN ROBINSON . . . . . .   "
THOMAS HENDERSON . . .   "
GEORGE T. HEMPHILL . . .   "
SAMUEL V. THOMSON . . .   "
B. W. ZEITZ . . . . . .   "
JOHN R. CANTLIN, JR. . . .   "
WILLIAM J. DILL . . . . .   "
JAMES E. GORMAN . . . .   "
JAMES AXFORD . . . . . .   "
GEORGE F. FIELDS . . . .   "
ALEXANDER FOSTER . . .   "
JOHN ENOCHS . . . . . .   "
J. NELSON ENOCHS . . . .   "
H. S. REGESTER . . . . . . Baltimore
MRS. H. S. REGESTER . . . .   "
JOHN W. BICKEL . . . . . Norristown
WM. A. CRIST . . . . . . Osceola Mills
MRS. WM. A. CRIST . . .   "
L. W. SPENCER . . . . . Curwensville
A. W. LEE . . . . Clearfield
BENJAMIN F. BROWN . . . Lock Haven
EMMET H. WELLS . . . . Wellsville, O.

➤⑤OMMITTEE◄

CLIFFORD P. ALLEN . . . . 1516 Marshall Street
WM. McINTYRE . . . . 4080½ Lancaster Avenue
GEO. KESSLER . . . . 1542 Franklin Street
CALEB J. BRINTON, Jr. . . . . 58 North Fourth Street
E. S. McDOWELL . . . . 1810 North Sixteenth Street
CHAS. W. MILLER (2) . . . . 511 North Third Street
WM. J. MILLIGAN . . . . 508 South Eleventh Street
ALEX. FOSTER . . . . 2418 Poplar Street
WM. McCOACH . . . . 2107 Fitzwater Street